This book is a work of fiction. Names, characters, places, and incidents are either the product of the author's imagination or are used fictitiously, and any resemblance to actual persons, living or dead, events, or locales is entirely coincidental.

The following story contains mature themes, strong language and sexual situations. It is intended for mature readers.

All characters are 18+ years of age and non-blood related, and all sexual acts are consensual.

Contents

Relentless

The Bertoli Crime Family Book One by Lauren Landish

Protecting her should be easy for a man like me . . .

When assigned as a bodyguard for Adriana Bertoli, I knew I was in for a world of trouble. With her fiery-red hair, sparkling green eyes, milky white skin, and lush, curvaceous body, she's a damn knockout.

But she also happens to be the niece of one of the most powerful mob bosses in the Seattle-Tacoma area, Don Carlo — ***my*** boss. And he's made it clear that none of his men are to lay a finger on Adriana.

The man to have that honor would have to be perfect — a warrior and a saint. **Sadly, I was no saint.**

It should be an easy order to follow. After all, I owed everything to the man, and I'd be nothing without him. But every moment in Adriana's presence is pure temptation. The longer I'm with her, the more I want her, and I fear it won't be long before I betray the man who's like the father I never had.

****Relentless is a full-length novel with an HEA and no cheating!**

Chapter 1

Adriana

"Hey honey, you wanna party with an APE?"

I rolled my eyes at the idiot standing in front of me, a young guy who looked like he was maybe nineteen and wearing a fraternity t-shirt. He was obviously approaching me as part of some sort of frat thing, although at least he had some taste. After all, he did have his choice of women to choose from—I don't go to a tiny school. "Are you doing this as a rush or something?"

The idiot's eyes wavered for a moment. He'd probably seen my paint-streaked clothes and mussed hair and correctly pegged me for an art student. Sadly enough, art students at my school have a bit of a reputation for being easy lays, and I guess he'd picked me out as an easy target. It took him a moment before he reassumed his false bravado.

"Come on, baby, you know APE's got the best parties and the best time for your weekend! Besides, you look like you could use a real APE, if you know what I mean."

I crossed my arms over my chest and stared at him, raising an eyebrow. This idiot certainly didn't know who I was, nor what I'd been through these past six months. Still, his grin didn't waver, and I pulled out an old nugget I'd picked up somewhere when I first came to campus. "You do realize that the average male gorilla has a penis size of only one and a half inches, right? Trust me, if I needed some dick, an APE's the last place I'd go looking. Run along, monkey boy."

The frat pledge, looking defeated, turned and walked away, quickly reassuming his cocky persona to hit on the next girl who came by and caught his eye. Laughing a much needed laugh under my breath, I readjusted my bag over my shoulder and kept walking, leaving the campus library and heading toward my apartment. As I walked, I kept my eyes open for Vincent, hoping he'd gotten the message. After months of harassment, which had left me frazzled and at the end of my wits, I'd taken out a restraining order against him the week prior. I hoped it would end the creepiness I'd been through for most of the past five months, even if my family thought otherwise. Uncle Carlo wanted to send a message *his* way, but I'd convinced him to let the legal authorities take care of my former sculpture teacher.

Uncle Carlo is old school Italian. Sicilian, in fact, and yes, that means exactly what you think it means. Carlo was in the family business, the Mafia, and worked his way up the ladder to become the Godfather of the Seattle-Tacoma area for the past fifteen years. After taking over for his murdered brother—my father—he'd quickly consolidated power, ruthlessly crushing his opposition and enacting revenge for his fallen sibling. Bloodthirsty, and certainly not a man to be trifled with. That was Uncle Carlo.

At the same time, he was a kind and generous family man who'd taken my mother and me into his house as soon as he could, caring for us like we were his own wife and daughter. Cancer had taken his wife when I was in sixth grade, so for most of my life, Uncle Carlo had been the male authority figure and his sons had practically been my brothers. He and Mom were in no way romantic. In fact, she filled an important role in his organization as one of his prime lieutenants.

Still, if anyone could talk Uncle Carlo out of a course of action, it was me, and he let me try it my way at first.

I went to the cops after Vincent started harassing me, getting a restraining order and having it delivered to the school as well, which removed me from the class next door to his in order to conduct an 'internal investigation'. That hadn't stopped his communication issues, though, and I'd gotten tired of his constant text messages, emails, and phone calls. Unfortunately, he knew my campus email, and that was one address I couldn't get changed.

To say it was a bit disheartening was an understatement. You would think that a restraining order and evidence of sexual harassment would have done something more than just a change of classrooms and an 'internal investigation'.

I was wondering what to do about it when I got back to my off-campus apartment that I shared with Angela. Angela—never Angie—had been roomies with me for two years, after she'd passed Uncle Carlo's discreet but thorough background check. Short, Asian, and alternatively perky and serious, she was the total opposite of me as a math major. However, for some reason, the two of us gelled, and for two years, we'd been the best of roommates.

The first threads of worry started to work their way through me when I saw the open window to our apartment. Angela had terrible allergies and insisted on keeping the windows of our apartment shut, even in the dead of summer. With ionic air filters and other anti-allergen devices running almost constantly, we racked up quite an electricity bill on a monthly basis, but thankfully, Uncle Carlo had no problems with footing that cost, and the nearly sterile air did mean that when I painted at the apartment, I never had to worry about some stray cat hair or something screwing up a canvas. For Angela to leave the window open was just not possible.

Hurrying to our door, I quickly unlocked the deadbolt, pushing the door open. "Angela? You home?"

Leaden, oppressive silence greeted my words, and I waved my hand in front of my face. The apartment was hot, and a sour, metallic smell was coming from Angela's bedroom. Setting my bag down, I walked carefully toward the room, calling out the whole time. "Angela? Hey, Anj? You here? You would have laughed your ass off. I ran into a pledge from Alpha Rho—"

The words dried in my throat as I entered Angela's bedroom and saw the carnage in front of me. Angela, dressed in her normal early semester apartment wear of a tank top and a pair of Seahawks shorts, was lying facedown on her bed, the back of her shirt ripped and torn, her shorts pulled down to expose her ass to the air. More important to me, though, was the spreading red pool underneath her and the drip of the blood from her bed and off her outflung arm. The wall next to her was splattered, red raindrops against the eggshell white drywall.

I don't remember much of the next hour or so. Everything was a bit of a haze. I must have screamed, or perhaps I'd maintained enough presence of mind to call 9-1-1. I do know that there were bright lights, and eventually a cop, who led me into the living room, handing me tissue after tissue as I cried my eyes out. Later on, the same cop—I think—led me to an ambulance, but I wasn't sure why, except that they wanted me to go to the hospital.

It wasn't until I was at the hospital and got an injection

from the doctor that I started to calm down—but in that detached, sort of loopy way that comes with some really decent drugs. I didn't really start to come to until that night, and I noticed that I was now in a room in the hospital. Everything was painted that sort of vomit-inducing color that looks like baby blue and mint green were mixed, and I was laying on one of those reclining beds. "Wha . . . What happened?"

"It's okay, Bella," Uncle Carlo said from my left, his voice soft and concerned. *Bella* was a nickname he often called me. I looked at him and took a deep breath. Carlo was wearing his dark blue suit, one of his suits that I associated with him and work. He must have come straight from the office, where he worked in his day job as owner of Bertoli's Pizza, the largest independent pizza delivery company in the state of Washington. Carlo had even once gotten on television with Guy Fieri, if you can dig that. He had other businesses, including Bertoli Trucking, Sicily Dry Cleaning, and a few others he was a minority investor in, but his day job was at the pizza company.

"Uncle . . . oh, it was so horrible!" I said, my voice still sounding slightly separated from my body. I felt like a little girl again, telling him about the monster under my bed or something. "There was so much blood!"

"I know," he replied, taking my hand in his. "I saw a little of the crime scene. The police didn't tell me they had brought you here until after I arrived. Tell me exactly what you saw."

I recounted my memory, starting with the APE and ending with my seeing Angela's body. It didn't take long. After all, until seeing the open window, everything had been a boring yet normal late summer day. I had just taken the last of my first sessions for the semester and had been looking forward to a good year. The only dark mark was Vincent Drake in the background, but I hadn't seen or heard from him at all that day.

I finished my recollection, waiting while Uncle Carlo sat back, nodding to himself. It's one of the things that makes him good at what he does, in my opinion. Regardless of how much of a storm he might be feeling emotionally, when it came time to make a decision, he forced himself to step back, setting his feelings aside for the moment.

"There were things you didn't see," he finally said, sitting forward. "The police haven't told me much, only what I was able to quickly see when I came to take you to the hospital, but I did overhear some things. Those fools never could keep their damn mouths shut."

"What did I miss?" I asked, starting to tremble. "Was it bad?"

He nodded. "The killer is most likely Vincent Drake. Tell me what you know about him."

I sighed, regretting limiting my actions to just a restraining order. Uncle Carlo had been right the first time. "I took Drake's class last fall semester. He was teaching Conceptual Sculpting. He always wore these cheap suits, the kind that you'd get at a Goodwill or something, and they always looked like they were about ten years out of date on his frame. I swear he bought himself a six pack of discount suits when he was thirty, and twenty years later, he was still working his way through them, waiting for the seams to give out or something."

Uncle Carlo chuckled at my description. "That's one of the things I love about you, Adriana. You've always been a born artist, with such great descriptions of people and things. Tell me about your relationship with him."

"What relationship? The guy was a loser from day one. I hated the course," I protested, a bit of my natural temper flaring up. I come from Sicilian and Scottish roots, so me not having a temper would have been a miracle. When he gave me a look, I sighed and fell back into my recollections. "For the first few classes, things were normal. He was creepy, but nothing I haven't had to handle before. It wasn't until the midterm project that he started to really focus on me. The sculpture I did wasn't the best, in my opinion, but it was special to me because I tried to carve Dad as if he'd survived all the years to now. I'd poured my heart into it and planned on giving it to Mom for her birthday before all this started and ruined it for me. For some reason, Vincent really took to it, and he started obsessing over me."

"Eventually, I filed a sexual harassment complaint against him with the school, but they did nothing, saying it wasn't enough to do anything against a tenured professor. They just warned him and told me to stay away."

"Adriana, why did you put so much trust in these incompetent fools? Have I not shown you how useless they are?"

"You have, and I don't know why," I said. "I guess . . . I guess because I know what you would've done. He has a family, after all—a wife and supposedly, a daughter."

"Had a family . . ." he said. "It was on the news while you were out. He killed his wife before coming to your apartment. Another stabbing. There's talk of some sort of letter or manifesto, but no details have been released. I have men working on it now. Good men."

I shivered again, finally realizing just how insane Vincent Drake was. "So what am I to do?"

He smiled, then patted my hand and stood up. "You're young and you're idealistic, my Bella. Part of that is my fault, part your mother's. Your artistic streak has made you fiercely independent, and we agreed to give you some free reign to try things your way. But now it's time to do things my way."

I gulped and nodded as he continued.

"You will stay the night here. I'll have a man posted outside your room, and then, starting tomorrow, Daniel will become your driver and your bodyguard."

"Daniel?" I asked, trying not to sound too excited or surprised. "Daniel Neiman?"

He nodded, but still caught the tone of my voice. "Be careful, Adriana. Daniel's a good man, and is as loyal a Soldier as any of my men, but he does have a weakness for pretty young women, as I'm sure you know. I won't tolerate anything going on between you two. Do you understand, Adriana? I've seen the way you look at him, and if it were anyone but you, I'd just assign someone else, but Daniel is the best at what he does."

I nodded, swallowing my objections. While Daniel was charming and there was a certain magnetism about him, he could also be a first-class bastard. My physical attraction stopped there. "I understand. You have nothing to worry about, trust me."

After Uncle Carlo left, I lay back, my mind whirling. As if I didn't already have enough on my mind, now I'd have to deal with Daniel around the clock. He was easy on the eyes. I'd have my hands full keeping myself from jumping his bones. He's got this Germanic or Nordic look about him, with piercing, amazing blue eyes to go along with blond hair, a square jaw and a chiseled physique.

He came to Uncle Carlo's house when his parents were murdered by a mobster who'd mistaken his family for someone else. I didn't even know his real name. Carlo had gotten him a fake identity in order to keep him safe from the Russians, who undoubtedly would've tried to hunt him down in order to eliminate all evidence of their screw-up. I'm not sure why Uncle felt it was his responsibility, but despite being the boss, he did have a heart. Daniel was raised in Uncle Carlo's house, and when I came, he was like one of the staff's children.

Now, at twenty-five, he looked like an Adonis, like someone who should have been making movies or causing housewives to have hot flashes on television rather than as a member of Uncle Carlo's organization. He'd gone to work for Carlo almost immediately after junior high school, starting as an errand boy before working his way up, not through brown nosing or anything, but through hard work and a level of dedication that was both frightening and inspiring.

Still, Daniel had his drawbacks, namely his cockiness. While most of the time it came across as good humor and banter, it annoyed the hell out of me. He knew he was hot, and he wasn't ashamed to flaunt it. He was God's gift to women, and I admit I'd fantasized about him more than once, which was probably why he sometimes got on my nerves.

But anything between Daniel and me would have to remain a fantasy. Uncle Carlo had made that clear *more* than once. He put up with Daniel's womanizing as long as I, his *Bella*, remained hands-off. That, and that it didn't interfere with his job.

And that's what worried me—now Daniel was assigned to me. The most efficient and dedicated operative in Uncle Carlo's organization, and one of the sexiest men on the planet, was to become my bodyguard and driver, by my side virtually twenty-four hours a day.

I shivered and lay back. Life was going to get very, very interesting.

Chapter 2

Daniel

The little Hispanic girl wiggled back and forth on my lap, trying her best to entice me with her moves. Unfortunately for her, I was distracted as the music just wasn't sexy at all. I get it. Bass heavy dance music gives the girl a chance to shake her ass, and the throb of the bass can reverberate through your body to add to the illusion of her touching you, but I can't stand it. Finally, I lost my patience and lifted her off me. "Not happening tonight, chica. Find yourself another disco stick."

"But yours is the biggest here, Papi," she complained, reaching down and cupping my crotch. She made contact, a clear violation of the club's rules, but I was still wearing my pants, and I was the sort of patron that the normal rules didn't apply to anyway. "Dios mio, you must be stuffing those pants."

Stuff my pants? Hardly. "Maybe you'll find out another time. Now beat it. I'm not in the mood."

She wiggled her tits, clearly surgically enhanced but an overall good job, then shrugged when she saw I was serious. She was a pro and knew when to back off. She smiled when I held out a twenty. "For your efforts. Just not tonight."

"Next time you're in here, just ask for Carmen. I'll make sure you get taken care of."

I nodded in understanding, and she walked off, knowing how to move her ass in the barely there miniskirt and high heels to make sure I got one last good look at her wares.

I downed the rest of my drink and got up from the seat, making sure my pants were unstained. Not seeing anything in the dim lights of the club, I shrugged and buttoned up my coat, making sure my tie and everything looked exactly as they should. Semi-satisfied, I turned and left the club, getting ready for the rest of the night's work.

Thankfully, I didn't have too many assignments that night. Don Bertoli knows exactly how much to push a man and when to give him some time off to unwind. After taking care of some problems with one of the local motorcycle clubs two weeks prior, Boss had put me on light duty. "Those gear heads may be as stupid as two ducks fucking, but they know how to swing a mean wrench," the Don explained when he'd visited me in my apartment, where I was healing from a swollen shut eye. The motorcyclists had fared far worse. "You handled yourself well, Daniel. Enjoy the time, and we'll work you back into the rotation when the time comes."

The time had started a week ago—nothing too extreme, just a few visits to the businesses that had relationships with Don Bertoli to make sure they were up to date with their payments. Sure, collection work was newbie shit, but it was easy, and it kept me from sitting around my apartment for too long. Tonight, on top of the strip club I'd just visited—with a nice wad of cash in my pocket for the efforts—I had two more stops to make before three in the morning.

I was in the parking lot when my cellphone rang. As only ten people in the world had the number to my work phone, I knew it had to be important and pulled it out. "Neiman," I greeted. "What's up?"

"Daniel, it's Carlo," a mid-tone, accented voice said in my ear, and I immediately stiffened. "I need your services."

"Of course, Don Bertoli," I said immediately, sliding behind the wheel of my car. "What do you need?"

"First, go home and get some sleep," he said. "I've asked another man to do the rest of your pickups for the night. What did you get done?"

"Williams' Market and the Starlight Club, sir. I was thinking of going to the others closer to closing time. Give them a chance to make sure they have the cash on hand."

I heard Don Bertoli's warm chuckle and was pleased. "You're wise beyond your young years, Daniel. But don't worry about that tonight. Tomorrow morning at six, I want you at Harborview Medical Center to pick up my niece."

"Adriana?" I asked. Adriana and I had been friends when I was a child, and while I couldn't say the same any longer, we still would run into each other from time to time. "What happened, Boss?"

"Some psycho piece of shit instructor is obsessed with her, stalked her, and killed her roommate this afternoon. Now don't worry. I have a man watching her room right now, but I know Adriana. She'll want to go back to classes, and you're the best man for the job. You're young enough that you won't stick out too much amongst the college students, but more importantly, I know that you are a man of honor. You'd never allow anyone to harm her."

"You have my word," I swore immediately. My benefactor had treated me well in the twenty-five years I'd been under his protection.

"Protect her like she's the most important person in the entire world. If you see Christ himself resurrected and saying Adriana is not one of the saved, you are to slay the Lamb, do you understand?"

"Absolutely. I'll be there at six."

There was a sigh on the other end of the line, and I could tell he had something difficult to say. "Daniel, what I say next is not because I don't love you like one of my own. You've been a better man than many of them, and I look upon you with the same pride that I do my own sons. You know that, right?"

"I do, sir. And I see you as the closest thing I'll ever have to a father. You know that."

"And I appreciate that, my boy. But Adriana, she's blood, and she is the closest thing I will ever have to a daughter. I won't have her with a man in this kind of business. So I'll say this again, even though I know you've heard it before, if only so that you know exactly where I'm coming from. If you so much as touch her, let alone do what you've done with all those other women, I will make sure that your cock is chopped off and stuffed up your ass *before* you die a miserable death. Understood?"

"Understood," I said, a fine sweat breaking out on my brow despite the coolness of the evening. "Perfectly."

"Good. Give me a call in the morning when you are at the hospital. Good night, Daniel."

"Good night, sir."

The phone went silent in my ear, and I closed it with a slightly trembling hand. I'd known Adriana from the first day she came to the Don's house, and for years, she'd been that one woman who was always untouchable. Don Bertoli had no problems with my sleeping around. He felt that young men should be virile, and if I was a one-time only bedmate, that was my choice. He'd even gifted me with some of the girls who worked for him from time to time, including a semi-famous actress who'd done a few science fiction shows in Vancouver—the sort of stuff that had a decent dedicated following of geeks, but didn't have a snowball's chance in hell of getting any awards.

From the beginning, Adriana had been off limits. Not just to me, but to everyone in the Don's organization, and it was spelled out to us in very clear terms. Touch Adriana Bertoli, and die.

The problem was, she was my weakness. In my twenty-five years on this Earth, I'd trained myself to ignore pain, to ignore exhaustion, and to ignore every temptation. Money meant almost nothing to me. I had enough from what the Don gave me, and he'd taught me how to invest it well so that I would have more than enough when I wanted it. Physical possessions, the same. The only reason I drove a BMW was because as a member of the Bertoli family, it was expected that I drive a nicer class of car than the average jackass on the road. Stylish, understated, and with a sense of power. That's what a Bertoli man drove, and that's what I drove.

But sex was both one of my most potent tools and also one of my biggest weaknesses. Oh, the average slut that I went to Pound Town with, I didn't even give a second thought to. I'd never felt guilty fucking just about any woman that caught my attention, and with my cock, who could blame me? It's not like they'd turn me down. It's not everyday that a woman gets to feel a legitimate nine inches of thick man meat inside them. I can't help I was blessed with size and endurance—give me five or ten, and I'll saddle up for round two and round three. Turning your regular Girl Next Door into a cock slut just so happened to be a hobby of mine.

Adriana, though . . . she was different. Sexy, intelligent, and self-assured in a way that no other woman I'd met was, she'd been the subject of some of my earliest masturbation fantasies back when I was in high school and needed to rub one out at least once a day. Where other women would melt at a look from my eyes and a smirk, she always returned my taunts with verve and spice, usually with something along the lines of once I had her, I'd be the one addicted to her and not the other way around. Not that I would've ever touched her if she acted like other women. I am rather fond of my balls, after all, and would prefer to keep them attached.

I started up my Beamer and turned on the lights, taking a deep breath as I put the stick shift into first and pulled out of the strip club's parking lot. I couldn't help but feel a little anxious. Adriana was the ultimate forbidden fruit, and I had to admit that my greatest goal in life was to have just one night with her.

"Just do your fucking duty," I reminded myself, hanging a right and driving uptown toward my apartment. It was going on ten thirty, and if I wanted to be fresh-faced and ready to guard Adriana, I had to get back to my apartment quickly and try and get some sleep.

Chapter 3

Adriana

I couldn't believe Daniel when he showed up the next morning at my room. I'd slept like crap, tossing and turning most of the night but not really dropping off until about two in the morning. Even still, a nightmare drove me from my sleep at about five. The morning light glowed in my window, and I decided to hell with it. Uncle Carlo had gotten me a private room, so for the next forty-five minutes, I gave myself a long sponge bath, sluicing away the dirt and bad feelings from the previous day before washing out my hair in the sink that was in the corner. The water was hot, at least, and as I pulled my clothes back on, I couldn't help but chuckle when I saw the streak of paint on my right thumbnail.

"Cheaper than a set of nails," I joked, thinking about my bad habit of not always cleaning paint off my clothes as well as I'd like. Rarely a day went by that I didn't find myself slapping my forehead over some missed streak of paint on a pair of pants, a shirt, or my body. I'd even once done a whole dinner with a rather cute guy with a streak of titanium white between my eyes. It wasn't until the dessert course and he asked if the mark was for Lent that I'd even realized it was there.

A few minutes later, Daniel knocked on the door, and I smoothed my hair back, checking my shirt and pants to make sure I didn't have anything hanging out or a water spot in an embarrassing place. "Come in."

"Good morning, Adriana. Long time no see."

"How're you doing, Dan—" I began, then I saw him in the mirror and broke down laughing. "What the hell are you wearing?"

"What?" he asked, slightly miffed. It wasn't that he didn't look handsome. He was debonair to a degree that few men could even hope to attain.

"Daniel, you look like you're about to go to work at a bank or in a law office," I said, turning to face him, crossing my arms, and leaning back against the sink. "Seriously, a slate gray suit with a tie?"

"Gray is better for daytime work," Daniel said simply, adjusting his tie, which was at least a tasteful purple. "I thought black or blue would be too dark for today."

I dropped my head and shook it back and forth, momentarily flummoxed. Daniel was the prototype for the perfect Bertoli man, but that didn't mean he was perfect for all times or situations. "Fine, for today only. But Daniel, you can't wear that if you plan on following me to all of my classes. Remember, I'm a college student, and an art student at that. You wear that monkey suit on campus, and you're going to stand out like a sore thumb."

He considered my words, then gave me a surly shrug. Even as kids, he'd hated being shown in error by anyone, especially me. "Fine. I wear this when I'm on duty, but I'll make an exception. What is it college students are wearing nowadays anyway?"

I gaped at him, then laughed. "Seriously? You dress in thousand-dollar suits all the time?"

"I don't mind a pair of jeans and a tank top on my day off, but when on duty, yes. There's no use putting fuzzy dice in the mirror of a Bentley," Daniel taunted, falling back into his old banter. "Especially when you've got the engine of a Ferrari like I do. Want a test drive?"

It was an old game between us, using supposedly innocent terms to banter back and forth sexually. It was fun most of the time, and I felt another smile coming on. It seemed that I needed the immature silliness. "If you even knew how to get that Ferrari out of the garage, I doubt you'd be able to do much more than first gear anyway. But seriously, what do you have for your non-work wear?"

Daniel thought, then brought his hand up to tick off his wardrobe. "I wear 5.11 for when I do my work at the range, Venum shorts for my martial arts practice, maybe some Under Armour sweats for colder days at the gym. You know, I work a lot—"

"Enough!" I laughed, glad he hadn't gone into his sock brands. "Just wear some jeans and a t-shirt, maybe a button-down."

Daniel shrugged dismissively. "I can do that."

"I'm sure you can," I said, trying not to laugh again, "and I doubt Uncle Carlo will mind. He's not the one who has to deal with any APEs."

"Apes?" Daniel asked, clearly perplexed. He held his hands up and shook his head. "Never mind, you can fill me in while we drive. So where am I supposed to go shopping for these button-downs? It's not really my style. I either go professional or as casual as it gets."

"How about Nordies, for one?" I asked. "You do know what Nordstrom's is, right?"

"Of course," Daniel replied with some defensive arrogance. I'd realized long ago that he was at his most sarcastic and verbally taunting when he felt threatened or insecure, although I didn't know what it was that caused him to act so around me more than other people. "It's where I like to get my dress shirts. They have some good labels there, ones the Don likes."

I rolled my eyes, knowing that regardless of what I said, there was nothing that would shake Daniel's devotion to my uncle. Daniel felt he owed his life to him and strove to be the best, most useful member of the organization possible. Considering he was only twenty-five, non-Italian, and being tasked with protecting me, I'd say he was doing a good job. "Come on, let's go."

"It's a little early, isn't it?" Daniel asked, checking his watch, which I noticed would have to go too. No college student—at least none on my campus—wore Bvlgari watches. "It's not even seven yet."

"Give me some time to get checked out, and then we can grab some McDonald's, or are you on a special diet too?"

"I try to eat healthy, but no, not really," Daniel casually said, as if men who looked like him ate fast food on a daily basis. "Let's go to an IHOP, though, if you want to eat like that. I can go to town on their pancakes."

Not even realizing it, I smiled and nodded. "No problem. Let's just get the doctor in here to get me checked out."

It actually took us until nearly eight, by which time I was starving, and as we left the hospital, I was actually looking forward to the day. We got into Daniel's BMW, and I had to remind myself that a lot of his taste was because of his desire to project the right image for Carlo. I wondered what the *real* Daniel Neiman would want, but then as I sat there, I realized it was probably *this* car. Gunmetal gray, it purred the whole time he drove, his eyes on the road and his hands at the ideal ten and two. Finally, after about two or three miles, I had to laugh. "Relax, Dan. You're not driving for the Indy 500, nor are your Jason Bourne skills necessary right now."

"Your uncle thought it was necessary, so I'd say my skills are more than needed right now," he replied tersely before cracking a cocky grin. "Well, most of my skills. You can't handle all of them."

"When you're done practicing with the girls and are ready for a woman, then I might give you a call," I shot back, laughing. That one had been too easy. He was out of practice. "Seriously, Dan. Thanks. It's good to see you. It's been a long time. When was the last time? Christmas?"

"Something like that," he said, relaxing a millimeter or so in his posture, but more so in his voice. I could start to hear the ghost of the guy I'd been friends with as a kid, the guy I actually liked. "Hey, there's IHOP up ahead, right next to the mall with the Nordstrom's. I have a feeling you're going to try to dress me up like an idiot, though."

"You're hardly an idiot. I could dress you like a Japanese boy band member, and you'd still look impressively heterosexual."

"Aura, Ade," he said, using the nickname we'd used among each other since we were kids, just as I was the only person who called him Dan—at least that I knew of. "Just can't help it."

We parked, and Daniel let me drag him inside the IHOP, where we both ate our fill. For his part, he was not so much tense as attentive, making sure we were seated in the area of the restaurant that gave him the best view of everyone both entering and exiting. When I tried to engage him in conversation, he was slightly distracted, his eyes constantly scanning the room and out the window while he forked his big stack of pancakes along with sausage and maple syrup, never looking down but amazingly never letting a single drop fall onto his suit. It was kind of like watching an android or something eat, and I was reminded again of the nickname one of the other Bertoli men had given him back when he was in high school. He was the Terminator.

Breakfast finished at about nine, and for the next three hours, until just before noon, I helped him with picking out and trying on different outfits, trying to find that right mix that said he was a college kid with enough cash to drive a late-model BMW, but not so stuck up that he looked like a douchebag. Of course, I got more than my fair share of eye candy too, and I was impressed when he came out in a printed t-shirt. "Jesus, Dan, you have any more veins in those biceps, and you're going to get kidnapped by the pre-meds to practice doing IVs on."

"Welcome to the gun show," he joked, giving me a small flex. "In more ways than one."

I saw the small bulge under the shirt on his right side, near his hip on the belt line. "Don't tell me . . . even inside the store?"

"I have my concealed carry permit," Daniel said with a chuckle. "After all, I'm a perfectly law-abiding citizen with no criminal record past two speeding tickets, one when I was a minor."

"Exactly how big is it?" I didn't realize until after the words were out of my mouth how deeply I'd stepped in it with the comment, but he let me go without too much of a retort.

Instead, he smirked and raised an eyebrow. "Wouldn't you like to know?"

While I waited for Daniel to get changed after paying—there was no way I was letting him continue wearing that hitman suit. There were enough rumors about the Bertoli name around campus as it was—I got a message on my phone from Uncle. The crime scene investigators had finished at the apartment and released it to me to get my things out. "Hey, Dan? Carlo just messaged me. He said that we can go by the apartment and get my things. Do you mind?"

He finished changing and came out, looking impressive in his jeans and polo. "Not at all. He told me that after getting your things, I was to help you move into a safe house, someplace that's in another name. I don't know where. I think he's having someone set it up right now."

"Then before we leave the mall, let's stop and get you a new watch," I said, noticing again the incongruity. "In fact, take that damn thing off and give it to me. I'll stash it in my bag."

"What's wrong with the watch?" Daniel said as he began to undo the leather band. At least he wasn't wearing one of those styles that came with gold metal bands. "Not college enough?"

"Not by a long shot," I said. "You're wearing a fifty-dollar pair of jeans, a thirty-dollar polo, hundred-dollar shoes, and a twelve-thousand-dollar watch. Which part of that strikes you as strange?"

"Fine, fine," he said, handing me the watch. "But if you scratch it, it's going on your bill. Come on."

Daniel turned to leave, and I just stared at him. "Excuse me?"

He turned back, lifting an eyebrow. "What?"

"The bags?" I asked, indicating the half-dozen bags we'd bought. "You know—put those muscles to work and all."

"My muscles work by making sure you're safe and protected," Daniel replied evenly. "Not by being your pack horse. Next time, don't buy so much crap, even if it's for me. It may not be chivalric, but you're going to have to carry your own damn bags."

It was a struggle, and I know that he could hear the muffled curses under my breath, but I knew he was right. We skipped the watch kiosk though, and I figured if Daniel really wanted to check the time, he could look at his phone like a lot of other people did. We went back to his BMW, filling most of the back seat with the bags, and I went around to the passenger seat, getting in. It was only then that Daniel relaxed enough to get in on his side, dropping into his low-slung bucket seat nearly silently. Closing the door, he looked at me.

"You're pissed off. I can tell. I'm sorry about that. I wish this were like when we were kids, but it isn't. I have a job to do, and even if you hate me every step of the way, I'm going to do it."

"Just drive," I said, rubbing at the lines in my palms left by the plastic handles of the bags. "Sure you have enough space for my stuff too?"

"I'll help you pack some suitcases," he said. "We'll get the clothes you need for the next week, and Don Carlo can send over someone else to clean out the rest."

We got to my apartment, and Daniel actually came around to open my door for me, not so much as a gentleman, but to tell me he thought the area was safe. We went to the door, which still had some little bits of crime scene tape stuck to the door jamb, which disturbed me but I felt prepared for.

Inside, though, my nervousness started to get the best of me, and I shuddered as I stayed behind Daniel, who'd produced his pistol from somewhere near his right hip and was sweeping it from left to right. We reached the living room and stopped. Daniel lowered the gun. "All right, where's your bedroom?"

"To the right," I said, pointing. The smell of blood still hung in the air, and I had to cover my nose and breathe only through my mouth to try and avoid getting sick. They may have finished with the investigation part, but the cleaners still hadn't been by—that was for sure. "Come on."

I hadn't gone into my bedroom the day before, and the sight that greeted us both when Daniel opened the door made me scream. Written on the walls in reddish black, the coppery smell confirming for me that it was most likely Angela's blood, was a message. It was song lyrics, and an immediate nauseous feeling came over me.

I fell back into the hallway, turning to run in a new panic when Daniel grabbed my arms and pulled me to him, holding me against his chest. I buried my face in his new shirt and shuddered, trying not to sob or scream. I didn't want to have to take any more drugs, even though it felt like my mind was breaking. "Wha . . . why weren't you told?"

"The cops probably didn't mention it, the idiots," Daniel said softly, his strong arms helping me feel safe and secure. "What was that message on the wall, anyway?"

"Genesis," I replied. "It's Vincent's favorite group. He subjected us to all sorts of that shit during the semester I was in his class. It's from a song called *Mama.* I fucking hated it even before he got creepy on me. In fact, Phil Collins is on my personal list of asses that I want to kick, just because of that damn class."

Daniel nodded then reached up, and with a hand that was both powerful and reassuring, stroked my hair. "Well, it's just some blood on the wall. I've dealt with that before, so tell you what. I'll go in there, get your suitcases, and pack the bags myself. As long as you don't mind me fooling around with your underwear."

His little joke didn't have the desired effect, and I pulled him closer to me, needing to feel strength and security for the moment. "Promise me something."

"What's that, Adriana?" he asked, his voice softer than I'd ever heard before. He sounded concerned, even tender.

"Promise me that you'll protect me from this psycho?"

He squeezed me tighter and hummed. "I promise, Adriana. I won't let him hurt you, no matter what. But, you're going to owe me for this. Big time."

His promise let me relax enough to hear his joke, and I slapped him in the chest, pushing him away. "Yeah right, Dan. Like I said, that Ferrari of yours isn't even getting out of the garage with me. Let alone to top speed."

He chuckled and nodded, holstering his pistol and stepping back. "We'll see, Adriana. We'll see. In the meantime, just remember that I'm going to know exactly what type of bras and panties you like."

"And if you're a good boy, maybe, just maybe, I'll let you fold them when you do the laundry for me. Now get going."

Chapter 4

Daniel

That evening at nine, after turning over Adriana's security to Julius Forze, I reported in to the Don. He raised an eyebrow when I walked into his house, setting aside his glass of Chianti. "Daniel, have you decided on casual Fridays or something?"

Realizing I hadn't changed clothes after leaving Adriana in her new apartment, I looked down, chagrined. "Sorry. Your niece felt that if I was to accompany her on campus, I had to blend in better with the average college student."

He looked me up and down, then chuckled. "Daniel, I doubt that regardless of how much you dress down, you'll look like the average college student. Men such as you and I, we've seen and done things that almost none of those bleating sheep can even begin to comprehend, and it shows in our faces and in the way we carry ourselves. We know the reality of life and of death. But if Bella wishes that you dress that way, I can only say to enjoy it. Please, have a seat and a glass of wine."

"Thank you, sir," I said, taking a seat in the leather chair. We were in the study, a richly decorated old-fashioned library, with oak paneling, deep leather chairs, and even a pool table in the corner, although I'd only been invited to play a game there once, one I'd intentionally lost. I poured myself a glass and took a measured sip. The Don values men who can appreciate a fine wine, but he appreciates men who don't get sloppy more. I quickly figured out exactly the right amount to drink and savored it for a few seconds before swallowing. "Fine vintage. New bottle?"

"Just imported from Castellina last week," the Don said. "Black Rooster."

"What can I do for you?" I asked, knowing there must be something.

He sat back, his chin seeming to disappear into his neck as he relaxed. It was a posture I'd seem him adopt countless times. If you were a confidant of his, he'd relax and slump into his chair when he was temporarily setting aside the distance between you and was inviting you to speak to him honestly, man to man. On the other hand, he also used the pose with strangers in order to let them underestimate him. I understood, as he wasn't the most physically imposing of men. Slumped like he was, a foolish stranger could easily mistake his nonchalance for lack of intelligence or strength, a mistake few had the opportunity to repeat.

In my case, at least, he was relaxing and letting me be more familiar with him. "You're going to have quite a challenge on your hands, Daniel. My niece, she's very willful."

"She is a strong woman," I agreed. "I believe that runs in the family."

He considered what I said, then chuckled. "Point taken, Daniel. Are you concerned that you'll have problems protecting her?"

"None. My only concern is that this Vincent Drake will be found quickly and brought to justice."

"I'm for the moment letting the police handle that side of things," Don Bertoli said sadly, "primarily because the other girl,

Angela—her parents are raising hell in the press. Her father is first generation from China, and he's the type who believes that the government is the solution to all our problems. Stupid man, but well intentioned."

"Would you like me to do some investigating? I'm sure I can be useful in that regard."

He shook his head, smiling. "Your entire life, you've always been an enigma, you know that? You came to my house when you were barely nine months old, and ever since you were out of diapers, you've been dedicated to learning whatever it is I ask of you."

"You could have abandoned me to the state orphanage," I replied, thinking back to my earliest memories. "You could have let me go to some foster home where I'd have grown up in a trailer park, or hacking it out in a Section 8 tenement. Or worse, I might have ended up adopted by some of the same people that you call fools. Instead, I was given a fine home and cared for. You made sure I was raised strong and well. I know we aren't blood, but you're the closest thing I have."

The Don smiled and reminisced for a moment. "You've comported yourself with honor and loyalty, more than anyone outside our line of work would understand. But now you have the most important task in your life. I'm counting on you, Daniel."

"I won't fail you, Boss."

"You never have."

After leaving Don Bertoli's house and returning to my apartment, I wasn't so sure. Keeping Adriana safe—that was nothing. I was sure that I could keep her safe from anything one man could throw at her. I'd probably even be able to keep her safe against a squad of professionals. I wasn't concerned with one fifty-three-year-old art teacher.

Instead, I thought as I got out of my shower and looked at myself in the mirror, the biggest threat to the successful completion of my mission was looking at me in the mirror. I was worried because when she was in my arms at her apartment, it had taken every bit of willpower I had to not think of all the dirty things I wanted to do to her. The way her breasts felt pressed against me, the fluttering of her heart, and the soft little voice she used when she asked me to protect her? I was surprised my cock didn't burst a seam on my jeans.

"Face it, No Man," I said, referring to my assumed last name as I talked to myself in the mirror. "You've wanted to fuck Adriana ever since you figured out what your dick was good for besides taking a piss with."

Adriana always had a special place in my mind, like the perfect template that all others were compared to, only to find them falling short. I'd never wanted any woman more than I wanted Adriana Bertoli.

Ten years later, standing in front of my own mirror naked, I shivered, both in desire and in fear. It had been at about that point that my typical banter with Adriana had taken on slightly sexual overtones, both of us becoming more brazen as she turned eighteen and finished up high school. Still, we both had that line that we were to never cross, even though I suspected that both of us wanted to.

Don Bertoli would never allow it. Adriana was his family, his blood. While I'd been loyal to him and served him well, and yes, loved him, I was an outsider, not even Italian. Besides, I wasn't the relationship type, and that's what she deserved. The rumors of me tagging the entire girl's volleyball team in my senior year were true. Come on, with those ass hugging shorts and all that jumping? Most of those girls were more than ready to put those ass muscles to work once they got a glimpse of what I was working with.

No girl ever got two nights, though, even after high school. It's probably what concerned Don Bertoli and was one of the main reasons I wasn't allowed to even think about being with Adriana. If I'd been the sort of guy who had a history of being loyal and dedicated to my woman, he *may* have considered it. He was a fair enough man. But a player who fucked and flew? No way.

Was it unfair? Sure. After all, the Don's two sons weren't any different. But men were allowed to be men, except for the man who was to be good enough for his Bella. That man would have to be perfect, a saint who was also a warrior. And sadly, I was no saint.

"Fuck it, just do your damn job and keep your dick in your pants," I said to my reflection. "Now get yourself to bed. You've got work tomorrow, remember?"

* * *

I was at Adriana's safe house the next morning at five forty-five, still wiping the sleep out of my eyes. I'd spent most of the past seven years since graduating high school working the night shift, and these early mornings were definitely not what my body was used to. Still, as I sucked down an energy drink, it could've been worse. After all, the Don had let me go early the night before, and I'd been able to get plenty of sleep, even if it was disturbed with dreams of Adriana.

"How'd the night go, Julius?"

Julius, an older man in his mid-thirties who'd been with Mr. Bertoli since I was in elementary school, stretched his arms over his head and groaned. "Not too bad. She had a few bad dreams, but I guess you'd expect that considering what she saw. I had more than a few myself after my first death scene."

"Since we caused our first death scenes, I think it's a little different," I replied with a slightly regretful sigh. "Is she still asleep?"

Julius nodded. "Yeah, she told me before she closed her door that she'd set her alarm for six thirty. She wants to be out of this place by seven thirty. Something about first class of the day, and this place being farther from campus than her old place. Hell if I know."

I wasn't surprised, considering that Julius was a high school dropout whose grandest idea of higher education was truck driving school. He was good in a fight, but pretty much dumb as a rock. Still, he was a good soldier and did his job well. "Okay. You had any breakfast?"

Julius shook his head. "Nope, I was thinking of grabbing some drive-through on the way back to my place. I know my old lady ain't left nothin' for me—never does."

Julius's wife was a former Bertoli whore who'd found herself unable to overcome the binge eating that came from her childhood history of growing up starving. Growing up on the wrong side of Seattle, where the time between meals sometimes counted in days rather than hours, did that to you.

On the other hand, she was a lot smarter than Julius, and

had at least gotten an associate's degree. She worked for the Don as an office assistant in his import/export business that operated out of SEATAC. "All right then, man, tell you what. Let me put together a little breakfast for the three of us, if you want to hang around an extra fifteen minutes."

"And save me ten bucks? You throw in some coffee, and it's a deal," Julius replied. He was even more of a skinflint that I was. "What're you making?"

"Let me look," I said, opening the fridge. I'd picked up some basic groceries with Adriana the afternoon before, so I was a little disappointed to find the cooling remains of a Papa John's box inside. "Yours or hers?"

"Mine," Julius said. "I was jonesing about eleven or so. Don't worry, the order was in my name and this place is in another. And I paid cash."

"Still," I said, wondering if I should say anything about it to the Don. I decided against it. Julius was normally a reliable man, and everyone gets the occasional urge for sausage pizza. "Well, on the good side, at least that means most of the stuff I bought yesterday is still here. Do you like spinach?"

"My mother used to make me eat that stuff three times a week—said it'd make me strong. Don't know if it worked or not, but I hate the shit now."

"All right then," I said, setting the baby spinach back inside. "Guess we'll go with an omelet."

I made one of my go-to breakfasts, a three egg white, one whole egg omelet with ham and cheese, cutting it into three pieces when I was finished before whipping out another one, knowing how much I tended to eat.

I heard the door to the back open, and Adriana poked her head out, her red hair tousled and her eyes still bleary. She looked adorable, and I had to remind myself to pay attention to my tea before I poured some on my hand. "Is that an omelet with cheese that I smell?"

"Yeah, you ready to join us?"

"Give me two minutes," she said, giving me a grateful smile that I appreciated more than I should have. "Thanks, and good morning."

"Good morning, Adriana."

Julius looked from me to her, then back at me as Adriana ducked her head back into her room and closed the door. "I've watched you two from time to time. Why didn't you two ever get together?"

I gave Julius a sideways glance and shook my head. Loyal, but dumb. Picking up the pan with the omelet, I started to plate. "You know exactly why. If it's all the same to you, I'd like my head to remain acquainted with my neck for as long as possible. If I mess around with Adriana, the odds of that become about the same as the Mariners winning the World Series this year."

"Gotcha, man. You're right. Well, if you don't mind, I'm gonna eat now and hit the road." Julius ate his breakfast in about five big, gulping bites, looking kind of like a shark swallowing a fish, but at least he rinsed the plate and dropped all his stuff in the dishwasher before wiping his mouth. "Take care, Daniel."

"Thanks, Julius. See you tonight."

He left just as Adriana opened her door and came out, dressed in jeans similar to the ones I'd chosen and a printed t-shirt that had a silk screening of Mt. St. Helens on it with the caption,

Look out, she's gonna blow! underneath it. I wondered if Adriana grasped the double meaning of a woman wearing such a shirt, then decided she knew exactly what she was doing. Rolling my eyes, I set her plate on the table. "Here you are. Coffee, tea, or orange juice?"

"OJ if it's still in there," she said, giving me another somewhat shy but enticing smile. "I didn't know you were a chef. This smells delicious."

I turned, trying to hide my reddening cheeks. "There are all sorts of skills of mine you don't know about. Maybe you'll get to see more of them."

"You show me yours, I show you mine," she teased back. "In another lifetime. Maybe when I'm desperate."

Chapter 5

Adriana

I'd like to say that I was able to throw myself back into my studies without any problems. I'd like to say that I was supported by everyone, who took me having an escort and bodyguard in tow with no problems. I'd like to say that the next week was productive and helpful, and that I was enjoying being an upperclassman in college.

I'd like to say all those things, but I can't. Instead, my first day back on campus ended within an hour of my arrival, with me jumping at nearly every snapped shut book or glittering object that came into my line of sight. Considering that I was walking around the arts building of a major university, that was a lot of books.

Finally, after my first two classes, I couldn't take it anymore. Both of the professors had given me the hairy eyeball when Daniel came in, to the point that I had to threaten to call the campus registrar about it with my photography professor. The other students stared, with more than a few whispered comments and understated conversations that I knew were about the murder, jacking up my stress levels even more. The final straw came when a door slammed, and I jumped nearly a foot in the air with a small scream in my throat before Daniel had me, holding me in one arm while his eyes constantly scanned the hallway around us. "Come on," he said, talking softly in my ear and walking me along.

We ended up going all the way out of Seattle and south a

little bit, stopping along the coastline at a random resort town and picking out a cafe. "You looked like you could use the break," Daniel said when he got on the Interstate. "There was no way you were getting any more learning done today, not with the way you're looking."

"Thanks, I guess," I said simply, resting my head against the headrest of my seat and letting him drive. I dozed off until we got off the Interstate and was charmed by his choice of where to take me. "Where'd you find this place?"

"I've never been here before, and I bet neither have you," he said. "You know the coastline is filled with little spots like this—there's gotta be a cake and coffee shop somewhere along here. It's something I learned in the past few years. If you really want to disappear, just do something you've never done before. You'd be surprised at how most people are just creatures of habit."

The shop was actually not all that great, with easily identifiable store-bought cake and coffee that looked and tasted like it had been found in a glass jar along with its freeze-dried cousins five minutes before we ordered it, but it was exactly what I needed. We sat on the back porch of the cafe, listening to the sound of the ocean in the distance. The sun was warm, and I felt myself relax as I sipped at the mug. "Thanks again, Daniel. How'd you know this would help me?"

"Part of what makes me good at what I do is judging people. See who would be worth giving a little bit of slack to, and who needs the stick. And of course, other things," he said evasively. I understood though. I knew what Daniel was and what he'd done. There was blood on his hands for sure.

"Can I ask you some questions about what you do for my

Uncle?" I asked. It wasn't that I was ignorant, but everyone liked to keep me at an arm's distance from the criminal side of the family. Despite Carlo's utter disregard for the law and those who enforced it, he knew that he led a life that ended with a high chance of death by violence. After what happened to my father, he didn't want that for me.

"I'll tell you, but not here," Daniel said simply, taking a forkful of his slice of cake.

I nodded, realizing it was probably a stupid question to ask in public.

We finished up and left our plates along with a fifty cent tip on them in order to hold down the napkins in the coastal breeze, driving the two blocks to the beach. Summer vacation was over, so it wasn't too crowded, and walking along the sand, we found a spot after ten minutes or so that was relatively isolated. "Here's fine," Daniel said, sitting down. "What is it that you want to know?"

"What exactly is your *duty* for my Uncle?" I had an idea, but I wanted to hear it rather than just assume.

"Any and everything he wants me to do," Daniel said simply. "Are you trying to ask if I've done hits for the Don?"

"Actually, I wanted to know how much you've done, or how many," I replied. "I figured by this point, you'd have messed at least a few people up."

"I have," he said, no guilt at all in his voice. Instead, he talked about it like any other sort of professional with a slightly distasteful job would talk about their work. "And more. I haven't kept count, but I've intentionally done four so far."

"So far?" I asked, shocked. "You're planning on having to

kill more?"

"If I'm asked to. I owe him my life, Adriana. And I will say, all four were not the sort of people who were worth much in terms of being noble members of society. All were people who deserved what they got, in my opinion. Don't take me wrong, Adriana. The Don is a ruthless, cold-blooded man when it comes to business. He's not a man to trifle with. But he's also a man of honor, and he will make sure that only those who are guilty of great crimes get a visit by men like me when our guns are hot. Even when he had me visit the motorcycle club up north a few weeks ago, it was only to intimidate, not to kill. The shots fired were because they decided to get aggressive when I'd only come to pass on a fair warning."

I turned and watched the ocean and the waves come in. Maybe it was low tide, or maybe the waves on that part of the coast weren't all that large, but it was calming, and I reflected on it. The more I did, the more I realized it didn't matter to me. I still loved Uncle Carlo, and despite his put upon arrogance, I liked Daniel too, blood on their hands or not. I only had one more question. "How far would you go to protect me?"

"I'd give up my life for you," he said immediately, with an undertone in his voice that left me wondering if he was saying that because of his sense of honor to my uncle or something else. "But I won't have to—not from a fifty-year-old professor."

I leaned against him, at ease. "All right then. Let's go back, and we can focus on getting me back to class. I can't exactly keep skipping out on it. Some of those teachers don't give a damn what happens in your life. An absence is an absence, and if you pick up enough of them, you fail the class."

Daniel grunted softly and jokingly elbowed me in the ribs. "Just give me their names, and I can pay them a visit."

I got up and dusted the sand off my shorts. "That's not necessary, but thanks."

* * *

For the next week, I slowly worked my way back into things. Daniel was with me every day, from sunup until nine at night, when another one of Carlo's men would take over, staying awake in the living room while I slept. Still, Daniel's presence was comforting. Saturday, he escorted me to Carlo's house, where I had a family dinner together with my mom.

"So how has your return to your studies gone?" Mom asked. She'd been out of town in New Jersey but was back now, and we'd spent hours just talking. It was nice to catch up with my mother, since we'd only had the chance to exchange quick phone calls in the time after the attack.

"The first day was rough, but by Thursday, I was able to get back to work decently enough. It helps to have Daniel there." I took another bite of my lasagna and reminded myself to use the house gym afterward. Mom could afford to eat spaghetti or lasagna every day. She's a widow with a grown daughter and no interest in remarrying. She hadn't blown up or anything, but she wasn't a size eight anymore either. I was a single college student who enjoyed maintaining her figure and didn't have the genetics of an Ashley Graham to be size fourteen with the weight in all the right places. "And before you ask, Mom, Daniel's been a perfect gentleman."

"Really? I was worried he'd have his eyes on you too much to focus on anyone else," Mom said. "But Carlo did vouch for him

. . ."

"When it's about business, he's as serious as it gets. He's a good man, like Uncle Carlo said."

"I'll mention it to him when he gets back into town. But still, like all good men, they are often nothing more than beasts under their skin. Be careful."

I nodded, if only to get her off the subject. We finished our dinner and I went upstairs to my old room. It was exactly as it had been the last time I stayed overnight. I found an old t-shirt and shorts and pulled them on, a little bit of nostalgia sweeping over me. Angela had gotten me the t-shirt, and I had to wipe away a tear as I thought about her. She'd been a good friend.

I went down to the house gym, which was somewhat of an anomaly and a carryover from my father's days. Uncle Carlo wasn't the athletic type, having decided early on that he didn't need to focus on what were, in his opinion, shallow pursuits. My father, on the other hand, had been the athlete of the two brothers and felt that physical fitness was important for both him and his men. So, the house had a complete fitness center, even if it was a bit dated. None of the main equipment was newer than twenty-five years old, two years before I'd been born. Still, Mom and Uncle Carlo kept it in pristine shape, and everything was in as good a condition as it had been twenty-five years ago.

Going in, I was shocked to find that I wasn't the only person to have the same idea, as Daniel was in the room already, wearing a pair of compression shorts and his undershirt. "Sorry, didn't mean to interrupt."

"It's your house more than mine," Daniel said with a shrug, turning his back to me and going over to the squat rack. "I just wanted to get a workout in while it was still a decent hour today. Forgive the outfit. I forgot to pack a bag and only had this in the trunk of my car."

"When have you been working out this past week?" I asked, knowing that as dedicated as Daniel was, he wasn't skipping his fitness just because he was babysitting me. "You look even more ripped than you were a week ago."

Daniel un-racked his bar, holding it in front of him before lowering himself down until his butt was nearly on his heels before exploding up, pushing the bar over his head at the end and locking it out before slowly lowering it and repeating the process. He didn't say anything during his work, but turned around when he was finished. "I have a membership to a twenty-four-hour gym," he explained. "It's my first stop after I leave your apartment. I go usually about five times a week and have a short routine that I can get done in forty minutes."

Impressed, I went over to the stretch mats on the side of the room and began my limbering up routine. I felt my eyes constantly pulled back toward Daniel, whose muscles rippled and flexed underneath his clothing. His tight compression shorts were enticing, as whether he knew it or not, he sported a bubble butt that would leave most women envious. It was all muscle, and I knew if I saw him nude I could probably see each individual muscle fiber at work each time he exploded up from his squatting position. The artist in me was amazed and intrigued and wondered if I had the skill to recreate such physical perfection in paint.

But the woman in me had much baser interests. I felt the heat first in the pit of my belly, a feeling that I hadn't felt in a long time, before spreading up and down my body until my eyes were nearly locked on Daniel's body. When he finished his work with the bar and went to take off the plates, I couldn't help but gasp when he turned sideways and the bulge in the front of his shorts became more noticeable. He was hung like a horse!

He must've noticed me staring, because he turned his eyes back to me, concern in his eyes. "Are you okay?"

I quickly wrenched my eyes from his crotch to his face, feeling the hot rush of blood to my face and certain that my nipples were imprinted on the thin cotton of my t-shirt. "I'm fine," I said, playing it off. "Just a little twinge. Guess I need to stretch out more often."

He dismissed it and finished his work. He went on to his next exercise, and I climbed off the stretch mat to get on the VersaClimber. At least that was what the sticker on the center post of the machine called it, but in my private moments, I called it the Stairway to Hell. Working both your arms and your legs at the same time like some sort of unending ladder, the machine is one of the hardest cardiovascular machines I've ever seen, and in fewer than five minutes, I was already sucking air. At fifteen minutes, I was gasping to the point that I could feel the blood pulse in my temples.

But the intensity of the machine wasn't why I chose it, I realized as I stepped down and wiped my sweating face. I'd chosen it because it allowed me to watch Daniel. I'd used the same bench—someone had once told me it was called a glute ham raise—to work my lower back and butt, but Daniel took it to the next level. Putting the pad closer to his knees than I did, he started with his head hanging down nearly all the way to the floor before he lifted himself in an arc, curling his knees at the top so that he ended up nearly vertical, then lowered himself at an agonizing slowness before repeating it again.

"You're working your butt and hamstrings today, aren't you?"

Daniel grunted his assent as he reached the top of his movement and nodded his head. "And quads. Leg strength is vital to running and fighting."

Of course. If it wasn't enough that he was built like a god, he was interested only in his ability to use his body in his duties, and maybe secondarily in his ability to seduce women. He wasn't trying to look the way he did. He just wanted to be more lethal in his work. That he was making me hotter than I'd been in years was beside the point.

I messed around with some of the equipment while he focused on his work, not really working all that hard but just getting a decent little workout while my eyes got to take in the display of human physical perfection in front of me. By the end of his last set, his shirt was soaked and his blond hair was a shade darker from sweat that ran down his skin in diamond rivulets, and I could feel that my panties were soaked, but not from sweat.

"I'm going to get changed," I said, getting up shakily from the leg extension machine I'd been on and wiping my forehead. "Do you think you can pick me up tomorrow at about eleven to go to Angela's grave?"

"That's fine," Daniel replied, wiping his own forehead. "I asked your mother, and she told me I could stay in a guest room tonight anyway. If you need me for anything, I'll be close by."

"Okay. Thanks. See you later, Daniel."

"Buona sera, Adriana."

I laughed and turned at the door, giving him a grin. "Twenty-five years in this house, and your Italian still absolutely sucks. You sound like you're hacking at the syllables with a machete."

He grinned back and ran his hand through his hair. "It's what you get when your tutors are a bunch of third-generation guidos. Besides, I'm much, much better with my French technique, if you ever want to find out."

I laughed and left the gym, forcing myself down the hallway because there was nothing more my body wanted to do than to turn around and find out exactly how good he was. I hoped that my desire would ease with distance, but instead, I was still overheated when I got back to my old room and fell into the soft mattress, groaning in frustration. "Fuck it. Time for a cold shower."

* * *

The next morning, precisely at eleven, I found Daniel waiting for me in the foyer, dressed not in the casual clothes he'd worn the last week for me, but instead in a black, somber suit, looking for all the world like a Secret Service agent. I'd also dressed for the trip, wearing a black dress that I'd always kept ready, knowing the sort of lifestyle my family had. Mob daughters have to go to funerals too often, in my opinion.

"Ready?" Daniel asked, standing up and buttoning his coat. I looked and was touched that next to him were a dozen roses in a basket, mixed white and red, ready for me. "I asked the gardening staff to pick out the best."

"Thank you," I said, my throat tight with emotion. He might have most of the time alternated in his personality between that of the Terminator or a cocky Lothario, but I too often forgot that he actually did have a tender, observant side to him. "They're beautiful, and I know Angela would have liked them. Come on. I'd like to save my tears for the graveside, if you don't mind."

Daniel drove me in his BMW, back in his silent mode but slightly more comforting than he'd been earlier in the week. When we got out, the bright sunlight dazzled me, and he silently offered me a pair of Ray-Bans from his inner coat pocket. I put them on and walked with him to the grave site.

It wasn't that hard to find. The dirt was still freshly turned and the Astroturf that had been laid on top screamed out against the dark, rich green of the surrounding grass. I had to resist the urge to reach down and tear the plastic off, at least tearing away the lie that under the turf wasn't just a pile of dirt but the body of my best friend.

"I hate the turf," Daniel said quietly, his hands crossed in front of him. "I remember that from Bucky Francetti's funeral last year. They'd lined the edges of the hole with it, and it looked to me like they were making a mockery of him with it."

"Some people are comforted by it, I guess," I said, kneeling and laying the flowers on top of the small mound. "Twenty-three years. She was too young and too good to end up like this."

"I didn't know her, but I saw her once when you brought her by the Don's house," Dan said softly. "She did seem like a good person. I'm sure you're right."

"I've spent the past week wishing that I'd gone to Uncle Carlo before that day, saying I needed help and protection. I was scared out of my mind, but putting on a front for everyone. If I had and you were there . . ."

"You can't beat yourself up about it, Ade. Besides, even if the Don had assigned me a week earlier or two weeks earlier, or whatever, it wouldn't have stopped what happened to her. My duty would be to keep you safe and protected, and I would've been with you, not back at the apartment with her."

I turned and stepped closer to Daniel, reaching up and putting my hand on his shoulder. "You have kept me safe, and I thank you. For the past week, I've felt more secure and safer than I have in months. Maybe in my entire life."

His hand came to rest on my hip, and we came closer until my body pressed against him. His lips lowered toward mine, and I tilted my head, wanting at that moment for nothing more than to feel his kiss. I could tell in his eyes that he wanted it too, when suddenly, he pushed me away, taking a step back. I nearly fell on my ass as I stepped back, the heel of my shoe catching on the edge of the Astroturf blanket on top of Angela's grave. "What the fuck?"

"We can't," Daniel said, stepping back again. He turned and scanned the area, his head moving like a radar dish. "For both of our sakes—we can't."

"What the hell are you talking about? Don't tell me that you don't want me," I hissed, stepping around to look him in the eye. "I saw it in your eyes just now, and I've seen it in your eyes before. Tell me you don't want me!"

"Of course I do," Daniel said, his eyes flickering with desperation and anger and something else. "But I can't, Adriana. Like I said, for both our sakes."

"What do you mean?" I asked softly, my anger fading as I saw the emotion in his icy blue eyes.

"It can never be just the two of us, Ade," Dan said, a tinge of sadness in his voice. "First—and I'm not bragging—I'd ruin you for other men. I've made that mistake in the past, and while I'm more than willing to fuck some skank and leave her wanting me for years afterward, you're better than that. I won't ruin your life, because no other man is going to compare to me."

"So why does there ever have to be anyone else?" I asked, putting my hand on his chest. "You and I, we've been eyeing each other for a long time. I think I can make my own decision about whether you're the type of man I want."

"You know nothing!" Daniel hissed, pushing my hand down. Seeing the hurt in my eyes, his face softened, filled now with more hurt, and for the first time in his life, fear. "If I ever touch you, if I ever do what I want to do, I'm a dead man. Don Bertoli has promised me that much. And I'm also worried about something more."

"What?"

"I'm worried that you're a dead woman as well," Daniel said softly. "I can face my own death, Ade. I've never had a life of my own, except what Carlo Bertoli has gifted me with. But I won't see you dead. I . . . I care about you too much for that."

Daniel blinked and reached into his coat pocket, pulling out another set of sunglasses, this time mirrored aviators. He slipped them on, obliterating my view of his blue eyes, and his face seemed to lose all traces of emotion, once again the perfect Terminator. "I'll wait a few rows away until you're done saying your farewells to Angela."

Chanter 6

Daniel

The next day, Monday night, after dropping off Adriana, I was back at the Starlight Club, wearing one of my suits. I was desperate and needed to do something to get my mind right.

Never, in the close to ten years that I'd been doing work for Don Bertoli, had I drifted so close to disobeying an order from him. And the rule I'd nearly broken wasn't some minor little thing like wearing the wrong type of tie or being a little short on a pickup from one of the businesses under his protection. Screw up like that, and you'd get a few words, and maybe be punished with making it up out of your own pocket. For someone with my rank within the Don's organization, I'd get a frown at most and be tasked with going back out to make sure things were rectified as soon as possible.

But what I almost did would be like breaking one of the Ten Commandments, a sin that could never be atoned for. Every man in Don Bertoli's organization, from the lowest lackey to even Pietro Columbu, his second in command, had been taken aside by the Don and told in no uncertain terms from the time she was eleven years old and started puberty—Adriana was not to be touched.

And the day before, I'd nearly lost it. Her lips had been so close, her green eyes so filled with soft desire, her generous curves so perfect pressed against me. I'd nearly damned us both. It had taken every ounce of my willpower to push her away and step back, and I'd tried the night before to get rid of my weakness by myself, jacking off until my cock ached and I felt like a guilty teenager again. It hadn't helped, and the next day, my desire had returned in full strength, fueled even more by the outfit she'd worn, her legs amazing in those tiny little shorts. I couldn't trust myself, being constantly distracted, and I knew I acted like a total asshole, barely talking at all through most of the day until we were both relieved when Julius showed up again, right on time to do his night shift.

So I found myself at the Starlight Club, one of my suits on like a suit of armor more than a layer of blended wool. If I couldn't be the man who could resist Adriana, then come hell or high water, I could remember that I was a Bertoli man, one of the best fucking Bertoli men there was. And Bertoli men were allowed—in fact, sometimes even encouraged—to do what I was about to do. I looked up at the sign and figured it was worth a try.

The Starlight Club was pretty quiet, but it was a Monday night, and there were only perhaps a dozen patrons inside, their sweaty faces looking slack and simian under the dim lights.

"Welcome, sir," the manager said, coming out from behind the bar to shake my hand. We'd known each other for a while, since I was the man most often tasked with the pickups at the club. The manager always had his payment on time and ready to go in a simple white envelope, and we'd enjoyed a couple of conversations in the spare time I had. "Business or pleasure?"

"Both," I said, distracted. When he gave me a concerned look, I waved it off. His cash was secure for tonight. "Not that type of business. Tell me, is there a girl named Carmen working tonight?"

"Yeah, she's scheduled for a dance in five," the manager said, relaxing. This sort of business he had no problems discussing. "She said you looked interested last time you were here."

"I am," I said, reaching into my coat and taking out two hundred-dollar bills folded together. I held them out, raising an eyebrow. "Think you might be able to reschedule the dance, let me have some private time with her?"

"What type of private time?" he asked while still making the money disappear. While ninety-nine percent of the customers probably suspected it, only the select few like me were permitted access to the other services the Starlight Club offered. "Carmen's one of my best. She's pretty pricey. She's selective as to who she gives private time to."

"I bet," I said, reaching back inside and showing the wad of cash I had with me. Bertoli rewarded his men handsomely, and I lived a frugal lifestyle. "Tell her if she's worth it, she's not going to need to dance for a month afterward if she wants."

"And what do I get? Sorry, business and all."

I raised an eyebrow at him, and he quavered a bit. He knew what I could do, and he'd be lucky that I didn't just destroy the entire club. I unbuttoned my coat, showing him the Beretta in a holster under my left arm, then reached into the pocket next to it and pulled out another hundred-dollar bill. "That's three, plus a bonus for you personally if Carmen's worth my time and money. Good enough?"

"Yes, sir," the manager stammered, stepping back. He reacquired his smile quickly though, and swept his arm to his left. "If you'll just follow me, I'll make sure you're comfortable before getting Carmen."

I shook my head, pushing past him. "I know where to go. Get Carmen and send up some bottle service. The good stuff, none of that fake label shit you pass off on the mooks."

I went into the VIP room and hung up my jacket, sitting on the reclining couch. I'd had my choice of places to go. Don Bertoli controlled most of the places like this in the Seattle-Tacoma area, but I didn't need whips, chains, or anything kinky. Not that I had anything against it, but my cock was more than enough for the women I dealt with.

Carmen was quick, coming in like a little pixie in her green silk robe and no heels. She was tiny, maybe five feet tall if you were being generous, with long, thick black hair and large doe eyes that I bet made most men think she was performing just for them when she was on stage or in a private dance. Her blindingly white teeth were perfectly even, and I wondered how a girl so pretty wasn't trying to make a living doing something else. But hell, I'm the last man who should judge anyone. Besides, I didn't know her or her circumstances.

"Hey, Papi," Carmen said, sauntering her way across the room and sitting next to me, placing a hand on my thigh where it lay light and warm, enticing. "When Terry came in and said you were out here, I was so excited I had to get here as quick as I could. I hope you don't mind that I forgot my heels."

I knew she was lying—it was part of her appeal, I was sure. On stage, the high heels added to the act, but in private, she could be the naughty young girl much more easily. "I bet. So I guess you've been thinking about me?"

"You have no idea," she said, turning more toward me and

rubbing her tiny little hand over my chest through my shirt. "I haven't been able to keep you out of my mind all week. In fact, I've done some naughty things while thinking about you."

I chuckled, trying to relax into the lying fantasy. With some of the women I'd been with, lies were necessary, and I certainly didn't want to know the truth in a lot of cases anyway. "So how about after the bottles get here, you and I talk about those naughty things some more?"

Carmen pouted, and I had to admit she could pull off the hurt, innocent look very well. "I'd like to show you if you'd let me."

I nodded and reached for the knot on her robe. "Perfect. But I have to warn you, Carmen. I'm not an easy man to please."

She let me undo the bow, leaving her robe held closed just by the simple crossing of her belt, a bit more of her cleavage becoming visible in the extra slack. "I know all about you. Two of the girls in the back tonight are hatin' on me right now. You're a legend, both for your generosity and your . . ."

The bottles arrived, and while it wasn't Dom Perignon, it wasn't cheap trash either. I let her pop the first cork and pour us both a glass, trying to grin as she let a little bit 'accidentally' splash on her robe, the thin fabric sticking to her skin. "Oops."

I waved it off and took a fifty-dollar bill out of my shirt pocket, where I'd transferred my stash for the night. "Here, you might need to have that dry cleaned."

"Mmm, you're generous. The girls said you'll ruin me, but as generous as you are, I may just have to risk it. You mind if I dance some for you?"

"Of course not," I said, gesturing with my glass toward the

tiny little dance area in the middle of the room. "But start with the robe on. It looks sexy on you."

She smiled at my compliment as she walked out, her ass swishing from side to side as she did. She went over to the sound system and punched in a song. The room's soundproofing took care of eliminating the crappy pop and bass-heavy hip-hop the main room had and replaced it with smooth, sexy Spanish-influenced cool jazz. I was surprised. "Not what I expected, but nice."

"The average jackass out there can't appreciate the finer things like you do," Carmen said, letting her body sway side to side as the music filled the room. She danced well, letting her clothes come off at a slow enough pace that she wasn't just peeling them off to get down to business.

Still, the whole time she danced, my eyes were glued more to the green of her robe than the ripe swell of her breasts, and to the red of her lipstick. The green was so much like Adriana's eyes, the lipstick so much like her hair. My cock twitched, starting to swell in my pants, but not because of the hot girl in front of me. *Shit.*

I blinked my eyes, throwing back the rest of my glass and grabbing the bottle by the neck, sucking deep from the green glass. Carmen smiled, a naughty angel smile as she saw my reaction, thinking it was because of her dance and her seduction skills. Bringing herself closer, she pulled off her bra, leaving her in a tissue paper-thick G-string and some little rhinestones that she'd attached around her right eye with spirit gum for decoration. "Mmm, I can't resist anymore," she said, climbing into my lap and grinding on my lap. "Isn't this where we were last time before we got so sadly interrupted?"

"Someplace like that," I said, reaching around and grabbing a handful of her ass in a last desperate attempt to put my focus on where it needed it to be, and not on the Italian-Scotch woman who was in the forefront of my mind. "Much better music, though."

"One thing," Carmen said, lifting her breast to my mouth. I sucked, letting my tongue flicker over her coffee-colored nipple, which hardened almost immediately in my mouth, and she threw her head back, moaning. "Oh shiiiit . . . but the rules."

"And the rules are?" I asked, letting go. My cock was hard, but I just wasn't into it, and the break in the flow wasn't helping. I'd hoped to let my instincts take over. After all, pussy is pussy. But her words irritated me.

She noticed and gave me her best attempt at a heart-stopping smile. "Nothing bad, Papi. Just we have to have protection. Do you have your own, or should I get some from my robe?"

"Of course. I have my own," I said, not minding the *rule*. I may have been with a few women, but I wasn't stupid. I always used protection. "That's fine. And nothing kinky. Not tonight."

"Mmm, you're too good to be true," Carmen said, rubbing back and forth. She kissed my nose, then around to my neck, licking and sucking while she dry-humped me.

I closed my eyes, trying to lose myself in the feeling of this spicy little sexual nymphet on my lap, but I couldn't get Adriana's face out of my mind. Groaning, I threw my head back, pushing Carmen away. "This just isn't going to work. Get off."

"But, why?" she whined, still climbing off. She knelt in

front of me, reaching out and cupping my cock through my pants. "Your big friend here says he wants me, and he's bigger than I've ever had. Please, Papi? You've got me so hot. I need it. A real man, for once in my life."

Carmen lowered her eyes and leaned forward, kissing the crotch of my pants. She was moaning, and I could tell she was serious about it. She would have fucked me even for no money by that point, but I couldn't. For the first time in my life, I had a willing, desperate woman there, ready for me to fuck her, and I couldn't do it. "No, Carmen. Go away."

"Come on, I need you," she said, reaching for my belt. Her hand froze and her eyes jerked up when she heard the click of the hammer on my Beretta.

"I said go, Carmen," I said evenly, with no inflection in my voice. It was my enforcer voice, the one that made men a lot more hardened than Carmen piss their pants in terror. The barrel pointed between her eyes, an inch from her forehead, probably looking like a cannon from her perspective. "Get the fuck out."

She whined in fear as she scooted back and ran from the room, not screaming but clearly scared out of her mind. I stared at the fucking gun in my hand and shuddered, lowering the hammer carefully before putting it on safe and placing it back in my holster. Had I really just done that? I must've been fucking losing it.

I grabbed my coat and put it on, not caring about if my tie was screwed up or not. Walking out, the manager looked at me with fear in his eyes, and I knew Carmen had told him what just happened. "For your troubles," I said, pulling out the rest of the bills I'd brought and handing them to him. "Tell Carmen . . . tell her I'm sorry."

His fingers shook as he took the pile from me, and he didn't even count it as he tucked it in his shirt. "Yes, sir," he stammered. "But sir—"

"You take five hundred for the trouble and half a bottle drunk, and give her the rest. Fair enough?"

He nodded, his eyes still wide in fear, and I left the club, stalking out into the night. I climbed into my BMW and started the engine, leaving twenty feet of black rubber on the pavement as I peeled out of the parking lot.

What the fuck had I been thinking? Pulling my pistol just because a girl wanted to suck my cock? The worst part was, I was ready to pull the trigger. All because it was Carmen who was on her knees and not who I needed. Fuck, it wasn't even that I *wanted* her anymore. I *needed* her. I needed Adriana.

And I couldn't tell Don Bertoli. If I went to him and told him that I couldn't continue to protect his niece because I wanted to fuck her more than anything else in the world, I wouldn't even be able to get the sentence all the way out of my mouth before my corpse hit the floor. I couldn't quit.

"You're in deep shit," I whispered to my reflection in the rearview mirror as I drove. "Deep shit indeed."

Chapter 7

Adriana

I was excited to be waiting in the parking circle of the house Wednesday when the long, black Cadillac pulled into the driveway and Uncle Carlo's driver got out, going around to the back and opening the door for him. Carlo had been out of town for nearly a week, soon after assigning Daniel to be my bodyguard, and I was glad to see him. "Uncle Carlo!"

"Bella!" he replied, letting me give him a big hug. "How is my little one?"

"Class today was a total bitch, but that's all over now," I said, smiling. He laughed and wiped at my hair with a chuckle.

"I can see that. Are you choosing to color parts of your hair green now, or is that just the result of your hard work?" he asked. He reached into the back of the Caddy and pulled out his personal bag, a habit he'd always had. The driver and staff might be permitted to handle his suitcases, but Carlo always kept certain personal effects in a tan leather bag that he carried with him nearly everywhere outside the house. "By the way, I got you something."

"Really? Cool!" I replied, immediately transported back to my teenage years. "What?"

"Well, a friend of mine knows of your appreciation for fine art, so he sent this along with me," he said, taking out a metal tube about two inches wide and just over a foot long. "He said this was the best way to transport them for you."

I popped the cap on the canister and carefully took out the lithographs, amazed by the photographic images. The first was a black and white photo of a mostly nude woman with her arms around her knees, hiding her body and looking at the camera with such pain in her eyes it was hard not to want to reach out and comfort her. The second was the same woman, this time from the collarbones up, her face turned to the sky and wearing such an expression of joy that you knew she was having the best moment of her life. "This is amazing."

"If you look on the back, all of them are signed by the artist," Carlo said. "I thought you'd appreciate that."

"I do. Thank you, Uncle," I said, not pausing to look through the rest of the images at the moment. "So you're back in town for a while?"

"I have nothing for at least the rest of the month," he replied. "But the first thing I want to do before I go into the office tomorrow and find out that the clerks have robbed me blind and left me penniless, is to have dinner with my favorite niece. Tell me you can spare the time tonight."

"Of course," I said, laughing. "I was planning on staying the night here in the mansion, actually. The apartment's nice and all, but it doesn't have the aura of family, you know?"

"I do, and like Judy Garland said long before even I was born, there's no place like home. Come, let's have dinner."

* * *

Dinner was actually light, some panzanella and salmon with vegetables that had me looking at Uncle Carlo in surprise. "Did you see your doctor recently or something?"

He laughed and cut into his salmon with his knife. "No,

Bella. But as I've gotten older, I've learned a few things about my body. After flying, I've come to understand that my stomach takes a while to settle down and can't handle the oregano, tomatoes and other things I normally enjoy. But I can at least still have my olive oil."

I laughed and took a bite of my salad, crunching on the crispy pieces of bread that had been sautéed in olive oil. "Food of the gods there—as you've told me my entire life."

"I spoke with your mother while I was on the plane. She says your readjustment has gone well?"

"It has. Thank you."

"And your classes? I hope they're teaching more than how to mix paint and slap it on some canvas."

"Oh no, they've done a little more than that," I teased, a glint in my eye. "They've taught us how to use our fingers to smear it on walls and paper, too. You should see your study; I've done some redecorating for you."

He laughed and took a careful bite of his fish. "Sorry, I went in there earlier before dinner or you might have gotten me. But seriously, Bella, how are your classes?"

"Pretty good. Actually, I'm signed up for a few business courses this semester," I said. "I put them off for a while, but the university thinks that it is important for us artists to have some business knowledge. So I'm taking a digital marketing course as well as business math this semester."

"That's good. Too many artists end up starving, not due to lack of talent, but lack of the ability to keep two pennies in their pocket," Carlo said. "Listen, I wanted to ask . . . have you been contacted again by that freak, Drake?"

It was one of the gray clouds hanging in the sky of my time, and one I wanted to be gone more than anything else. So far, the police hadn't found a single clue as to the whereabouts of Vincent Drake. "Not so far. The police detective in charge of the investigation called me yesterday and said that they are doing their best to find him. They think he might have fled the country, but he wouldn't say why they think that."

"There's a chance of that," Uncle Carlo said. He sighed and set his silverware down. "I've had some of my people looking into his background. It was surprising, considering your description of him, but he's a scary man."

"Besides being a psychopath? He's a fifty-year-old man with a tub gut and bad taste in clothing and music. What else is there to worry about now that you're on to him?"

Uncle Carlo shook his head, sighing. "Vincent Drake is more than that, sadly enough, and he's fifty-three. I'm not surprised the police didn't tell you, or perhaps the fucking morons don't know yet, but Vincent Drake is former military. His public service record is fairly tame. He was in the Army for eight years, getting out just after the first Iraq War. According to the public record, he was a Public Relations Specialist, and reached the rank of Staff Sergeant before an honorable discharge."

"You say that like he's more than just a former journalist," I said, my mouth going a bit dry. I took a sip of my water, trying to clear the knot in my throat. "What is it?"

"The posts that he was assigned—they don't have media specialists," Carlo said simply. "My sources dug some more, and found that Vincent Drake was more than that. He was in the Psychological Warfare division and was involved in the capture and interrogation of Noriega back in the Panama invasion. He was Special Operations, Bella. We don't know exactly what training he went through, or what it did to him, but the man is not some artsy palooka who just went off his rocker."

I shuddered, my appetite suddenly lost. "That's not good news, but I'm confident Daniel will keep me safe."

Uncle Carlo nodded, taking another bite of his fish. "Your mother and I talked about this yesterday on the phone. She told me how highly you spoke about Daniel, and she was a bit worried. After a phone call I got this morning, I am too."

"Why are you worried?" I asked. "I mean, me being at odds with Daniel would only make things more difficult."

"Getting along is good, but you sounded to your mother like a girl with the beginnings of a crush," he said. "I have to caution you on that."

"Uncle," I said, trying not to whine. I took a deep breath. "Okay, I'll admit, Daniel's a handsome man. But I don't have a crush on him. Even if I did, is that really a bad thing? You said yourself that he is a man of honor, and I could probably do a lot worse."

Uncle Carlo sighed and rested his forehead in his hands, shaking his head back and forth. "Bella, I know what you're saying, but Daniel, at least when it comes to ladies, is not to be trusted. And even if that wasn't the case, it won't change what he does for a living . . ."

I sat there, fuming, feeling like I was being talked down to, and not liking it too much. Godfather or not, leader of the Sea-Tac families or not, I was a twenty-three-year-old woman, not a twelve-year-old-girl saying she had a crush on some television heartthrob. "Well, maybe he can change. And he doesn't have to do that for the rest of his life . . ."

He shook his head. "If it was anyone other than Daniel, I'd have pulled him from the job already. But with what I've learned about the man who's stalking you, I can't afford to have anyone other than the best of my men protecting you. In terms of doing his duty to protect you, I can trust him, and his honor will make sure that he does the right thing. But outside of that, Adriana, he knows the rules. No man under Bertoli family employ is to touch you. They do, and they will pay with their lives, very simply. I won't compromise on this, nor will I listen to any arguments otherwise. Now, I would like to finish my dinner. Is this conversation finished?"

"Yes, Uncle," I said, staring a hole in my fish. I waited for him to finish his, then wiped my mouth with my napkin. "May I be excused?"

He gave me a long look, then nodded. "I'm sorry that I have to be so strict on this, Bella, but it is for your own good. Thank you for the meal."

* * *

In my room, I lay on my bed, staring at the ceiling. It was too early to think about going to sleep, barely past eight in the evening, but I didn't know what else to do. I didn't want to go to the family room. There was nothing I wanted to watch on TV, and the odds were that either Uncle Carlo or Mom would be there. After what Carlo said, I didn't want to talk to either of them, not with the way they were trying to run my life. I wasn't in the mood to work out, either, as just the thought of the gym sent memories of Daniel's body in his tight workout gear through my mind, and I was aroused enough around him as it was.

Was I really developing a crush on Daniel? I wondered. We'd known each other for most of our lives, and I knew as kids we'd played together. In a house with a lot of Italian men with a slightly skewed view on social rules, he was one of the few kids in the house. He'd been the kid who'd helped me learn how to ride a bike for the first time, and he'd even shown me how to shoot a basketball. Sure, after we hit our teens, we'd drifted apart, but it wasn't like he was a stranger.

But I couldn't deny that even thinking about him was making my body yearn for things, sensual things that made me want to touch my body. I knew it could put us both in danger, him more so than me, but I couldn't help myself. Maybe it was selfish, but the urge was strong.

My hands took on a life of their own as I imagined Daniel, his muscles hard under my hands, his sensuous lips tasting my skin, kissing down my neck to my breasts. I could hear the muffled gasps and moans of our passion as if it were real, stifled only because we knew the risk we were taking but didn't care. His fire for me was too much, unable to be denied, and it fueled us both, driving us crazy with lust. I let my fingers run down my neck to the V of my shirt, stroking the suddenly hypersensitive erogenous zones and adding to the heat burning inside me.

In a semi-trance, I lifted my shirt and bra up, cupping my right breast in my hand and rubbing the stiff nipple until I was moaning, unable to stop the deep cry in my throat. I wanted him so badly, I wanted to feel what it was that made his name a whispered legend. "Daniel . . ." I whispered as my right hand stroked down my stomach to creep inside my pants. "Oh yes . . ."

My panties were soaked, and I shivered as my questing fingers rubbed over my wet lips, the friction sending sparks of heat up and down my legs. It had been months since the last time I'd had sex, a side effect of the creepy behavior from Vincent, and I needed a man, a man like Daniel so badly that I could taste it. Daniel was all that and more, and the thought of him left my head spinning.

Pushing my panties to the side, I imagined Daniel's cock, how hard and huge it must have been when he got aroused. I imagined holding it in my hand, the warmth and steel rigidity as we would kiss, his strong hands crushing me to him as he held me tight, whispering in my ear that he's always there to protect me and to take care of me. My legs parted as I fantasized that it was for him that I was opening myself. Fear and desire mixed as my mind's eye imagined the intimidating presence of his manhood, but I needed it so badly.

My finger was a poor substitute, I knew, but still, the feeling of penetration knocked all the breath out of my body. My hips lifted to meet my middle finger and I stroked in and out, the heel of my hand rubbing against my clit in slow circles. My finger pumped in and out, now rubbing over the tip of my clit, soaked in my own juices and reducing the friction to an amazing lightness that made me bite my lip. It felt so good. I shuddered, imagining Daniel's hard stomach dragging over my clit as he pulled out, teasing me momentarily before he lowered his head to between my legs. He had such a sensuous tongue, I was sure it would feel amazing on my skin, and the image of his mouth fastened over my pussy drove me the rest of the way up.

My mind went into rapid-fire slide-show fantasy mode, and

images of Daniel naked, fucking me in every position imaginable, using his tongue, his hands, his amazing cock everywhere he could flashed through my mind as I trembled on the edge of coming. Then, in a voice so clear I swore it was the real thing and not just my imagination, I heard Daniel whisper in my ear, "Come for me, Ade. Come for me."

I clenched, my pussy clamping around my finger as my hand ground against my clit, gritting my teeth as I rode out my orgasm. Daniel's blue eyes were in my mind the whole time, his little cocky smile that promised me more pleasure than I'd ever felt in my life, and as my hips slowly sank back into the bed, I knew that I was in trouble. Crush or not, I knew I wanted Daniel, and bad.

I lay there for a while, the smell of my sex heavy in the air, wishing it was more than just the solitary musk of my masturbation. I wanted to smell the salty sweet tang of a man's body with mine, and I knew there was only one man whose aroma I wanted to smell.

Sighing, I looked over at my clock. Eight forty-five. Still far too early to go to sleep. I decided to get out of bed and try and do some homework. I had some marketing homework I could prep for, even if the class was pretty much a cakewalk.

I opened my laptop, pulling up my school email. There were three messages, the first two normal class notes and announcements that I quickly read and noted in my mental itinerary. The third was a personal message, supposedly from another student at the university, a Mike Rutherford. The title was "Strength in your time of sadness." Curious, I opened it.

The screen of my laptop flashed, and the normal desktop

was replaced by a slide show of some kind. Music started, and I immediately started backing away as Phil Collins' voice started. It was the song “In Too Deep.”

The slide show changed from the lyrics of the song to images from my apartment, of Angela being stabbed, and her blood being smeared on the walls. I screamed, hysteria taking over for me as Phil's voice launched into the chorus of the song.

I screamed again, and suddenly, Uncle Carlo was at my side, with Mom next to him, holding me and rocking me gently. He looked at the computer, which was looping around to the chorus again with its grisly imagery, and he slammed the lid shut. Still, the song wouldn't stop, still audible through the built-in speakers, and I sobbed, panic stricken and desperate. He pulled the plug out of the wall and flipped the computer over, picking it up. He held it over his head for a moment, and I could read in his body language the desire to smash the offending chunk of metal and plastic down on my desk, but in the end, he set it down, savagely flipping the tabs that let him yank the battery out. Once all power had been cut, the computer shut down, and the three of us looked at the laptop, my sobs still racking my body while Mom held me. “It was him,” I wailed, pointing at the computer. “Vincent. He's still out there!”

“Not for long,” Uncle Carlo said. He picked up my laptop and put it under his arm. “I'm sorry, Bella, but I'm going to have to take this. Is there any information you need for your classes?”

“Carlo, she's hysterical,” Mom said, stroking my hair. “Ask her in an hour.”

He looked at Mom, his eyes flashing in anger, then nodded, agreeing. “You're right, of course, Margaret. Still, I will make calls.

When the expert gets here, he's going to start going through it. In the meantime, I have another call to make."

"Who?" I asked, sniffling. With the music gone, I could at least focus some, and I was recovering from my scare.

"Daniel," Uncle Carlo said. "He needs to know. And I'm going to make sure he doesn't leave your side."

Chapter 8

Daniel

I found Carlo, Margaret, and Adriana in the main living room. I was still in my exercise gear, coming straight from the dojo where I'd been trying to relieve my stress and tension via sparring. I think a few of the guys were glad that I'd gotten the phone call. I'd already put two guys down in the time we'd been at it, one with a leg that was already turning purple from my kicks, and another with a concussion.

"What happened?" I asked, seeing Adriana's still frightened face. I realized how I'd spoken, and I quickly took a deep breath, reasserting control of myself. "Apologies. How can I help?"

"Adriana was in her room, trying to do some homework or something, when she got an email from that piece of shit, Drake," Don Bertoli said, seething. I'd seen him pissed off before, but never to this degree. He almost never cursed in front of Adriana or Margaret that I'd seen. "I need your services, of course."

I nodded, looking straight at Adriana, who still was huddled on the couch, her arms wrapped around her knees and her eyes haunted. "Whatever you need, sir."

He took a deep breath, regaining some of his famous self-control. "First, go by her apartment and sweep it. I want to know if that asshole has found her new place. Second, clear out Adriana's things. She's moving back here until he's caught and dealt with."

I licked my lips, working up the courage to do something I'd never done before as an idea rushed through my mind. "No offense, sir, but I think my skills could be used better in another pursuit."

"Explain yourself," Margaret said, her voice calm and perceptive. "It's not often that people contradict Carlo."

"Apologies, Mrs. Bertoli, but I only speak because I want to ensure your daughter's safety," I said, intentionally keeping any comments I made directed not at Adriana. With the way that the Don was about Adriana, I had to show that I was emotionally detached, professional. "It is just that while I can do the things that Don Bertoli asks, I think I'd be much more useful in trying to find this Drake."

Carlo relaxed, and I was glad he wasn't offended. "What do you have in mind?" he asked.

"I can possibly track back how Drake was able to send his message," I said, wanting to sit down and show how on a piece of paper, but staying on my feet. I hadn't been invited to sit, after all. Actually, at the moment, the one thing I wanted to do most was hold Adriana and run my fingers through her beautiful flame-red hair, reassuring her that it was okay and that she'd be safe. But I couldn't, that was for sure. "If so, I can start to hunt this man down."

"He's more dangerous than we first believed, Daniel," Don Bertoli said, gesturing to the chair on his left. I took a seat, making sure to not let my sweat-soaked shirt touch the leather. "He has military training. Special Operations training. He might be more than you can handle."

"With all due respect, even a psychopath with military

training is within my capabilities," I said. "Especially if he doesn't know that I am hunting him. He probably expects a bodyguard, if he's seen Adriana since the murder, not a man of my talents. It is more difficult to defend against an enemy that you don't know is coming."

"You want the stalker to become the stalked," Margaret said, her voice bloodthirsty. "And if you find him?"

"I have some things I'd like to do, but that would be at your discretion. First, though, I have to find him."

Carlo considered the idea, then nodded. "Agreed. First, I'll let you look at Adriana's computer. It's in my study. Second, tomorrow morning, you will go to the school and start your hunt. Adriana's security here isn't a problem."

"Actually, first, I think Daniel needs to take a shower and get dressed," Margaret said with a small laugh. "He looks like hell. What were you doing, getting into fights?"

"Actually, that is exactly what I was doing," I said, rubbing at the pink spot on my arm where I'd blocked a kick. "Sparring practice. But I'd like to look at the computer first and find out what I can. Then I'll speak with some of my contacts, men who I can trust to go and get the information we need. Thank you."

* * *

I didn't have a suit or anything at the Bertoli house, so I had to drive back to my apartment, leaving the computer for later analysis. My mind whirled as I thought about how incompetent and stupid the police and school administration had been. Seriously, online harassment is both pernicious but also relatively easy to stop. The key is changing things. Changing email addresses, IP addresses, and other things can be a pain in the ass, but it stops most electronic harassment. In Drake's case, I wasn't sure, but considering the look I'd seen on Adriana's face, I was filled with anger.

It was Adriana who had me the angriest. The look in her eyes, like the entire world was unsafe and that she was just a little hunted animal angered me. That any man, even a psycho like Vincent Drake, would want to drive a young woman to such a state was despicable.

I'd killed people, I admit. I'd told Adriana as much. But I'd never intentionally tried to terrorize or harm an innocent person. The closest I'd come was the night before, with Carmen at the Starlight Club, and I apologized for that one. The fact was, Drake and Adriana were both getting to me. I could take care of both by finding Drake. After that, I'd talk with Don Bertoli. As much as it pained me, I couldn't work with Adriana again, not without breaking his rules. Maybe the Don had connections out of the Seattle-Tacoma area that I could work with. Maybe there was a way I could keep my honor and my life intact at the same time.

First, though, I had to track down Vincent Drake. Of course, I'd tell Carlo that he had first choice on killing Drake, but if the opportunity presented itself, I was going to put a pistol to that bastard's head and pull the trigger until the hammer dry-clicked a few times.

I got to my apartment, still trying to figure out what to do. An idea popped into my mind while I scrubbed the sweat off my body, and I felt a bit of lightness coming to my mood for the first time in a while. "Adam. He can help."

Adam Kane was someone I'd met through a job that Don Bertoli had given to me. Not in the employ of the Don, he was a freelance private investigator whose morals were reasonably flexible enough that he didn't mind it when I would sometimes come to him with Bertoli business—somewhat of a moral anarchist, if you will. He was loyal to an employer, though, and good at what he did.

Grabbing my phone, I called up Adam. "Yo, Kane."

"Daniel, it's good to hear your voice," Adam answered in his normal high-pitched whine. It wasn't his most endearing feature. In fact, Adam was the sort of guy who probably didn't get a woman in bed unless he paid for it handsomely first. Short, dumpy-looking, with a good case of acne scars and the tendency to collect blackheads that could have starred on YouTube videos, he was still a smart guy with a good sense of humor and loyal to those he cared about. A lot of women could do worse than him. "What can I do for you?"

"I've got a situation that could use your services," I said. "I hope you aren't busy."

"Nah, just your standard following cheating husband cases," Adam said with a chuckle. "Nothing I can't pass off to my assistant. Considering you always bring me interesting things, I can clear my schedule. When would you like to meet?"

"Meet me at midnight at the boat ramp on 14th Street," I said. "Bring your computer gear."

I hung up my phone and looked in my closet. The relatively empty space was divided into two sections. On the right, I had my normal clothes, suits that Don Bertoli would approve of. On the left, my casual stuff that Adriana requested I wear. All of them were hung up on wooden hangers—which prevent lines from developing in the shoulders of your coats or shirts—or clipped at the waist on pants hangers. I reached for one of my suits, then stopped. This job had gotten personal, whether I wanted it to or not. In fact, the more I tried to avoid it, the more mistakes I made. I should have anticipated the emails. I should have seen it coming. Instead, I was so caught up in trying not to break down and take her to bed that I was making stupid mistakes and overlooking things.

"Fuck it," I said, my hand drifting to a sport coat that I had hanging to the right of my closet. I hadn't worn it in a while—before I'd really started doing heavy work for the Don and had been trying to scrape together whatever I could. I pulled it off its hanger and gave it a sniff, happy that it still smelled all right.

I grabbed my Beretta, this time choosing a belt holster that wouldn't imprint too much under the sport coat, and pulled the coat on. Checking myself in the mirror, I thought I looked good.

I met Adam at five after twelve, having to wait the five minutes for him before he approached me. He's good at private investigation, but not so much with keeping time. "Good to see you, Daniel. Couldn't you have picked a more picturesque location?"

"It's the middle of the night, Adam," I said, gesturing around us. "Did you really think we could meet up in a fashionable nightspot or something?"

"Well, I figured that with who you work for and what you do, you'd at least be able to get me drinks and maybe a pretty girl to look at after we finish business," Adam said with a chuckle. A notorious horndog, I wondered just how many gigabytes of porn was saved on his computer at home. In a moment of reflection, I realized that Carmen at the Starlight Club would have been right down his alley.

"Not tonight, Adam. No offense, but I need you focused on the job right away. Your perks can come later."

Adam spread his hands and cracked his knuckles. "Whatcha need, D-man?"

"I hate when you call me that," I remarked for what was perhaps the hundredth time in our working relationship. Like Don Bertoli, I rarely allowed people to talk to me in a disrespectful manner, but Adam was competent and professional in most other ways. I could use his skills. Besides, he did have a disarming charm to go along with his sense of humor, and I liked the man despite his perpetual tardiness and screwing around with my name.

"I know. But seriously, man, you're looking and sounding like you've got a bug up your ass the size of a football. Does this have anything to do with the Bertoli girl?"

In an instant, I had him by his shirt, shoving him against my car. "What do you know, Adam?"

"Whoa, Daniel, chill," he said, lifting his hands. "The case has been in the news for over a week now, remember? Pretty college co-ed, a pair of murder scenes that looked like they were straight out of *The Silence of the Lambs*, a crazy ex-professor? Come on, even with the details the media is keeping silent, the whole thing is capturing people's attention. Once I heard the name Adriana Bertoli in one of the news reports, well . . . people talk. Some of your normal pickups have noticed you aren't the one doing the weekly cash rounds right now. I'm just putting two and two together. That's all."

I let him go, dusting off his shirt. "Sorry. Just, the police are about as worthless as a box of dildos to me right now, and I'm not able to put my full skills toward finding this asshole. Either I take the time to protect Adriana, or I take the time to find and hunt this asshole. I don't have the time to do both."

"Which is why you gave me a call," he said. "What do you need?"

"I want you to find Vincent Drake for me," I said. "Don Bertoli told me that he's former Special Operations. He obviously knows how to do at least basic computer hacking or something. His most recent harassing message was in an email, sent in the name of Mike Rutherford."

"And should I know who Mike Rutherford is?" Adam asked. Considering I had to look it up, I wasn't offended.

"He's one of the key members of the band, Genesis," I answered for him. "Plays guitar. This Drake character happens to have a major affinity for the band."

"Gotcha," Adam said. I reached into my coat and pulled out a thumb drive, which I passed over to him. "What's this?"

"A copy of the email, along with what I know about Vincent Drake. Bertoli's men don't operate in the same digital world you do, so it's only a simple text file."

"It's enough to get started," he said, taking the drive and making it disappear into his pants pocket. "You got a timeline on this?"

"Make it your primary case until this asshole is in my hands. If you find him, let me know immediately. This guy . . . he's mine."

He lifted his eyebrow, giving me a long look. "You're not turning him over to the cops? You know that girl's family is going to want justice."

"They'll learn about it," I said quietly. "But this fucker belongs to me."

"What about your boss? He's not going to like that."

I sighed, knowing I'd fucked up again. My private thoughts might be different, but I had to make sure my public face was constant. "Of course, he belongs to the Don. But I'm the one to hand him over."

Adam nodded. "Deal. Consider this a favor though, Daniel. You've brought me enough money that I'm grateful, and this case . . . it's the sort of thing you don't chase down for money. You do it because it's the right thing to do. Even men like me know there are some basic rights and wrongs the world's gotta follow."

He turned and walked off into the darkness. Just as I was about to get back into my BMW, and he was nothing more than a black shape against the slightly less dark of the surrounding area, he turned back. "Hey, D-man?"

"Yeah?"

"I like the new look. Makes you look less stuffy, more like a badass. I bet the ladies like it too."

"Fuck off, Adam," I said with a good-natured wave. "Now excuse me. I have to get to work myself."

Chapter 9

Adriana

I'd recovered from my scare, but I was going stir-crazy. The college administration, still more worried about covering their asses than trying to stop Vincent from harassing me, wasn't very helpful when Mom went in to talk to them the day after the threatening email. They said that without direct evidence that the message was sent by Vincent, there was little they could do. Mom at least got them to agree to let me take the rest of the week off, forwarding my assignments to my school email. Since I didn't have any tests for the next two weeks, I was okay there at least.

Still, being kept in the house, even one as luxurious as the Bertoli mansion, was driving me nuts. Everywhere I looked, I saw the same faces, the same people, the same things that I'd seen a million times before in my life. To make it worse, Uncle Carlo took away my phone and computer, telling me that Daniel would now have screening of my communication added to his duties. So I was stuck watching daytime TV, reading books in the library, and trying not to be bored out of my mind. I wasn't even allowed outside, except to the small garden that was built into a section of the mansion that was surrounded by other buildings. I was being kept a prisoner for my own damn protection.

Friday, though, Daniel was back, and after a long, private conversation with Uncle Carlo, he found me in the gym. "Well, it looks like you're giving it a bit more effort than you were the last time I saw you in here," he said as I heaved my way through another set of chest presses. "Trying to beef up on me?"

"More like I'm bored and pissed, and this is the best way to work it off," I said, pushing. The handles of the machine moved away from my chest for a second before pausing, stuck at the halfway-point. I gritted my teeth and grunted, very unladylike and totally unavoidable, but I couldn't complete the motion. The handles crashed back to the stop point as gravity won out over my muscles, and I hissed in frustration. "Shit."

"Listen, I just wanted to tell you that I'm sorry about yesterday. I'm back to sticking by your side now, but you're not going to like one thing."

"What's that?" I said, rolling my shoulders. I didn't lift very often, and I knew I'd be sore the next day because of it, but I didn't really care. It was better than being bored out of my skull. Actually, just having Daniel nearby helped.

"Carlo told me that you're to live in the house. So starting next week, when you go back to classes, we're going to have to leave earlier to make it on time."

"What about you?" I asked. "It's going to be even more of a pain in the ass for you."

Daniel shook his head. "Actually, I'll be getting a bit more sleep, since I'm going to be staying here too. The housekeeper's making up my old room."

"That thing? It's the size of a broom closet!" I protested. "Seriously, the pantry is bigger than that!"

Daniel shrugged it off. "I don't need it for much more than a mattress and to store a few clothes. We've got a shower over here, after all. Speaking of which, if you just happen to wander down here at six fifteen in the morning and hear the hot water running, feel free to join whoever is in there."

"Yeah, right. Knowing my luck, it'd be the gardener. No thanks."

Daniel laughed and turned to go, when I stopped him. "Dan?"

"Yeah, Ade?"

"Are you busy tonight? I'm going batshit crazy around here, there's far too many men in dark suits, and I need a break from all this heaviness."

Daniel sighed and turned back. "We're here to protect you, Ade. He could never get in this place."

"Still, I need to get out of here, even if it's just for a few hours. Think of it as mental therapy," I said. I went over to my next machine and adjusted the seat and pins, readying myself. "Come on, don't make me order you."

Daniel chuckled. "I think you'd prefer me ordering *you* around. But I have to say no either way. Your mother wants me to do something. Also, I have some restitution to take care of. I don't like saying it, but I didn't exactly behave well the last time I stopped by the Starlight Club."

I was surprised at the flare of anger and jealousy at the mention of the Starlight Club. I knew what sort of business that was, and I didn't like the idea of Daniel going there, regardless of whether it was his job. "You should frequent a better class of business, Daniel."

"It's my job, Ade. In either case, I'm going to be leaving around six and won't be back until after midnight."

"Fine. Then tomorrow night, you're protecting me while I

go out to dinner and a movie. I need a few hours to feel like a normal girl, and not a fucking victim." I sat down at the machine and started, pulling the handles this time instead of pushing them. "Got a problem with that?"

I think it was the first time I'd seen Daniel uncomfortable in a long time. Sure, he'd been hesitant in the graveyard, but not uncomfortable. He wanted to say no, but another part of him wanted to say yes. "Fine. What time?"

"I'll tell you tomorrow," I said with a smile. "It'll be fun."

I don't think he knew that I heard his next comment. He was trying to keep it under his breath, but it still made me smile, knowing I was affecting him the same way he was affecting me. "It'll be my fucking funeral, more like it."

* * *

Mom and Uncle Carlo weren't happy about it, but they understood after enough convincing on my part. So, at six thirty Saturday night, I was dressed in my best jeans and t-shirt, freshly scrubbed. I'd taken the time to make sure that I didn't have any paint on my clothes or in my hair, even though I'd spent four hours that afternoon painting in the library, letting my stress out through the use of oils. The painting was shit, dark and violent and not at all like what I preferred to do, but it helped. It let me pour out my emotions in a safe and familiar way. At least Vincent's fuckery hadn't robbed me of one of my primary joys.

Daniel met me in the foyer, looking for all the world like some of the guys who'd come to pick me up for dates back in high school. Well, except for the small bulge on his left side where he had his pistol under his shirt. "You ready?"

"Of course," I said, trying not to skip down the steps.

Mom stood there watching, her eyes filled with concern. "I'll be back by eleven."

She looked at me, then at Daniel, and gestured with her head. Daniel nodded silently and stepped outside, his keys in his hand. Mom used the opportunity to lean in close. "You behave yourself, young lady. Do you understand?"

"I'll be fine," I said, giving her my best innocent smile. "It's not a date. I doubt you'd want me to go alone—not that I'd want to—but I need to get out."

"It had better not be, for both of your sakes," Mom whispered. "Be careful."

I kissed her on the cheek and gave her a hug, patting her back. "I will. Thanks, Mom."

Daniel was already outside, standing next to his car, holding the passenger door open for me. "Should I ask what she said?"

"You're smart enough to know," I replied with a smile, sliding into the passenger seat. We drove, heading out of town. I'd chosen a mall outside of Seattle, purely for the fact that we'd never been there before.

As we drove, Daniel relaxed bit by bit as we put miles between us and the house. "Dan?"

"Yeah, Ade?" he asked. He reached out with a thumb, jabbing the power button on his car stereo, and I was surprised as relaxing, mellow instrumental music, not jazz but something else, filled the car. "Just downloaded it today. Thought you could use the relaxation."

"Thanks," I said, leaning back into the leather seats. "I just wanted to let you know, this dinner is for you too. I know you've been doing your best, and you've been showing a few signs of stress too. Also, I shouldn't have snapped at you about the Starlight Club. I know it's part of your job."

"Thanks, but you didn't need to," Daniel replied. "Last night was purely business. I met my private eye there. He's helping me with tracking down Drake."

"No more on Vincent tonight, please? For the next four and a half hours, I don't want to hear or even think about that man."

"Deal," Daniel said. "Just dinner and a movie for a stressed out girl. Too much cobalt blue and titanium white or something."

I laughed. "Something like that. Although after today's painting, I think I need a few more tubes of black and gray."

I was surprised when he nodded. "I saw. I liked it."

"Really? I thought it was terrible," I said. "Not realistic at all—too dark, just . . . not me."

"Maybe not, but it's got a lot of intensity. You really poured a lot of yourself into it, and I guess it speaks to me that way."

"Then it's yours," I said immediately. "The best way to get through to an artist is to say you like their work, even if the she hates it herself."

The restaurant lived up to the reviews, with some of the best burgers I'd had in a long time. Daniel enjoyed as well, and ended up licking the barbecue sauce from his bacon barbecue burger off his fingertips, something I'd never seen him do before. At home, he'd always been the epitome of decorum, wiping his hands and mouth with his napkin even if everyone else was nearly under the table drunk. "Worth the thirty-minute drive, that's for sure," he said. "What did you think?"

"Great. You know the only downer in this?"

"What's that?"

I took a sip of my soda and set my glass down. "You and I were good friends for about five years there, after I came to Uncle Carlo's house. But then we were kept apart."

"For good reason, Ade. I haven't been the type of man who's supposed to be friends with a classy girl like you."

"I think I'm old enough now to pick who my friends are and who I want to spend time with," I said simply, but I was touched by his compliment. "I guess what I'm saying is, when this is finished, I don't want you to drift away again. I know Uncle Carlo doesn't like it, but I want to talk to him about it later."

"You can talk all you want, but he's not going to listen. I'm not worthy of you in his eyes." Daniel lowered his eyes to the table, and I could tell he wished it weren't the case.

"And what do you think?" I asked, then shook my head. "Nevermind. That's an unfair question. Come on, let's see the movie. After all the terror of the past week, I need some fictional scares to put all of it in perspective."

The movie was a remake of a Japanese horror flick, *The Ring vs. The Grudge*, and had plenty of creepy atmosphere. Sure, it was an amalgamation of two pretty worn out movies, but it was still fun. As the tension built, I pulled my legs up underneath me, my eyes wide and staring at the screen. The first time the ghost popped out to scare the first victim to death, I'll admit I jumped, a little bit of popcorn bouncing out of my tub to rain down on my lap, some of it falling onto Daniel's lap as well. "Thanks," he said blithely, picking up a kernel and tossing it into his mouth. "You okay?"

"Yeah," I whispered back. "It's why we came anyway. It's therapeutic."

When the next scare happened, I shrieked loud enough for those around me to jump too. Daniel put his arm around my shoulder, not saying a word.

I fidgeted some, the hard plastic of the arm rest in my ribs preventing me from getting comfortable before I realized that the arm rest lifted. Scooting to the side, I pulled it up and out of the way, snuggling back in closer to Daniel, who rested his arm on my shoulder for the rest of the movie. With his strong arm holding me lightly, I didn't have to jump for the rest of the movie, but I certainly enjoyed some of the scares that were left, and by the end, I was laughing at some of the cheesiness of the two ghostly characters and the idiotic people caught between them.

As the credits rolled and the lights rose, I reached up and gave Daniel's hand a squeeze. "Thanks, I needed that."

"No problem," he said, removing his arm, "but I think you and I need to set some ground rules. For our safety, especially mine."

I nodded, reality poking its ugly head in, and sighed. "I guess so, but can we at least save it until we get to the car?"

Daniel looked like he was about to protest, then just nodded. He reached over and took my hand, entwining our fingers. "Let's go."

The three hundred and twenty-three steps from the theater to Daniel's car were the best part of the evening, as for the first time in nearly a year, I felt totally like a normal girl, free from all the stress and worry of what I'd been through. I imagined that it was like what girls who weren't Mafia princesses felt like most Saturday nights when they were out with a cute guy.

Daniel held my door open and got in afterward, sticking his key in the ignition. "Did you enjoy yourself?"

"I did," I said with a smile. "You know, Daniel, when you want to be, you're a pretty decent guy."

"Don't let the secret out," he said with a chuckle. "But Ade, we're pushing a very dangerous line, one that I don't think we should cross."

"I know," I said, sighing and looking out the windshield. "The problem is, I like spending time with you. Beyond what that could mean, I'm just saying that going out with you is a lot of fun. Even when we've been bumming around campus, just you taking me to classes and stuff, I've enjoyed myself. I keep wishing you were an actual student."

Daniel's short laugh and nod told me both that he agreed but also felt it was impossible. "Ade, I don't even know my real last name. The Social Security number I used to get my concealed carry permit is invalid, connected to a man who died a decade ago overseas in Zimbabwe and therefore cannot for certain be declared dead. Besides, while I learn what your uncle asks me to, I'm more of a hands-on type of man. But yes, I've enjoyed my duty for the past two weeks."

"Has it been just duty?" I asked quietly, stopping him. Daniel stared at me, his mouth working silently for a moment, and I could see the answer in his eyes. "That's what I thought. Your duty and honor is stopping you . . . stopping us."

"It is what it is. We can enjoy this time, the times when we can be friends . . . but nothing more," Daniel said, the last words said between tightly-clenched teeth. He started his car and put it in reverse. “If it means anything, I wish things were different.”

“Yeah . . .” I replied, looking out the passenger window so he couldn't see me cry. “Me too.”

Chapter 10

Daniel

I took Adriana back to classes, the two of us leaving early enough that we got to her first class twenty minutes early. I went inside and did a security check of the room while she sat quietly in her spot next to the emergency exit. The professor, a bespectacled woman who looked like she probably worshiped Annie Leibowitz, looked on with mixed emotions. She wanted to support Adriana as a female and a victim of violence, but at the same time, she didn't like that I was there. "Young man," she said as I checked under her podium for any listening devices, "I don't think that—"

"That's exactly your and everyone else's problem at this school," I said quietly, low enough that Adriana couldn't hear me. "You don't think. You're more worried about your political leanings, your bureaucracy, and covering your asses, and you've forgotten that there is a very scared, very threatened young woman involved in all of this. But I haven't. I've pledged to keep her safe, and lady, if I were you, I wouldn't get in my way."

She blanched, then nodded. "Just be quick about it, okay?"

"I'll be done by the time your class starts," I replied, continuing my search. When I sat down next to Adriana, she looked at me questioningly. "Just a disagreement about Picasso's Blue Period."

"Uh-huh. And that's why she's staring at you in abject fear right now?" she asked, amused.

I shrugged. "I have that kind of an effect on people sometimes."

The class started, and it was one of Adriana's more boring classes really, a lecture class that only went to labs and actual production during the last few sessions of the semester. Until then, the teacher wanted the students to supposedly focus, to draw inspiration from the life around them.

In my opinion, it was all bullshit. You want inspiration? Look around you. The world is a beautiful and fucked up place. Inspiration existed in almost every moment of every day. You didn't need to focus to find an inspiration.

As an example, I did my first hit for Don Bertoli when I was nineteen, soon after I'd completed high school. The guy I was to take out was a piece of shit meth dealer who'd not only stiffed Don Bertoli on his payments, but had also been caught more than once dealing bad shit, which could cause the police to poke around more than normal. Nobody wants that, and so I was sent in.

I found the dealer in the parking lot of a Pizza Hut that he used for a lot of his business. I was wearing all black and a face mask, but still in my suit. I was supposed to make sure a message was sent.

I'd been training for years already, a decade spent preparing myself, knowing that the day would come that Don Bertoli would ask me to start repaying the generosity he'd heaped upon me for taking care of me all those years. Walking across the parking lot, the throwaway S&W 9mm I was going to use felt heavy in my hand, when suddenly, things started to go wrong.

The target, supposedly a tweaker who never carried anything on him, spun at the sound of my approaching footsteps. Seeing the suit, he knew exactly who I worked for, and instead of running like I'd suspected he'd do, he reached for a pistol in the waistband of his pants. I barely got my gun up in time before he squeezed off a round, which ricocheted off the pavement, nicking my right leg as it whined by. I pulled the trigger, and his chest nearly exploded, blood bursting from his back in a massive spray that painted the side of the Pizza Hut in a crimson Rorschach diagram.

The next day, after getting my leg bandaged up, was the most beautiful day I'd ever had. Each bite of my breakfast was the greatest meal I'd ever feasted upon, and each breath was sweet and perfect in my lungs. You want inspiration? I had inspiration, forty-five caliber inspiration that came in semi-automatic.

When the lecture was over, Adriana had an hour to wait before her next class, a painting lab that almost always left her covered in enough paint that I thought she looked like she was trying out for a clown spot in the local circus. We hung out in the university library, where we could at least grab a quiet corner and I could keep an eye on the comings and goings. Adriana picked out a romance novel, of all things, and sat down reading. "Really?" I asked, seeing the illustration on the cover. "I figured you for a better quality of literature than that."

"Don't knock it until you try it," Adriana said. "Besides, at least it lets me live vicariously."

I didn't know if her comment was aimed at me or just a general complaint about the situation she was in, so I didn't reply. Instead, I looked at my phone, wishing Adam would call. He was normally much more involved in keeping me updated, but other than the once-daily messages that boiled down to 'no news yet,' I'd gotten nothing.

"Hey, Dan?" Adriana asked, shaking me from my thoughts and focusing my attention back on her. "Sorry."

"Don't worry about it," I said. "Is there something you

need?"

"I know you're screening my emails, so can you pull up my system and see if I got any new ones? I'm expecting a message from my marketing professor on an assignment he gave while I was at home."

Nodding, I took the laptop, a brand new one that was scrubbed of any viruses that Vincent Drake's last message could have downloaded. The new one ran every email in a virtual box setup that was supposedly foolproof, although I bet that Adam could get past it if we had enough time.

I pulled up the email client, which downloaded three messages. "Let's see—one from a Dr. Roberts, that's the one you want, I assume, a message from the university saying that if you want tickets to the next home football game you need to turn in your request for student section tickets by Friday, and . . . shit."

"What?"

"Peter Gabriel," I said. "Do I even need to tell you who that is?"

Adriana shook her head. She knew the members and former members of Genesis even better than I did by now, and turned pointedly away from me, picking up her book from her lap and pretending to read. I stuck a headphone into the sound jack and opened the mail in the virtual box, hoping the system would hold. I didn't want to have to tell Carlo that we had to buy another new computer.

The music was unfamiliar, and I'd spent the time over the past week listening to most of Genesis's famous songs. This one was different. The sound was more classic rock than what I'd expected, and the lead singer certainly wasn't Phil Collins. I assumed it was Peter Gabriel—I wasn't sure. The song was hacked and cut, the lyrics blended from different parts of the same song with a clumsy homemade transition, probably put together quickly on a laptop.

It took me a second with how the lyrics were jumbled, but then it came to me. It was of course a song from Genesis — called "Am I Very Wrong." The images were like before, shots of the lyrics crawling by karaoke style with stills of Drake's crimes in between, but this time, interspersed with the blood-soaked shots of Angela's murder, were photos of Adriana herself, taken within the past two weeks around campus. I knew that for sure, because I saw myself in three of them and knew exactly when they'd been taken.

The last slide of the show wasn't a picture, but a single normal PowerPoint-type slide that read,

"I do hope the new beefcake doesn't mean I'm not number one in your heart, my Adriana. I'd hate to have to hurt him."

The son of a bitch had been on campus. He must've been good to be coming around campus and have no one notice him. Closing the virtual box, I shut the computer down and took a deep breath. My job just became a lot harder, and I wasn't sure what I could do about it, not until Adam or one of the Don's men got me some information to work with. Until then, the only thing I could do would be to stay by Adriana's side and make sure that if Drake did go all the way over the edge and into direct attack, he'd never get within twenty feet of her.

"Wait right here. I'm going to the edge of the room to

make a phone call," I told Adriana, who nodded without a word. I walked the ten feet away to give me enough privacy so that she couldn't overhear, and dialed Don Bertoli.

"Hello, Daniel," he said, his voice mellow and cultured like he'd been expecting my call. I could hear a bit of the background noise and knew he was at the office, dealing with the legal side of his empire. "Is there anything I can do for you?"

"Yes, sir. Adriana received another email from Vincent Drake. If you have your men access the email, it's in a message supposedly from Peter Gabriel."

"Peter Gabriel?" Don Bertoli said, sounding surprised. In the past two weeks, we'd all become at least passably acquainted with the discography of the group, although the Don himself and Margaret had admitted that at one point, they'd liked them when they were younger. I doubted either of them would be buying tickets to a reunion tour any time soon, not that it was the actual group's fault. "Anything of particular interest to report?"

"Yes, sir," I said, lowering my voice. "Sir, I suspect that Drake has been on campus. There were pictures of Adriana and myself on campus going to classes, taken within the past two weeks. While they're telephoto, they are also clear enough that he was most likely within a couple of hundred yards."

The silence on the other end told me everything I needed to know. "Okay, Daniel. When you bring Adriana home tonight, make sure your car is clean, and I'll have someone standing by to install some new security measures on it overnight. Anything else?"

"No, sir. I need to get Adriana to her next class now."

"We'll talk when you get home. Goodbye."

I hung up my phone and walked back over to Adriana, who was still staring at her book but hadn't turned a page yet. Kneeling down, I looked her in the eyes. "Are you okay?"

She blinked, her eyes wide and frightened, and shook her head softly. "I just want this to end." She took a deep, shuddering breath. "Let's go now. I don't want to go to my next class."

* * *

After dinner, which I ate by myself in the kitchen while Adriana ate with her family, I went out to meet with Adam, this time at the Starlight Club. The manager, cued in to my coming, met me at the door. "Sir, it is good to see you."

"Bullshit," I said with a small chuckle and an apologetic shrug. "You're just worried that I'm going to do something stupid again."

I took off my coat and unbuttoned my shirt, showing him I wasn't carrying a pistol. I'd left it locked inside the borrowed Lexus that I was driving while Don Bertoli's expert worked on my car. They'd already gone over it in the few hours we'd been home and assured me that nobody had left anything inside, but after they were done, anyone even touching my car would end up recorded, and I'd get a message about it.

The manager of the Starlight Club looked me over, then nodded. "I'll be honest, you had us scared last time."

"Yeah, me too," I said, thinking back to the lack of control I'd shown. That might work for your average street gangster, but not for one of Don Bertoli's men. "Is Carmen okay?"

"She took a few days off, but she's back to work," the man said. "In fact, she's working tonight. Would you like to say hello? No private rooms though."

"Not right now," I replied, taking out a small pack of hundred-dollar bills. "Actually, I have a friend coming. He's doing some work for me, and I'd like to reward him with a little private dance from Carmen. She's just his type. After I leave, of course. Think she could schedule him in?"

He looked at the bills, greed flaring in his eyes. In the world of the Starlight Club, sex and money ruled everything. "I think that could be arranged. Your friend knows how to follow the rules?"

"He's much better behaved than I am. Let me grab a table, and I'll call you over when he arrives."

He nodded, and I found a table in the quietest corner of the club. The bouncer, a big moose of a guy named Shawn, who I knew was more look and aura than actual ability, kept his eye on me, but I just gave him a nod of understanding. I was there to stay under control and get some business done.

Adam showed up, amazingly, right on time, his face flushed as he walked in the door. On stage, a rather flexible, surgically enhanced blonde by the name of Tammy Twister was showing the crowd exactly how she'd earned her stage name.

"God damn, you think I'm going to be able to focus with that going on in the background?" Adam said as he sat down. His eyes were so fixed on Tammy that he nearly missed the chair before finding his seat.

"If you can focus, there's a certain young lady I'd like to introduce you to later," I said by way of enticement. "I must say, though, that I've been a little disturbed by your lack of progress."

He pulled his eyes away from the stage as Tammy's music ended and she collected her few articles of clothing and left the stage with a little wave of her fingers to the crowd. Reflecting on what I'd just said, he shrugged. "What can I say, man? You're right. This Drake character has got some skills that go beyond the normal level of scum that you and I have dealt with."

"No shit," I said, reaching into my coat and pulling out another thumb drive. "He sent this today, complete with photos taken within the past two weeks—close enough to easily be within rifle shot. Those shots are at ground level too. It's not like he was on top of a building or in a hotel across the street or anything."

Adam nodded and put the thumb drive into his shirt pocket. He pulled out another drive, the same one I'd given him before, and handed it to me. "That jives with what little I've been able to find out. I copied what I could find, but most of it is just background."

"Give me the run down, so I can tell Carlo when I get back. I can look over the details later."

Adam gestured to the waitress, ordering a Jack and Coke. I asked for just mineral water. I didn't want any issues with alcohol right then. The waitress walked off, her ass swaying side to side, Adam getting himself an eye full before turning back to me. "This guy is scary, Daniel. I can't get the exact operational details, but I was able to find some people who were willing to talk generalities with me. After enlisting, he specialized in what some people would call enhanced interrogation techniques, teaching some of those skills to groups who later on were accused of human rights violations and were taken before international courts."

"Shit," I commented, nodding to the waitress when she gave us our drinks. I took a sip of my mineral water, wishing for a moment I'd asked for a whiskey instead—I could've used it. "So how'd this fucker get a job teaching sculpting at a major art college?"

"Apparently, Drake took a little vacation from reality right after the first Gulf War," Adam said. "The military, of course, kept it hush-hush. It isn't good for a Spec Ops guy who was just teaching at the School of the Americas only six months prior to go off his nut. From the one source that was able to talk to me, the hospital they sent him to used a lot of—get this—artistic therapy. Knowing they'd never let him back into service, the military rehabbed him and even paid for him to attend college, where of course, he became an artist. Financially, he did pretty well too, which is probably why he got the job he did. Looking over who bought his pieces, though, a trend emerged."

"What?"

Adam took a drink of his Jack and coke and sat back. "The only people who bought his shit were government sources or military contractors. I saw a picture of a statue he did for Fort Drum, up in New York. I think my little cousin did better last month with his fucking Play-Doh."

I sighed, shaking my head. "And the military never thought to check up to see if their little wind-up toy stayed repaired?"

"Hey, it'd been twenty-two years since he got out of the hospital," Adam said. "Guess they figured they'd done their bit for him, and that whatever was fixed would stay fixed. Most of the people who felt they owed him a debt of gratitude were either retired or dead, and the new generation of brass just wants to forget the bad side of it all. Besides, who the fuck knew he was breaking down again until he snapped? The first sign was the sexual harassment claim by Adriana, and a lot of people hadn't believed her, dismissing it as an oversensitive college girl's whine."

"And now everyone who caused this asshole to become what he became is just hoping he gets himself captured or killed before he gives the military a black eye," I finished. "Is there even an investigation?"

Adam shook his head. "Doubt it. They might be providing some background support to the Seattle police, but with only two murders, graphic as they are, there's no real cause for the FBI or anyone else with the Feds to try and step in. There's no Colonel Trautman coming to try and pull this Rambo out of the woods this time. This is in the hands of the locals."

"Who can't even stop a rampaging preschooler on a sugar rush," I replied with no amusement. "And your efforts to find him?"

"He's picked up some computer skills somewhere. That first email that you handed to me, I dissected the code. It had some decent work involved. He knows well enough how to use the Deep Web and mask his steps, at least. Combine that with his military skill at blending in, and he's going to be tough to track. He's going to have to make a mistake, I think."

"I can't stay by Adriana's side forever," I said, though I wished I could. "I don't think Mr. Bertoli would like it if we spent the rest of her life attached at the hip."

"Bet you would, though," Adam said, setting his drink down when I shot him a dirty look. "What? She's a beautiful girl."

"Still, don't even joke that way," I warned him. I finished off my drink, then sighed. "All right, well, I still want you on this. He's got to have made a mistake somewhere."

"I'll do my best," Adam said, polishing off his Jack and

Coke. "Daniel, I know this one's important to you. I'm serious that I'm going to do my best."

I nodded, then rubbed my hands together, trying to relieve my tension. It was time for me to get back to where I wanted to be, next to Adriana, making sure she was safe. "And I appreciate it. In fact, I thought I'd give you a little preview of my appreciation. Wait right here."

I signaled to the manager, who nodded in understanding and disappeared to the back while I went up to the bar. Carmen came out a minute later, a professional smile on her face but still a hint of concern on her face. "Hi, Carmen."

"I heard you wanted me to spend some time with a friend of yours?" she said, leaning against the bar. I didn't think she was trying to give me a preview of her boobs, but with my height and her clothes, that was what happened. This time, though, she was professional, not seductive. "That him over there?"

"That he is," I said. "I just wanted to say I'm sorry about last time."

She shrugged it off, a true pro. "I've been doing this for three years. I've seen stressed out men before. You did scare the hell out of me, but you seem like a decent guy."

"People keep telling me that recently, for some fucking reason," I replied, getting her to smile a little bit. Leaning in, keeping my elbows and hands on the bar and clear of Carmen so as not to scare her, I lowered my voice. "Be nice, okay? Don't play him and milk him for everything he's got." I motioned over to Adam. "Come with me."

We walked over, and Adam's eyes nearly bugged out of his skull when the little Latina came around in front of him, her hair pulled back into hasty pigtails and her outfit actually helping with the look. "Adam, this is Carmen, a friend of mine. Carmen, this is Adam. I have to go, but you two have fun."

"Th . . . thanks," he said, his eyes fixed not on Carmen's chest, but on her face. She did have a pretty face, I had to agree, but still, she was taken aback to the point that she blushed a little and gave a genuine smile. She was probably used to her customers never looking higher than her breasts. "Hi. Would you like to sit down?"

I turned and left, waving the manager over. "Make sure they both have a good time, okay? Call me if there's a problem later."

"Okay, sir. And thank you."

"Don't mention it."

Driving back to the Bertoli estate, I had to smile as I thought of the look that passed between Carmen and Adam. I didn't know much about the girl, to be honest, but she seemed okay—just doing what she needed to do to survive.

When I got back, I was shocked to find Margaret Bertoli standing in the foyer, concern written on her face. "Mrs. Bertoli, what's wrong?"

"Adriana," she said, her eyes filled with worry. "She's been trying to go to sleep, but she's woken up twice now in the past hour, panicked and screaming. Daniel, I know you're trying, but you need to deal with this man who's doing this to her."

I nodded and took the thumb drive Adam had given me out of my jacket. "I got this tonight. Later on, I'll give it to Mr. Bertoli. It's more background information on Vincent Drake. I'll take a look at it after I talk to Adriana."

"Daniel . . ." she said, then nodded. "Fine. See if you can assure her that she's safe. Carlo and I certainly can't right now, it seems."

I rushed over to Adriana's bedroom, finding her sitting up in bed, her eyes haunted and her hands in her lap. "Dan . . . where were you?"

"Talking to my private investigator," I said. "Don't worry, I'm back."

"I'm having problems going to sleep," she said.

"You're scared," I said simply. Margaret was still in the room with us, so instead of taking her hand, I simply knelt down on the floor next to her bed. "Ade, you don't have to worry. I'm going to make sure you're safe."

"How? He got close enough to take those photos," Adriana said, revealing that she'd seen the email. I cursed under my breath at whatever dumb fuck had let her see them, then nodded.

"I know. But he won't get anywhere near you here, especially since I'm going to stay right here, sitting in a chair outside your room all night. Nobody's going to get by me."

Adriana nodded, her eyes filled with trust. "Daniel . . . thank you."

"Get some sleep, Ade. You've got that math class tomorrow, remember? Don't worry."

Margaret spoke with her daughter for a little while as I went down the hall and grabbed a chair from the library, arranging it and my laptop next to Adriana's door. I was just sitting down when Mrs. Bertoli came out. "Do you really plan on staying here all night?"

"Yes," I said simply. "If she calls out, I'll be there before she can even fully wake up."

She looked at me for a moment, then patted my shoulder. "Thank you, Daniel. After this . . . you and I should have a talk."

"About what, ma'am?"

She smiled. "About my brother-in-law's rules, and how sometimes they need to be changed. Good night, Daniel."

"Good night, Mrs. Bertoli. Sleep well."

She went down the hallway, and I looked to my left and right. Adriana's temporary room was buried in the interior of the house, with no windows to the outside, on the first floor in a relatively unused part of the guest wing. The house was quiet, and I sighed. Opening my laptop, I fired it up and decided that I could do a little bit of reading up on the information Adam had given me before I closed my eyes.

Chapter 11

Adriana

If there was one thing that was supposed to be a benefit of the new threat from Vincent, it was that the university's IT department finally agreed to change my student email. With how persistent he was, I don't know how much it would help, but it certainly wouldn't hurt.

Walking out of the IT building that afternoon with Daniel next to me, I smiled and stretched my arms over my head. The weather was great, and it was just one of those days where it was hard to feel bad, regardless of what was going on. "Well, score one for the good guys."

"*If* we're the good guys, that is," Daniel said with a smirk. "I don't think I make anyone's list of good guys."

"We can call you the anti-hero then," I replied with a punch to the shoulder. "You know, the bad guy with a giant redemptive streak."

"I can live with that," Daniel said, then shook his head a moment later. "Check that. I guess I've gotten used to people calling me at least decent over the past few days. It feels a bit strange. I'm used to being called a heartless bastard, or a similar sentiment."

"Okay, how about the good guy who sometimes does the hard thing?" I said instead as we walked down the stone steps and out into the quad. "I think that's a pretty good guy, actually, a lot better than most of the so-called good guys out there who aren't strong enough to stand up for what they believe in. And there's no way you could be called a heartless bastard."

"Much better. So what do you want to do between now and your last class? Which, by the way, I hate. The professor keeps staring at me while you guys fuck around on your computers doing Photoshop or whatever."

I laughed, realizing that Daniel didn't understand. "Dan, Professor Wilson's gay. He probably thinks you're hot. Or haven't you noticed that you have an effect on quite a few members of the student body?"

"Not concerned in how the rest of the student body reacts to me," Daniel said. He was scanning the quad again in his Terminator mode, more personable than he'd been the first day, but still focused on his job above all else. "I'm worried about you."

I knew what he was saying, but I blushed anyway. It had been touching that morning to find Daniel, still in his suit from the night before, sitting in the chair outside my room, his eyes open and looking to me when I cracked my door open.

Now, after a morning class and going to the administration office, he looked more than slightly worn out. He may be the Terminator, but he wasn't quite Superman. "Tell you what, let's go over to the student union and get you some coffee. It's not the best, but you need a shot of caffeine or something, and the place is busy enough that Drake wouldn't dare show his face. You can slack off for an hour while I keep my eyes open. We can even sit with my back to the wall."

Daniel smiled, then yawned. "Is it that obvious?"

"My math class is boring, but I've never seen your head

droop before today," I said. I stepped in front of him and put my hand on his chest, stopping him. "You're an amazing guy who's busted your ass for the past few weeks, but you're not invincible. You need sleep, too."

"I'll take twenty-four hours to do nothing but sleep after I ensure that Drake is in the ground," Daniel replied.

I knew for sure he was exhausted. He hadn't even made a sexual joke about taking me to bed with him. I was starting to miss the little game we played, even though neither of us ever acted on it. I patted his chest and turned around. "Come on, Dan. For the next sixty minutes, you're on break. I'll buy you the coffee after you close your eyes for a while. Trust me, I know exactly where to go."

The student union of my university has some pretty cool little areas, one of which was the so-called *Student Performance Center* on the second floor. Created and funded by a grant from one of the local tech giants, it had a lot of stuff that was supposed to help students relax, study, or just get their minds together better. A lot of it was junk, in my opinion, but there was one that would be useful at the moment.

"What's this?" Daniel asked as I led him inside, bouncing on the slightly squishy padding on the floor. "I'm tired, not insane. I don't need a padded room."

"It's a sensory isolation room," I said with a laugh, closing the door and locking it. "It's not totally secure. The staff can unlock the door from outside, but it cuts off the outside noise, and the floor is pretty comfortable. Oh, also about the staff—they have a video camera that was installed after these places got a reputation as a hook up spot. They get involved if any clothes come off."

"Hope they scrubbed the mats down then," Daniel said with a chuckle and set his bag down. He took a seat on the cushion and sighed, stretching out his legs. "It is pretty soft, though. I could see why people would want to have sex in a spot like this. Plenty comfortable standing, sitting, or laying down, I bet."

"It's comfortable enough that you can get a nap," I replied, ignoring the images that flashed through my mind of Daniel wearing a lot fewer clothes. "Go ahead. I'll be fine."

Daniel nodded gratefully and closed his eyes, leaning his head against the corner of the room. Within a minute, he was breathing deeply, and within five minutes, he was snoring lightly, his mouth open and his face looking calm and innocent. If Daniel was handsome when he was awake, asleep, he was absolutely stunning.

Shaking my head at the injustice that a man so rough could have such delicate eyelashes, I pulled out my math book, hoping to get a jump on my study for the test I had coming up the next week. Thankfully, the concepts were pretty straightforward. Business mathematics is almost all basic algebra, just applied in specific situations, and I thought I had a good grasp of things.

I was just working through how to do inventory depreciation calculations when I heard Daniel rearrange himself, moving into a more comfortable position. I looked over and smiled at the position he'd taken, stretching out almost the entire length of the small booth, his head pillowed against his bicep. His snoring stopped, and he breathed slowly and steadily. I wanted to stretch out next to him, to feel at least for a moment what it was like to be next to him like that, but I knew it was a bad idea.

"Ade . . ." Daniel mumbled in his sleep, his face relaxing even as I saw the quick flutter of his eyes behind his eyelids that told me he was in deep REM sleep, dreaming. "My Ade . . ."

I felt guilty, like I was spying on him in his most intimate moments, and I closed my book. I wanted to reach over and wake him, but I also knew that REM sleep is the type of sleep that the brain needs most. Instead, I put my book away and moved to the far side of the booth, trying to think of a way to distract myself without prying into his dreams.

Daniel mumbled again, this time unintelligible. His eyes were tight, and his free hand clenched at his chest. ". . . love you . . ."

His words sent a lightning bolt through my body, and I knew I was blushing. In the course of my life, I'd had men tell me they loved me before, and I'd said the same to them, but never had I heard such a heartfelt cry, and not from a man who didn't even know he was saying it. It was honestly the most romantic thing I'd ever felt in my entire life.

I still felt like I was prying, but I also knew I'd promised him that I would stay in the room until his nap was finished. If he woke up and I wasn't there, he'd be worried sick and I'd never be able to explain myself.

Instead, I sat back and pulled out my phone. The deprivation rooms were built with a sort of mesh in them that stopped cell and Wi-Fi signals, but that didn't mean I couldn't set my alarm. I sat back and closed my eyes, not really needing to go to sleep, but a little nap never hurt.

I must have dozed, however, because the next thing I

knew, I heard Daniel squirming on the floor, a weird sound coming from him. I opened my eyes and saw that his dream must've changed into a nightmare. His face was drawn and shocked, his eyes now open but unseeing, not realizing what was going on. He was locked in his mind, caught up in the trap of his own dreams. “No . . . no!”

Daniel's eyes widened again, and he scrambled to his feet, blinking and gasping as he was startled awake. “What the hell happened?”

“You had a bad dream, I think. Do you remember what it was?”

Daniel's mouth opened, then closed, and he shook his head. “No, not really. Uh, did I say anything while I was asleep?”

I shook my head. He didn't need to know, and I didn't need to tell him. My alarm went off, and I picked up my phone, shutting it off. “Well, if you're going to have a bad dream, at least you had good timing with it,” I said, chuckling. “Come on, we've got just enough time for us to grab some coffee before my next class.”

“I don't know if I should. If I look awake and perky, your professor might just eye fuck me for the entire period. If I look sleepy and surly, maybe he'll leave me alone,” Daniel grumped, then he shook his head and dragged his hand through his hair. “Oh well, fuck it. Let him stare.”

I smiled. “Good decision. Come on, let's get that coffee.”

Class went well, and Daniel and I were in a good mood when we got back to the house, even though it was Julius's turn to take over for a few hours. “Sorry, the nap was nice, but I need more if I'm going to be good for tonight,” Daniel said as he stood at the base of the stairs. "Sure you'll be okay?"

"We'll be fine, won't we, Julius?" I asked, grinning at the older enforcer. "You can help me with mixing my paints for my project I'm working on."

* * *

Daniel slept from six until ten, waking up a bit after Mom and Uncle Carlo got home.

"Well, I'm glad he'll be up in time for the night watch," Mom said, giving me a meaningful look. "And how are you feeling?"

"The new email is good, even though I know it's kind of a bit of window dressing," I said. "And I know things are at a standstill on other fronts, but I'm taking progress where I can."

Mom gave me a look. "Is your good mood from the email, or from something else? *Someone* else?"

"Mom, let's not go there," I said. "Not now. Not yet."

"All right, dear. I just want you to know, I was thinking of talking with Carlo after all this mess is done. I'd like you to have a little freedom to make your own choices, Adriana."

"Thank you, Mom. I appreciate it, no matter how futile your speaking to Carlo is. But for now, I think I'm going to go to bed."

Mom nodded, looking at the doorway where Julius was sitting in the other room, slightly sprawled in his chair and reading a Sports Illustrated. "Okay. You aren't going to stay awake until Daniel can sit outside the door?"

"I guess," I said, grinning. "Think you might want to catch some TV with me to kill some time?"

We had just gotten to the TV room when my phone

buzzed in my pocket and I pulled it out. It was a text message, and I pulled it up.

There must be some misunderstanding.
- You Know Who

"Damn, not again," I whispered under my breath. It's like he knew exactly when Daniel didn't have my phone.

"What is it, honey?" Mom asked, turning white when she saw the text. "Are you okay?"

"I'm not going to let him terrorize me," I said. "He's twisted up my life, made me a prisoner in my own home, and I need to be babysat everywhere. I'm going to set this aside. We can tell Uncle Carlo and Daniel about it later, but for the next hour or so, let's just watch some TV."

I *thought* I had put it out of my mind, even casually mentioning it to Daniel when he woke up and met Mom and me in the living room. Going to bed in my room, I even closed my eyes with a smile, thinking not only of what Mom had told me, but the little smile of approval she gave me as Daniel escorted me to my room.

Everything changed as I slept, and the fear I'd been repressing slipped out from under the tight control I'd been keeping myself in. I don't know what had caused it—perhaps it was seeing Daniel frightened earlier, maybe it was Vincent's text message, but most likely, it was the combination of the two.

In my dream, I was in Daniel's car with him, the two of us pulling into the parking lot at school. As Daniel was coming around to let me out, suddenly, something burst out of the bushes, tackling him from behind and driving him to the ground. I couldn't see exactly what happened, except for the gout of blood that geysered up into the air, in the sort of dream-state unimaginable amount that looked like it was a foot wide and spewing in gallons per second.

I screamed in my dream, ripping open the door to the car and running. "Mama, come here, mama," whoever was chasing me said in Vincent Drake's voice. "Come and feel my invisible touch."

I tried to run faster, but of course, as this was a dream, I was going nowhere. Instead, I could feel him gaining on me, his stench filling the air with the reek of blood and death.

My feet tangled up, sending me tumbling to the turf. I screamed, certain that I was going to die, when I was jostled awake, finding Daniel staring at me. "Shh, Ade, shh . . ." Daniel whispered, holding me close. I could hear the hammering of his heart in my ear as he hugged me against his chest. "It's just a dream, I'm right here, it's just a dream."

"He got you," I whispered, watching as the door to my room finished closing from the momentum of Daniel's throwing it open to come in my room. "He killed you, then was going to kill me."

"I'm still here," Daniel promised me. "And I won't die without knowing you're safe."

I clung to him, his strength and now familiar scent giving me comfort. My terror changed, my desire for comfort becoming an overwhelming desire for reassurance, for human contact. Nuzzling against him, I lifted my lips up, brushing them over the warm skin of his throat. "Ade."

"Shut up," I said, tasting his skin for the first time. "I need a man tonight, not a bodyguard."

He stiffened for a moment, then pushed me back, the hunger in his eyes matching the fire that was building inside me. For so long, we'd flirted with each other, both aware of the other but not doing anything about it other than some words, and we were at the point of no return. He pushed me onto my back, pausing above to look at me with an expression on his face I'd never seen a man give me before. It was like he knew what he was about to do was suicide, but he didn't care. I needed him, he needed me, and the rest of the world didn't matter.

His lips were soft but strong as we kissed for the first time, our tongues immediately coming into contact and tasting each other. I'd never been kissed with such fierce passion before, all consuming and powerful. His tongue caressed mine as his hands found the hem of my t-shirt, pushing it up and grabbing my breast, his fingers squeezing and kneading the skin until I was gasping. My nipple was teased and tweaked with every movement of his hand, and he let go of my lips to run the tip of his tongue around the curve of my ear and inside, sending sparks of pleasure down my body. "Daniel . . ."

He stopped for a second to look me in my eyes. "Don't worry, I won't hurt you."

"I want you to hurt me. Hurt me in a good way."

Reaching down, I ran my left hand over the bulge in his pants, and it was intimidating. "Ade."

"I know," I said simply, looking him in the eye. "I didn't tell you before, but you talked in your sleep during your nap."

He nodded, accepting my statement, and reached into the pocket of his pants. He took out his wallet and set it on the nightstand next to me. Climbing off, he opened up the billfold and took out a foil packet. "For later," he said, showing me the condom. I was shocked. The diameter was huge. "Safety first."

Daniel's grin broadened, and he peeled off his shirt. He folded it up carefully, setting in on the floor before pushing his shoes off with his toes and taking off his pants. I wasn't sure what to think. I just lay there with a sense of destiny as I undid the drawstring on my pajamas and pushed them down my hips. I still had my panties on when Daniel reached forward, taking my wrists in his iron grip, and froze me. "What?"

"Not so fast. I want to take those off myself."

He climbed onto the bed, still wearing his boxer briefs that bulged out obscenely, barely hiding what was contained inside. His chest was chiseled in the dim light of the bedside lamp he'd flipped on when he came in to comfort me, and I reached forward, tracing the muscles under my fingertips. "You're amazing."

"No," he replied, kissing me again before working his way down, his mouth finding my nipple and sucking on it strongly. "You're amazing."

He kissed his way down to the waistband of my panties, and with agonizing slowness, started rolling them down. I could feel the anticipation build as he kissed each fraction of an inch of freshly exposed skin, smiling all the while.

I reached down and ran my hand over his scalp, lifting my hips slightly to let him finish pulling my panties off, where he set them down on the mattress next to my hip. I was nearly begging him to use that amazing tongue on me, and he hadn't even touched me yet.

Daniel grinned up at me as he opened his mouth and let his tongue hang out wolfishly. "You're never going to be the same."

"Good," I whispered back. "I don't want to be."

He lowered his tongue, and the first trace of him up the lips of my pussy left me paralyzed in pure pleasure. I'd never felt anything like it before, like every nerve in my body was lit up at the same time, all of them screaming in joy. When he reached the top, Daniel looked in my face and smiled, this time not with arrogance but with happiness. "I think you like it."

"More. Please, more." I couldn't help it. Normally, I was the forceful one in bed, but Daniel had me asking and practically begging.

He smiled at me, lowering his head once again. All thought other than pleasure was driven from my mind by the first touch of his tongue on my pussy again. Energy and light flooded my body, my thighs trembling and wanting more of his amazing, electric tongue. My spine shivered as he kept going, my hips quivering as I started to grind upward into his hungry mouth and tongue, unable to control myself. I'd never felt this much pleasure before, such a pure ball of sexual excitement building within me, and I wanted more and more.

Dimly, in the back of my mind, I was aware that Daniel had slipped his fingers inside me, working them back and forth both to open me up for his cock and to add to whatever voodoo his tongue was doing to me. All I knew was that I was in heaven and that I didn't think it would ever stop.

Suddenly, his tongue moved directly to my clit, and what I thought was heaven before increased tenfold. I clutched at my sheets, balling them in my hands as something exploded inside me, silent and joyful and amazing all at the same time. My heels drummed into his strong back, uncontrolled and desperate. Daniel held my hips tight, pushing with his hand on my pussy as I rode whatever the hell it was out, until I collapsed into the bed, spent. "What the hell was that?"

"Don't tell me you've never had an orgasm before," Daniel said in disbelief as he crawled up between my legs, kissing my lips. The musk of my juices stained his mouth, and I loved it. It meant nothing would ever be the same between us again, and I was glad for it.

"Of course, dummy. But nothing like that before," I said, thinking back. After experiencing that, no wonder some women became nymphomaniacs. "Never in my life."

"It gets better," he promised, kissing me softly. "Want to help me with the condom?"

"What I want is to forget the damn thing and totally feel you inside me," I said while reaching over to grab the packet.

He got to his knees and pulled down his shorts. His cock jumped out, bobbing in the soft light, and I gasped at its perfection. Long, thick, with a flared head that I knew would thrill every nerve inside me. I was suddenly struck with the urge to bend over and suck it, even though I had my doubts I could even get it all the way into my mouth. He was power and sex personified, a deity in the flesh.

Hesitantly, I reached out with my hand, wrapping it around his shaft, or at least trying to. It was hot, steely hard but silky, like he knew the impressive tool was too much for a lot of women to accept, so it did its best to ease the penetration. And that is what this was for, there was no doubt. Daniel, from his bubble butt to his ripped abs to the thick cock, was a man built for sex. "Dan . .

.”

“I know,” he reassured me. “Don't worry.”

I looked up at him, and suddenly I didn't. I trusted him with my life, and I was ready to trust him with more. Instead, I gently stroked his cock and handed him the condom packet. “Take it out, and I'll put it on.”

Even with the obvious larger size, Daniel's cock was nearly too large for the condom, and he grimaced slightly as I rolled it down to the base. I gasped, kissing his chest and nuzzling under his jawline.

He ran his hands up and down my back and kissed my neck. We were on our knees, his cock trapped between us, hot and throbbing and demanding my attention.

I adjusted myself and laid back, spreading my legs as far as I could, accepting him in between and on top of me. “Change me. Make me yours.”

There was a moment of fear as his cock slid inside me, spreading me open. I thought he was in, but I felt myself being opened wider, wider than I'd ever thought I could be, and still I didn't think the head of his cock was fully inside me. My body rebelled, pushing back at the too-large intruder, when somehow, he slipped inside, all the resistance disappearing in a rush of fullness.

“Just know one thing, Ade.”

“What?”

Daniel paused his hips and looked me in the eye. “I've wanted this my whole life.”

I pulled him to me, our lips meeting to seal our bond. I moaned into his mouth as he began thrusting, filling me slowly, making me his. I realized the truth as he filled me more and more, that his words were absolutely true. He may have been with other women, he may have fucked them raw and left them begging for more, but I was the one he *really* wanted.

I cried out when Daniel's hips met mine for the first time, and he grimaced, his face tight. "No!" he whispered urgently, bringing his fingers to my lips and shushing me. "Your uncle is sleeping upstairs, remember?"

"I can't help it," I groaned as he pulled back, biting my lip as he pushed forward again. I tried with all my might, but I cried out again, a little less loudly this time, but still loud enough that Daniel looked away, panicked. Not wanting to lose him, to lose the moment, I looked wildly to my left and right, seeing my night shirt still on the bed. I grabbed it. "Here. Use this."

Daniel considered it for a moment, then nodded. "Only if I have to."

Lowering his lips to mine, he kissed me again while he thrust, his mouth swallowing my moans and adding to the sensation. I'd never been stretched this way, and I wanted it again and again. My hips tried to rise up to meet his thrusts as his cock slid in and out, but he was so powerful, I was hammered down to the mattress even before I had a chance to move.

I held on desperately, my body racked with feeling as Daniel pounded me. I knew he was unleashing years, perhaps even as he said, a lifetime's worth of pent up passion and desire, and I wanted it all. I wanted to be his, to give myself to him every night of my life, if only he'd make me feel this way again.

"Daniel . . ." I groaned in his ear. "I'm going to come."

"Me too," he grunted back, taking the wadded up cotton of

my shirt and shoving it in my mouth. He had to, pulling back so that he could get the great gulps of air he needed to thrust into me, his body shimmering in sweat and his face intent on mine. His arms were planted in my pillow on each side of my head, and he stared into my eyes as we crashed over the edge.

I had thought the sensation of his tongue had been the most ecstasy a woman could feel and not die, but I was wrong. My second climax crushed the first like it was just a small tickle, my scream muffled by the cotton I bit down on even as my hands clawed at his back. I felt his flesh give way under my short fingernails, and I watched as he shuddered, his cock expanding before twitching, his climax crashing over him and leaving me feeling more of a woman than ever. I had caused this wonderful man to lose that much control. I had drawn it out of him, and I was proud of the fact.

Daniel took the cloth from my mouth, kissing me tenderly, completing the act of making love. What we'd done left one thought in my mind as I was chased down into my sleep and my dreams. "I'm yours . . . be mine . . ."

Chapter 12

Daniel

I awoke after my doze with my damnation in my arms, and for the moment, I couldn't have been happier. If I was to be damned, there were a lot worse ways to go than to wake up with Adriana Bertoli nestled in my arms, her fiery hair cascading over my left arm and chest, the soft weight of her right breast resting in my palm, her hips snuggled up against me. In the soft glow of her bedside lamp, she was an angel, even with her eyes closed.

I sighed and kissed her forehead, knowing how much had changed for me, even with just that one time. First, I was damned, a dead man walking. The reason was simple. There was no way in the world I could even think of not wanting her again. Her final whispered words as she fell asleep captured me more than her body had, as perfect as it was.

If I couldn't resist her, then I knew it was only a matter of time before Don Bertoli found out. We could be together on only the third Tuesday of each month in a random hotel a thousand miles from Seattle, and still, somehow, he would find out. That's just the way things happened with him, and part of the reason he was such a good boss. And once the Don found out I'd been with Adriana, regardless of whether Margaret approved of it, I'd be found dead within twenty-four hours.

The second thing that surprised me as I held her in the quiet hours of the night was that I didn't feel the immediate need to wake her for another round. My cock wanted it. I could feel it hardening against her ass. It was rip, roaring, and ready to go. It wanted this moment for as long as I could remember, and just once wouldn't do. Even still, I didn't feel the emotional need. Normally, I was a sexual-timed all-you-can-eat buffet, seeing just how much I could get done in the amount of time before the woman's body gave out into utter exhaustion. With Adriana, though, I felt differently. Let her rest, my heart said. She's special. There will be more to come.

With a start, I wondered what time it was. Twisting my neck painfully to look behind me, I saw that it was nearly three thirty in the morning. I'd been out for a while. The staff would start to wake in an hour or so, but more importantly to me was that the outdoor patrols hadn't come back in yet. They were under strict orders. Once the doors were locked and the security system was armed, nobody went in or came out until the morning staff went on duty at five. There were even outdoor bathrooms if someone had to take a piss. Still, I couldn't be sure someone didn't have a case of insomnia.

With regret, I eased myself away from Adriana, my heart breaking when she mumbled in her sleep. "No . . ."

"Shh, I'm just going to stretch a bit," I whispered softly, kissing her hair. I found the edge of the blanket and folded it over her, confident that nobody would disturb her sleep and find her gloriously naked underneath the blanket. Easing my way around the room, I was glad I'd taken the time to fold up my clothes neatly, even finding my socks still stuffed inside my shoes. I looked around after I finished dressing and nearly smacked my head as I saw two pieces of incriminating evidence: the condom wrapper and the condom itself. I gathered both of them and reminded myself to dispose of them.

Slipping out of Adriana's room, I paused at the door, sparing a look back at her sleeping figure on the bed. Memories flashed through my head, and I couldn't help but smile.

I heard footsteps coming down the corridor, and I nearly jumped out of the room, closing her door behind me. I had only a second to slide down into the chair when one of the morning staff, a cook named Kathy who I'd once hooked up with, came down the hallway. "Good morning, Daniel. Still awake?"

"Of course," I said, pulling my laptop in front of me and hoping she didn't notice I was just turning it on now. "What's got you up so early? Trying to get a sunrise yoga session in or something?"

"Indigestion, actually," she said. "Since all this stuff kicked off with Princess Firecrotch in there, I can't get a full night's sleep. Someone told me you were staying outside in the hall recently, and I was thinking that seeing if you were up would be a better use of my time than tossing back and forth, debating if I wanted to try and chew on a Rolaid before faking another hour and a half of sleep or not."

Kathy's mouth was one of the main reasons I'd both fucked her and hated dealing with her. While she was a talented cook, she was disrespectful of nearly everyone else besides the Don, especially Adriana. She never missed an opportunity to talk down about her, with a list of nicknames that ranged from merely disrespectful to downright disgusting. Princess Firecrotch was one of the milder ones.

"Kathy, you know I hate it when you disrespect the

Bertolis," I admonished. "Seriously." I figured she wasn't as careless with her tongue around anyone else, and that she thought since I slept with her in the past, I could be trusted.

"Well, what does she have that I don't have, besides a last name and some bigger tits?" Kathy said with a sneer. "She's an art student with some double Ds. At least I went to culinary school before going to work."

I didn't want to be drawn into an argument. My lovemaking with Adriana was so near at hand that I wasn't sure I'd maintain my objectivity. "Kathy, I know your feelings. But I'm a Bertoli man, you know that. I'm asking you to cut the comments around me. Now, if you'll excuse me, I have some work to do."

She crossed her arms and gave me a dirty look. "She's got you whipped, and she hasn't even given you any pussy yet. And to think, you could have been having me this whole time."

"I've had better," I said evenly, looking her in the eye. "Much better. Is there anything else?"

"Fuck off, Oliver," Kathy hissed back, turning and stomping away. I chuckled under my breath and wondered if she knew that her attempt at giving me a nickname hadn't gone over my head. While I had stopped at a high school education, I'd read *Oliver Twist* back when I was in junior high. I mean, come on, orphan boy gets involved with criminals before making good? What kid in my position in life wouldn't want to read it? Between that and *Great Expectations,* I was fully educated in Dickenson's ideas on what could happen to orphans. So far, reality was far different from fiction.

I shook my head, thanking my luck that I had gotten out of Adriana's room when I did, and turned my attention to the laptop.

I hadn't been totally lying. I did want to complete some work, mainly on analysis of the photos that Vincent Drake had sent in his most recent harassing email. There was something about them that tickled my brain, and I wanted to see if my sleep-induced theory was right.

Pulling up the message, I made sure my volume was turned off and started to dissect the email. The slide show had been pretty basic, what you could put together with a typical office suite program, and by doing a little splicing of code, I was able to pull out the actual slide show itself from the surrounding programming. It surprised me somewhat that a man who had the programming skills to do a desktop hack would be so lazy as to use just an office suite for the video itself, but it was a bit of good luck for me. Perhaps he wasn't as skilled as I thought, but just knew how to use ready-made code you could pull off the right websites if you knew what they were.

Once I had the slides isolated, I took a look at the pictures that were taken with me in them. I soon saw that all of them were taken from the same area of the campus, although they'd been taken on different days. With that hint, I looked at Google Maps, using the satellite overhead shot to identify the areas of campus that he had most likely taken the photographs from. I hoped that it would be something easy, like a single apartment building or something equally stupid. In fact, the most likely area was a narrow band of woods that bordered one edge of campus, planted about forty years ago to help separate the campus from the busy street on the other side. It stretched for nearly a half-mile, and on the other side was a major street. While it helped me in that it eased my fears of Drake bringing a rifle to the same spot in order to take a shot, I still wasn't totally at ease.

I shrugged and sent the information to Adam in an email. He said in his last message that he had some feelers out on Drake's cyber trail, going through the photography equipment he'd used. Apparently, the market for such items is pretty small, and Adam had some ideas.

The gray light of pre-dawn started lighting up the sky, and I sighed, stretching in my chair. There were still at least two hours before I had to wake Adriana up, and until then, I couldn't even go get coffee, which I desperately needed. Sure, I was damned, but even the damned could protect an angel, and that was what I was going to do.

Chapter 13

Adriana

I woke up in the morning, immediately feeling like I was missing something. I reached out with my arm, pushing the blanket on top of me aside, and realized what it was. Daniel. Where was he?

"Daniel?" I said, keeping my voice down to avoid being overheard. I opened my eyes and looked around, trying not to be sad but failing when I found that I was alone.

Had it all been a dream, a morphing of my nightmare into a fantasy? I closed my eyes and knew by the pleasant ache down below that it couldn't have been. Even the smell in the air of the small room wasn't that of a wet dream or a masturbatory fantasy. There was the distinct smell of male sweat and sex in the air, and I knew it had all been real. The kiss, the tasting, the mind blowing sex, all of it.

Getting out of bed, I found my pajamas still lying where I'd left them, except for my t-shirt, of course, and I picked everything up and put it in my laundry bag. The motion must have created some noise outside the door, because seconds later, I heard a knock. "Adriana?"

It was Daniel. "Daniel?"

"Are you dressed?" he asked, his voice professional and lacking any of the passion or tenderness he'd shown me last night. Swallowing my sudden tears, I grabbed my bathrobe off the hook next to the door and pulled it on, belting it quickly. "I am now. Come in."

He opened the door, looking in with the friendly but not enamored look that he'd had the night before. "Hey, glad you're up. We're running a bit late this morning, so I asked one of the other guys to take you to breakfast while I run and grab a shower and change. I'll see you in the car."

"Dan . . ." I started, but his eyes silenced me, and he gave me a shake of his head that could have been measured in millimeters. "Later."

"At school," he said and turned, leaving. Julius waited for me in the hallway, looking tired but not overly concerned. He'd been on outdoor patrol and probably had a very boring night.

"Good morning, Julius. Shouldn't you be heading home now?"

"Eh, I'll do that in about a half-hour or so. Just going to take you to breakfast, then grab my things and go. How'd you sleep?"

"It was . . . different," I said, sighing. There was no other way to describe it without giving myself away. "Anyway, let me grab my shower and then you can take me to breakfast. Give me ten minutes?"

"No problem."

The entire drive to school, Daniel was reluctant to talk, at least about what I wanted to talk about. Instead, he insisted on talking about the weather, the people driving by, the song on the radio, the normal chit-chat that I thought we'd worked past. When we pulled into the parking lot at school, I didn't even give him a chance to open my door before I was out and slamming it, nearly catching his fingers in the process.

"Can we talk now?" I seethed, angry but not really knowing why. "Or do you want to discuss if Icon for Hire is going to be putting out another new single in the next few weeks or not?"

Daniel glanced at his watch, a cheap little G-shock knockoff that he'd picked up from the campus bookstore, then pointed at the student union. "Study booth," he said, his voice both soft and hard at the same time. He could tell I was pissed, but there was no room for argument in his voice. It wasn't a request. It was a command. "We've got ten, fifteen minutes at most."

Thankfully, the early morning meant few people were using the booths, and as Daniel closed the door and locked it behind him, I turned, trying not to yell. "What the hell? I knew you were the type for casual sex, but I hoped after what you said last night . . . I didn't think that's all it was. I hoped . . ."

Daniel cut my words off, pulling me to him and kissing me hard, his hands crushing our bodies together as he pushed me against the wall. His tongue was electric, leaving my lips to trace around my ear again, lighting me up in ways that, until the night before, I didn't even know existed. In fewer than ten seconds, I'd gone from pissed to so aroused that I'd have had sex with him right there, regardless of the fact that I knew the booths were monitored by security cameras for preventing that exact thing.

"Dan . . ." I sighed, wrapping my arms around his neck and holding him gently as he let me go, his hands still resting on my hips, his eyes full of tenderness. "Why?"

"Why did I kiss you right now, or why did I leave you this

morning to wake up alone?" he asked softly, his eyes warm and his voice tender.

"How about both?" I replied, enjoying the feeling of being forehead to forehead like this, like a couple dancing without moving. "You pissed me off."

"I know, and I'm sorry about that. It wasn't my intention," he said, his fingers tracing patterns on my lower back. "But I kissed you because I didn't want you going off in a rant that I knew I could explain if you just gave me a chance. I kissed you because for the past two hours, it's been the only thing I've wanted to do, ever since opening the door to your room and seeing you in that bathrobe, looking lost and scared. I wanted to tell you that you're different, that I don't want this to be only one night. But that's also why I didn't say anything at the house, and why I had to leave your room at the same time."

"Uncle Carlo," I said, realizing. "The rules."

Daniel nodded, sadness in his eyes. "Ade, last night I wrote my own death warrant, and I don't regret it. Even though I was nearly caught sneaking out of your room, I don't regret it. The only regret I have is that the chances of us having real happiness, the future that I can see in your eyes and in the way you talked last night . . . the odds of that are slim to none. I'm Neiman, *no man*, an orphan with no family. No name, nothing but my wits, a decent gun, and what Carlo Bertoli has given me. You're his niece, the only child of his murdered brother. You're more precious to him than a daughter, Adriana. And Carlo has told me twice now, if I ever did what happened this morning, I was a dead man. Do you know your uncle to be a man who's willing to compromise?"

I blinked, tears in my eyes. "No," I whispered. "But Daniel

. . . maybe it can still happen. Mom said she'd talk to him. Her and I together, maybe?"

He kissed me again, his lips soft and silencing. When we parted, he smiled. "I doubt it. It's okay though. You're worth it. You know, my only worry as I sat out there in the hallway was that I know if we keep doing this, doing what I have so wanted to do for years, that I'd be breaking your heart? Not because I'll leave you on my own, but because you're going to have to bury me."

"Not going to happen," I replied, my anger coming back but not directed at him. "You've spent weeks protecting me, and I know you'll give Vincent what he deserves. I need you to put some faith in me, too."

"How so?" he asked, a smile on his face even as uncertainty flashed in his eyes.

"Let me protect *you*. You keep me safe from Drake, and I'll keep you safe from Uncle Carlo."

Daniel's eyes were still concerned, but he nodded. "Okay. But we do have to have rules. Rule one is, no expressions of affection or our new situation in public. Not even here at the university."

"And this study room?" I asked, pulling him closer this time. "Please tell me I can spend at least my study time in this sort of room with you, kissing those bewitching, seductive lips if nothing else?"

He took his hand off my hip long enough to glance at his watch, then nodded. "For another two minutes at least. Then we might have to take a break until after your second class of the day. You've got that meeting with your Renaissance professor at three this afternoon. That's a gap of nearly two hours."

I pulled his head down, my lips hungry and eager for one last kiss. "Two hours . . . I can make do with that."

* * *

Getting home that night, I was happier than I'd ever been before. The two hours with Daniel hadn't happened in a study booth. Those had all been taken up when we got back to the student union after my second class, but instead, in a little used section of the library, where we kissed and made out like teenagers in between stacks of musty books that I doubted had been taken off the shelves in years. I'd actually been two minutes late for my meeting with my professor, apologizing but not overly concerned. Artists normally have a reputation for not being on time anyway.

At dinner, even Uncle Carlo noticed my newfound happiness. "You look better than you have in weeks, Bella," he remarked as he sipped at his wine. "What's going on?"

"Just classes went well, Uncle," I said, not liking lying to him but knowing how important it was. "And I had a good meeting with a professor. Besides, the weather today was great, and just before dinner, I had a nice session in the pool. How could I not feel better?"

He nodded and took another drink. "I understand. I'm glad to see that you are adapting well. You know, I had a period, before you were born, when I had to go everywhere with a bodyguard as well."

"Really?" I asked, intrigued. "What happened?"

"Eh, this was back in the late eighties, when the Japanese were trying to buy up Seattle," Carlo said, reminiscing. "Your father was in charge then, but I was the one in charge of talking with some Japanese who came in from Osaka, wanting to muscle in on our turf. They thought they could go through the port without cooperating with the local groups. In negotiations between us and them, things quickly broke down as they thought they could bring in some Yakuza muscle and just take what they wanted without providing the proper respect. Things got quite heated for a little while, and there was a month or so in the middle when Johnny and I both went around with bodyguards."

It was rare that he talked about my father, and even less often that he used Dad's name. Gianni "Johnny" Bertoli had been his closest friend and protector growing up, and it was nice to hear Uncle Carlo talk about him. "How'd it get resolved?"

"In ways that are not for the dinner table discussion," Uncle Carlo said with a cryptic smile.

* * *

After dinner, I worked on my painting for the night. Daniel woke from his nap in time to watch me finish. "It's changing," he remarked. "It's not as dark as it was before."

"I've got reasons to feel more positive about the world," I said, carefully avoiding saying what I meant. "Still, it is pretty dark for me."

I washed up, changing into my pajamas and going to my bedroom, where Daniel's chair and new side table for his computer were already waiting for him. I paused at the door, turning around. "Come tuck me in?" I whispered, leaning in close. "Or maybe check under my bed for monsters?"

"If I do that, the only monster will be in your bed," he growled sexily in reply, his breath tickling my ear. "Are you sure you want that?"

"More than anything," I replied. Disregarding the risk, I

leaned in and kissed him on the cheek. "Maybe later, when everyone is asleep."

I heard footsteps in the hallway and pulled back just as Kathy walked by, her clogs squeaking on the hallway tile. "Well, good night, Daniel. I hope you can get your work done," I said, maybe a touch too loudly. Kathy disappeared around the corner, and I blushed. "Sorry."

"My fault," Daniel whispered, his eyes flicking left and right before focusing on me, their icy blueness softening to angelic warmth. "Good night, beautiful lady."

Chapter 14

Daniel

Three days later, I was still walking in heaven, but I was also seriously pissed off. I was in heaven because I'd never had such a sensual, exciting time before in my life. Every moment with Adriana was pure, agonizing bliss. We found little ways to sneak in shared contact and moments, like her resting her hand on the console of my car while I drove her anywhere. When I could, I'd reach over and lay my right hand on hers, just resting there until I had to make a turn.

Adriana started coming to the house gym not once or twice a week, but each of the past three days. It was motivating and sexy to work out in front of her, something I'd never experienced before. Exercise was for fitness and performance, not foreplay. At least, that's what I'd thought until Adriana started doing hip bridges in short, tight shorts—supposedly to tighten her backside, but in the meantime, giving me one hell of a show.

Mostly though, we found private places around campus in the form of closed classrooms or private nooks in the library where we could hold each other. In those spaces, there was no Bertoli or Neiman, and there was no danger. It was our own private little world, where I was able to feast on her kisses, to run my fingers through her hair, and even when we were feeling super frisky, caress the soft weight of her breast through her shirt while she cupped my balls through my shorts. Teenager stuff, but I was still enthralled.

The second night I'd gone into Adriana's room, just after two in the morning, I found her sitting up, nervous. "I was afraid you wouldn't come," she whispered, climbing out of bed and walking over to me. "I was going crazy in here."

We didn't just fuck, but instead we made love, even if it was hasty. Each night, Adriana gave herself to me while I taught her what her body was really capable of feeling.

"I'm drunk from our time together, and I want to explore more with you."

I was drunk too, knowing the risks each night when I opened her door, and each night, not caring as she kissed me for the first time. I needed Adriana like I needed air and water. I couldn't stop.

I was happy in a way I'd never felt before. But, three days later, I was seriously pissed off. Not at Adriana, but at Adam. He hadn't messaged me in two days, not even his normal message of 'nothing new.' With Drake still out there, I was getting annoyed.

That morning, as we drove to school, Adriana noticed. "What's wrong?" she asked, her hand resting on mine. While we couldn't be sure my car wasn't bugged by Don Bertoli himself—after all, it had been his men who'd *secured* my car—we could still talk about other things. "You're looking more tense than normal today."

"Haven't heard from Adam in a few days. I hope he isn't slacking off," I growled, pulling my hand away to make a right turn. "I need his help."

"I'm sure he's doing his best," she replied, trying to reassure me. "Have you tried calling his office?"

I shook my head. “He's kind of a one-man operation. He says he has assistants, but what he means is that he has people he sometimes shops out work to. Your case, though, he was handling personally. And the only contacts I have for him are his cellphone and email.”

“Well then, have you tried calling him?” Adriana asked with a chuckle. “I mean, that's what I'd do.”

“Of course, but he's not picking up. I left him a message. I was going to give some other people a call this afternoon and see if he'd been by. He was giving the girl at that Starlight Club quite the look when I last saw him. Knowing Adam, he's gone back at least once.”

“She's that hot, huh?”

“Men will do stupid and dangerous things for women they're attracted to,” I replied, giving her a meaningful look, which she returned with a smile. It was the closest we came to saying how we felt in the car. “So I'll wait until the club is open, then give them a call.”

After lunch, I did just that, sitting next to Adriana in the cafeteria while I dialed. The phone rang a few times, and I was just getting ready to leave a message when Terry, the manager, picked up, sounding out of breath. “Starlight Club, what can I do for you?”

“Terry, it's Daniel Neiman,” I said, giving him a second to adjust. “How's it going?”

As usual, Terry semi-freaked out when he heard my voice. I didn't know why. Other than the incident with Carmen, I'd never even had to threaten the man. He was always on time with his payments and had never given the Bertolis any reason to be concerned about him. He even threw in some free extras to Bertoli men from time to time, but he still acted like we were about to burn the place down whenever we even talked. "Good afternoon, sir. What can I do for you today, sir?"

I rolled my eyes, letting Adriana listen in some, and she covered her mouth, laughing silently at the overabundance of the word sir. "Terry, I'm calling for some information, nothing more. My friend I brought by the other night, Adam . . . has he come by the club again recently? I'm trying to get a hold of him."

"He was here last night, actually," Terry said, relief in his voice. "Uhm, I don't know if you would approve sir, but he and Carmen left the club. I think they may have gone on a date."

I nearly dropped my phone, I was so surprised. "A date? No offense, but doesn't that break the rules?"

"It does, but Carmen is quite taken with him for some reason. I don't have any leverage on her. She's clean and sober, totally debt free. She dances by choice. And from what she told me, Adam doesn't have a problem if she continues to dance. There's little I can do to stop them."

"Never mind. Good for Adam," I said, dismissing it with a small laugh. "Listen, can you please give Carmen a call? I doubt you want to give me her number, but just tell her that if she's in contact with Adam, I need to speak to him immediately. Think you can do that?"

"Of course, sir. However, Carmen should be in at three o'clock today, if that's okay."

"Okay, but please call me back no later than five. Thanks, Terry."

"It is no problem, sir. Uhm, one thing though."

"What's that?" I asked. Adriana sat back, and I pulled the phone to my ear.

"About the first meeting between the two and the matter of the bill. It isn't much, only a thousand, but I was wondering when we might be able to settle it?"

I chuckled and looked at Adriana, who gave me an innocent look. Now that we were *together*, if you could even call it that, it seemed that she wasn't as upset about the other side of my work any longer. "I can stop by this evening, say around nine or so. If Carmen is around then, I need to talk with her. Professionally. Maybe backstage?"

"A VIP would be better, sir. The other girls will be preparing for work, and your reputation precedes you. But I'll let her know."

"Thank you, Terry. Goodbye."

I hung up my phone and noticed Adriana's look, a small, affectionate smile of amusement. "What?"

"You asked a dynamite stripper to wear clothes for a conversation," she said with a proud little smirk. "I guess I am having an effect on you."

* * *

The VIP lounge was quiet. I'd turned on some Samuel Barber music to drown out the outside noise when Carmen came in, looking totally different than I'd ever seen her before. Out of her stripper clothes, she looked like one of the girls I'd seen running around the college campus the past few weeks—or even younger. When she noticed that I was looking at her strangely, she blushed and looked down. "What, Papi?"

"Just . . . I know this sounds strange, but you look a lot

different, Carmen. Better, if you can dig it."

"I can," she said, even sounding different from the Latina seductress I'd known her as. "And thank you. Most of the guys I dance for seem to only think of me in that short skirt with my boobs hanging out. I doubt any of them give a damn otherwise."

"Except it seems Adam does," I said, using her comment to broach the subject of my visit. "Can I ask?"

Carmen laughed, giving me a genuine smile. "Well, he definitely was disarmingly charming—not like the type that usually comes in here. So when he asked if he could see me again, I said yes, and without him asking, I gave him my phone number. I figured he'd never call, but he did, and we've been out twice since. Breakfast both times—we tend to work hours that preclude romantic dinners and such."

"That's kind of what I wanted to ask you about," I said. "I'm sure you know I work for Don Bertoli."

"Of course I know. Everyone does," Carmen said, her voice serious. Carlo Bertoli was not a man most people wanted to joke about. "Honestly, it's why you scared me so much that night you lost control. You're the sort of man who could blow my brains out and not face any repercussions."

"I don't know about that, but I'm still sorry about that. You didn't deserve what I did, that's for sure. You were a bit . . . how shall we put it?"

Carmen laughed. "Let's just put that behind us—how about that? So what's your question?"

"Recently, the Bertoli family has been threatened. I've been assigned as bodyguard to his niece, and I asked Adam to look into the person coming after her. He was giving me daily updates until two days ago. Do you know what happened?"

Carmen thought, then blushed slightly. "I know what happened two nights ago," she said with a smile.

"Well, that explains that night," I said, "but what happened since?"

"I don't know. I haven't heard from him, and it seemed like he really liked me."

I thought for a moment, perplexed. She must've really put him off his game. I wanted him to have fun, but I didn't want it interfering with his work. I waved it off and finished my drink. "Okay. Thanks, Carmen. Look, if you hear from Adam, tell him I need to talk to him immediately. Let me ask—how much would you make if you worked the rest of your shift?"

She sat back and thought, tapping at her lip with her perfectly sculpted gel nail. "Easy. Tonight's a Thursday, so we'd only get some of the early college boy crowd and the diehards. Not too good, honestly. Maybe three or four hundred at most?"

I pulled out my billfold and took out five hundred. "Here. Take the rest of the night off, and after my current duties with the Bertoli family are wrapped up, let me talk to the Don. He's always looking for smart people who can do more than just shake their ass in sweaty guys' faces."

Carmen smiled. "You know, even girls like me have dreams."

"What's that"

Carmen sighed and looked down at her feet. "I want to open my own dance studio. I went to the International Dance Academy for ten years until my father died and I had to give it up. I don't have the turnout to be a professional ballerina either way, but I would still love to teach."

"Who knows? Maybe that can still happen," I said. I opened the door to the VIP room and turned back. "Recently, I've had changes in my life's outlook too."

Leaving her behind, I went to the bar and offered Terry a hundred-dollar bill. "Thanks, and Carmen's taking the rest of the night off," I said.

"Okay, sir," the manager said. I barely heard him, leaving the bar and heading off into the night. Where the hell was Adam?

I had more questions than answers when I got back to the Bertoli estate and was surprised to find Adriana still up and in the living room. "Can't sleep?"

"Remember, we start late tomorrow. I was just enjoying time with Mom and Uncle Carlo," Adriana said, stretching out on the sofa, knowing exactly what the look of her legs was doing to me. "Have a nice trip to the strip club?"

"Very funny. It was just business," I replied. "Still, questions abound, and I'm not pleased about it."

"Oh, tell me," she said, pointing at the chair next to her. It was still close enough that we could easily see each other without sharing the same seat. It was safe.

I told her about my conversation with Carmen. Her eyes twinkled when I got to the part about Carmen and Adam seeing each other, as if she actually knew them and was happy. "Seriously? That's awesome!"

"Ade, you don't even know them," I reminded her. "Why would you even care?"

"Guess I'm just feeling romantic," Adriana said with a smile. "And besides, why can't I cheer for people I don't know?"

I was about to answer when my phone rang, and I pulled it out of my pocket. "Speak of the devil," I said in a pleasantly good mood. I was planning to only curse him out a little bit when I saw that the call was a video call. "Hmm, this is new."

I hit the button, and the first image was of a plastic-tiled ceiling. The panels and grate on top were only slightly identifiable. There was a glaring light off to the upper left corner of the screen, and I could hear someone breathing. "Adam, tilt the camera, man," I said with a laugh. "You can't video call for shit."

The breathing intensified, and I grew worried. That didn't sound like him at all. "Beefcake. Hard to see you at this angle, but I wanted to keep the surprise going a while longer."

I looked at Adriana, who had dropped her feet over the side of the couch, her face turning pasty white. "Drake," she whispered. "I'd know that voice anywhere."

"What do you want, Vincent? And how'd you get this phone?" I asked, not letting on that Adriana was in the room. "I know it's you."

The camera angle spun and twisted nauseatingly, and suddenly, I saw him. By now, I was familiar with his image. I'd studied the photographs I could find of him extensively, and I could see where Adriana was right. He looked the part of a loser.

The scary thing was that his face looked like that of an accountant who had gone insane. There was a baleful glint to his eyes, a certain shine that I'd seen before in Bertoli men who had gotten a little too close to the line in terms of committing crimes and killing others. I killed because I had to; men like Drake killed because they liked to. "Ah, there we are. I assume you know what I look like, Beefcake. You probably know a lot about me."

"I know a little bit, Staff Sergeant Vincent Drake. I know you're a fucking psycho who got his rocks off raping and murdering an innocent girl. They didn't put that in the papers, but I know the truth. You tried, didn't you?"

"Did more than try, dumb shit," Drake said. "Say hello, baby. I can see that red hair of yours on the side of the screen. Don't be shy; you've got your big strong protector right there next to you."

I glanced at Adriana, who shook her head. "No way. Fuck this guy."

"But that's all you had to do," he said with a maniacal giggle. "I told you, you and I are meant to be together forever."

"So you kill and terrorize, and do it all to Genesis lyrics?" I yelled, barely controlling my voice. "I swear, I'll tear your heart from your fucking chest if you ever come near her."

"I doubt that very much, beefcake. You're just some stupid mob muscle. I'd wear your guts for a belt and not even break a sweat," Drake said.

I heard another sound, something muffled in the background. "What is that? You can cut the corny movie bad guy lines now."

Drake giggled again and smiled into the camera. "Just a warning, or maybe a preview of what's coming to you, beefcake. Or should I say, D-man?"

"Are you going to show me, or are you going to bullshit some more?"

"You mean like this?" he asked, turning the phone around. I could see more of the room. It looked like he was in some sort of meat locker, but from the lack of frost and other things, one that had long been unused except for the single hook in the middle. Hanging from the hook, his ankles tied together and his arms tied underneath him to what looked like some big gym-style dumbbells, was Adam, his eyes wide and his mouth covered with duct tape.

"Shit," I whispered softly, disgusted. I knew exactly why he'd been hung that way. By turning him upside down, all the blood was rushing to his head, keeping him conscious longer during torture. The plates would pull on his shoulders and ankles, adding to the pain he was feeling. It was like being racked, except that the pain was longer, less traumatic. The torture was more mental and exhausting. "You son of a bitch."

"Oh, you should see what comes next," Drake laughed, the camera jostling as he positioned it somewhere. "Excuse the angle. I don't have a tripod for this, after all. It's not like the phone's mine."

"Turn away," I said to Adriana, whose eyes were fixed on the image on the screen. "You don't need to see this."

Drake knelt and ripped the tape off Adam's mouth, balling it up and tossing it aside. "Howdy, Mr. Private Dick! You can say something to the camera if you want."

"Fuck you," Adam gasped dryly, his face etched in agony. "I'm not going to beg for you. Fuck you."

"What, you don't want to say hello to D-man?" Drake said with a laugh. "Why not?"

"I said everything I needed to say to him in my last email. He's going to hunt you down. He'll find you, and you'll get what you deserve. That's what he does. That's who he is." Adam's eyes were wide with pain, but still, I could see what he was trying to tell me. I promised myself that I would remember his courage and conviction. Even facing his death, he was trying to nail the bastard who'd gotten to him.

Without another word, Drake walked to the camera and cut the call. I set my phone down with shaking hands and turned to Adriana. I'd expected her to be nearly catatonic. After all, the man had been mentally torturing her for months. Instead, she was lucid, aware, and looking me in the eyes with newfound strength. "You're going to take him down," she said.

I nodded. "I need to wake up your mother and uncle," I said. "I need to get to Adam's apartment before Drake does."

"Why?" Adriana said, standing up. She was a bit shaky and her face was pale, but she was still there.

"Adam was trying to tell me something. I think he had some more information he was going to send me on his computer. We tended to exchange thumb drives, not emails. After all, the NSA can't tap a thumb drive. But if Drake was paying attention, he's going to want that computer too."

Adriana nodded, then kissed me on the cheek. "I'll go to my mother's room and wake her up. You go and get that information. And be careful."

"I will," I said, turning to go. At the door, she called my name one more time, and I stopped, turning back. "Yes?"

"Be careful," she said.

"I will. I'll be back before you know it."

Chapter 15

Adriana

I was still awake when Daniel came back with a computer tower under his arm. “I grabbed this and ran. There was no thumb drive that I could find. Glad I remembered how to pick locks. I didn't have time to get his spare key.”

Uncle Carlo, who was sitting up with me in the living room along with Mom, gave the computer a measured look. “Daniel, I applaud your bravery, but what good is just the computer base?”

Daniel took a deep breath, knowing he needed to make sure he was being respectful without being condescending. Carlo was what some liked to call 'computer illiterate'. “I can plug everything else I need into it and use it just fine. To be honest, all I really need is the hard drive inside.”

“I must be getting too old," my mom interjected. "Just do what you need to do, Daniel.”

“If we could get everything set up, I can do it right outside Adriana's room while she tries to get some sleep.”

“Sleep? What the hell do you mean, sleep?” I asked, slightly outraged. “Do you really think that after that call, I'm even thinking of going in to class tomorrow?”

“Well, you would be safer here, but at the same time, we don't want to let him run your life," I responded.

“I can stay here, work on my painting, and still get plenty of things done." I stopped and took a deep breath. “Sorry, I didn't mean to snap like that. I just want to know and be involved in what's going on."

"No apology necessary, Ade. I know you want him caught."

I quickly wiped away the smile that came with Daniel's words and looked at Mom. "Well, Mom, think you can get him set up?"

As a matter of fact, we did have a desktop computer, an older one that Mom used to have for her personal usage. She still had it taking up a corner of her room, and with my help, the two of us dragged it down to the hallway in front of my room. "Forgot how heavy all this stuff is," Mom griped as she lugged the monitor and keyboard. "Would you believe that they used to be bigger?"

"Mom, I do happen to remember the old style computer monitors, you know," I said with a laugh. "The ones that were about the size of a microwave?"

"Even bigger," she said. We reached Daniel's table, and Mom set down the flat panel monitor, looking at the tiny card table. "Sure this will be big enough?"

"He'll make it work," I replied.

I watched for a few minutes as Daniel took apart Adam's computer, removing the hard drive.

Mom watched in concern, then shook her head in acceptance. "I guess I shouldn't be surprised. I'm going to go back to bed. Good night."

"See you in the morning, Mom," I said, giving her a kiss on the cheek. "Thanks."

"It's nothing, honey. Sleep well."

Once she left, I checked up and down the hallway, and

seeing that we were alone, leaned over and kissed Daniel's cheek.

I smiled and ran my hand through his hair, relishing the feeling. "I enjoy that you care so much and that you know me so well. Think you can finish your work in time for a little bit of time with me?"

"We shouldn't," Daniel whispered back, clearly reluctant. "It's already after midnight, and I can't expect Carlo or your mother to not wake up and check on us. Also, I'm a bit worried about that cook, Kathy. She suspects something. I'm sure of it. It's just too risky. I'm sorry."

"You're probably right," I said. "Tomorrow night then. It'll be Friday, and a lot of the staff have the next day off so they go out or sleep late, and we can make love over and over . . ."

"Shh," Daniel said, reaching up and taking my hand in his. He brought my fingers to his lips and kissed them, then let go. "You keep talking like that, and I'm going to be sitting out here with an erection all night."

"Now that would be noticeable," I chuckled, pleased. "All right, I'll try and get some sleep. Good night."

"Good night, Adriana."

It wasn't what I wanted, but it was enough to know he was nearby, and I slept through the night without any bad dreams. The next morning, I found Daniel still hard at work, typing away at Mom's computer. "Good morning," I greeted him, resisting the urge to kiss him on the cheek again. "Still working?"

"Trying to process all the information now," Daniel said, giving me a little smile. "You slept well."

"No dreams," I replied, "so I'll take that as a good thing. Tell me what's going on."

"Adam had just gotten an information dump, so I don't think he'd even begun to do his own analysis. I'll turn a copy of this over to your uncle. What's on your agenda today?"

"IHOP, actually," I said with a chuckle. "Think you can handle some pancakes?"

"Of course. But we'll need to hurry if you're going to make the first class."

"Give me ten minutes. Think you can be ready by then?"

Daniel sniffed at his armpits and looked at his shirt. "What the hell, I'm supposed to be copying a college student. Might as well do the two-day dress job too. Give me five and I'll be good."

Daniel got up and stretched, then gave a huge yawn. "Okay, I'll meet you in the foyer in ten minutes."

I showered quickly. Daniel wasn't the only one who was willing to do the college slum-bum act for a day, and we left after saying goodbye to Mom, who'd gotten up early and looked impeccable in her business suit. She even gave us a little wistful smile as we left. "Think she knows there's something going on between us?" Daniel whispered as we approached his car.

"She's got good intuition," I replied. "But I think she's fine with it."

We ate a relaxed breakfast, Daniel still scanning the restaurant the entire time. "You know, this is the third time we've been out to eat together," he said with a chuckle in between bites of bacon maple pancakes. "When can we just admit that we're going on dates?"

"I'd say this is our second," I replied, licking whipped cream off my spoon. I'd indulged and gotten the whipped cream and chocolate sauce. "The burger joint was our first, and I'd say I did a halfway decent job of bullshitting Uncle Carlo and Mom about it."

"Hmm, if you say so," Daniel replied with a smirk. "Didn't fool me though. Not that I didn't enjoy it. In fact, if we can ever get out of the shadows with this, I'm planning on doing that again."

I chuckled and sat back. "Tell me, Daniel, what sort of dates did you go on with other women?"

"Dates?" he asked incredulously. "I didn't go on dates. I haven't been on a real 'date' since I was a high school junior. Until you."

"Then what'd you do?" I asked, curious.

"I think you're smart enough that I don't need to spell it out for you. I like to think it was easy because of my looks, but I think who I work for helps."

I reached over and took his hand, squeezing it. "We're both totally screwed up in the head, you know that?"

"I do," he replied, before seeing his watch. "We need to get going. Thanks for the idea. I enjoyed this."

* * *

That night, after everyone else had gone to sleep, I got out of bed, not willing to wait anymore. I needed him, even if people suspected. I crept to my door and quietly opened it, seeing him looking at his laptop. "Daniel."

He heard the desire and need in my voice and closed his computer without even looking back, standing up quietly to come into my room. As soon as the door was closed, I was in his arms, pulling him toward the bed. "This is so dangerous," Daniel whispered, his hands still coming up to start unbuttoning my pajama top. "We're going to get caught."

"I need you," I said, shrugging off my top. I turned him around and pushed him to sit on the bed, reaching for his pants. "I need this."

Freeing his cock, I knelt, looking him in the eyes. "Another new thing for me," I teased, leaning forward and licking the silky-soft head. It was delicious and wonderful, and I was even more aroused by the look on his face as I sucked the head of his cock into my mouth, my tongue running around the ridges and tracing the blunt arrowhead. Fueled by another fantasy of mine, I lifted my boobs, wrapping them around his cock and massaging them back and forth.

Daniel opened his mouth to say something when the door to my room burst open and two people came storming in. One was Julius Forze, and the other was Pietro Marconi, Uncle Carlo's second in command. I turned around, the question out of my mouth even as I knew the answer. "What the fuck?"

"Don't move, Daniel," Pietro said, temporarily ignoring me. "Adriana, cover yourself."

I barely had time to get my top on before Uncle Carlo came into the room, his face a mix of rage and sadness. "Adriana . . . my Bella . . . why?"

"Uncle . . ." I said, before finding my strength. I stood and crossed the room to look him in the eyes. "I'm twenty-three, and I can choose who I fall in love with. I'm not one of your men. You can't command *me*."

Carlo's eyes flared, and he lifted his hand to slap me, but I didn't move and didn't flinch away. His hand froze, and I stared him in the eyes, daring him to do it. If his men hadn't been there, I would have said something too. But I still loved my uncle, even if I was pissed at him and outraged that he would violate my privacy. I didn't need to return the humiliation.

Carlo's hand trembled, and he lowered it slowly. "Because you are my blood, I will forgive that disrespect," he hissed. "And because you supposedly love him, I won't kill him. Now leave and go to your mother's room. I will speak with you both later."

In the hallway, I saw Kathy, who I'd seen going by my room frequently over the past few days. She had a smug look on her face, and I knew who'd sold us out. Saying nothing, knowing my time would come, I left, sparing a look back at Daniel. He was still on the bed, his pants pulled up. His face was filled with shame, concern, and pain. I turned to go back and he shook his head slowly, pointing with his nose. I understood and left the room, hating myself every step of the way.

Chapter 16

Daniel

I was grateful to Mr. Bertoli for at least letting me pull my pants up before he had Julius and Pietro lead me from Adriana's bedroom. He looked to see if I was going to fight, but when I stood without argument, he turned his attention to Pietro. "Take him to the garage. I'll speak with Margaret and my niece first."

"Yes, Godfather," Pietro said. A long time Bertoli man, Pietro Marconi was a second-generation member of the Bertoli crime family and was as tough as nails. Another man I'd looked up to when I was growing up, he'd also moved from an enforcer role to something else, but I knew his skills were still sharp. There was no way I could get the drop on him, even if I wanted to.

Carlo looked at me for a moment. The anger he'd kept under control while Adriana was in the room broke free as he crossed the room, and his fist caught me straight in the nose. My head rocked back and blood flowed, but I could tell it wasn't broken. Carlo is great at what he does, but he's not a fighter. "You betraying piece of shit," he literally spat into my face. "I loved you like one of my own sons."

Carlo whirled and left the room, leaving me with Julius and Pietro, both of them still holding their guns trained on me. The room was suddenly quiet, and Pietro took the time to finally say something. "Are you going to come easily, Daniel?"

"I won't fight you," I said simply, my heart breaking. I

knew I'd betrayed Carlo's trust even as I opened my heart to Adriana. In the Mafia, there is room for only one true love, and I had let someone else take the place of my Godfather. "Can I ask a favor though, even though I don't deserve it?"

"You can ask," Pietro said. "Doesn't mean I am going do anything about it."

"Can you have someone just pack my backpack and have the keys by the door? If Don Bertoli is going to let me live, I'd like to leave without the shame of rooting for my fucking keys."

"If you still have that BMW afterward," Pietro said. "Come on."

Julius led the way out, with me in the middle while Pietro pulled up the rear. In the hallway, I saw Kathy leaning against the wall with a triumphant smirk on her face. "Guess you won't be fucking Firecrotch anymore."

"Fuck you, Kathy," I replied evenly. "She's a better class of woman than you will ever be, you miserable bitch."

"Come on," Pietro said, poking me in the back with his pistol before Kathy could say anything back. We went to the garage, where Pietro tied my hands together. He tossed the other end of the rope over an overhanging beam and started to pull it tight.

I thought back to the image of Adam. "Not overhead."

Pietro nodded and pulled the rope down. Instead, he tied the rope to the support column, then stepped back. "Just to let you know," he said as he assumed his position by the door, "Kathy is gone, as of the morning. Nobody talks about the Bertoli family like that."

I nodded in gratitude and stood quietly, waiting for Carlo.

Even though the weather was still warm, a hint of chill was in the night air, and I shivered. Julius, who wasn't as disciplined as Pietro, looked me over, even stepping closer to talk. "Why, Daniel?"

I stood straight and tall and looked Julius in the eye. "We've always been attracted to each other. Being with her so much, we were destined to fail. She said we were in love, and maybe we were, but it was too soon to know for sure."

Julius looked at me with newfound respect, and even Pietro's stance softened. Julius stepped back, and we waited in silence until Carlo came in with two more of his men, thick-muscled moose whom I knew more for their brawn than their brains.

He didn't even greet me, and gone was the cultured, slightly affable middle-aged man who charmed as much as he analyzed. Instead, I was facing Cutthroat Carlo Bertoli, the man who'd started as one of the most cold-blooded men in the entire Bertoli family. "You motherfucker," he nearly screamed, storming across the floor of the garage and backhanding me. One of the moose, a thickly muscled guy named Lorenzo, noticed that I wasn't trussed up overhead and opened his mouth, but he closed it when Pietro gave him a look. He knew that Pietro was nearly as merciless as Carlo was. "You seducing son of a bitch!"

Carlo's next strike was a kick to my nuts, which I didn't have to fake being doubled over by. Pain radiated sickly up my body from my offended testicles, and I had to force myself to keep my eyes open as he started kicking me over and over. I curled into a ball, silent. My silence seemed to infuriate him more. "Why? Why won't you scream and cry?"

He paused, shaking out his aching leg. I used the

opportunity to get back to my knees, but nothing more. Instead, I kept my silence as Carlo crossed the room, rooting around in a closet that I knew contained gardening equipment before finding what he wanted, coming out with a gardening shovel. "Lorenzo, make sure he feels it, but no edges, and nothing to the head," Carlo said, handing the moose the shovel. "And make sure he can walk."

You don't really know pain until you get beaten with the flat head of a garden shovel, I learned, as Lorenzo started tooling off on me. The first shot was to my chest, right in the middle between my pectoral muscles. I was barely able to jerk my head to the side in time to avoid catching the handle in the mouth. The second shot was to my back, driving me back down to the floor. As he began systematically beating me, Carlo yelled.

"Daniel, I raised you! I gave you a home, a family, and a life! I didn't ask too much, just that you be an honorable man, and I don't have too many rules, do I? No. But you had to go and break the one that was closest to my heart. Stealing from me, lying to me, those I can understand, and maybe even forgive, can't I, Pietro?"

"Yes, Don Bertoli," Pietro said immediately, his gun now put away and his hands clasped in front of him like he was having a prayer in church or something. "Very forgiving, sir."

"Damn right," Carlo said, turning back to me. "So why did this piece of trash have to go and break the one rule I hold sacrosanct? You're lucky that I love my niece, Daniel. I promised her upstairs that you'd live and that you'd walk out of here tonight. It was a moment of weakness on my part, because I love her so much. But I swear this to you. If you ever, and I mean ever, set foot in Seattle again, I'm going to make sure your cock is fed to Pietro's dogs while it's still attached to your body."

He knelt and spit in my face, then got up and turned away. "Tune him up some more, Lorenzo. But remember what I said—he walks out tonight."

Carlo left the garage, and I turned my face to look at Lorenzo, who set the shovel aside with a grin. "Don Bertoli said you have to walk out," he growled, cracking the ham hocks he called knuckles. "He didn't say anything about you having to look good doing it."

I don't know how long the beating went on, as Lorenzo's second hit rocked my head pretty hard and things went kind of swimmy for a while. I do know that the entire time, I didn't say a word, except for the times his knee caught me in the stomach and I grunted as the air was forced from my lungs. In the end, I was bleeding from quite a few places, and while I had all my teeth, I was pretty sure my nose was broken.

"Lorenzo," Pietro, who'd stayed behind the whole time to watch the beating, said after I coughed up some blood onto the floor, "that's enough."

Lorenzo, who'd worked up a pretty good sweat in the course of kicking my ass, stepped back, panting slightly. "Okay, Mr. Marconi. I think I need a drink of water anyway."

He left, and it was just me and Pietro in the garage. I struggled back to my knees and tried to get to my feet, but failed, losing my balance. Before I could hit the concrete again, Pietro was there, holding me and helping me up. "That took a lot of balls, kid," he said in a low voice as he cut the now bloodstained ropes that held my hands together. "Why'd you not say anything?"

"I deserved it," I mumbled, my lips swollen but still understandable. "I betrayed the man who was like a father to me."

He nodded, then slung my arm around his shoulder. "All right. I had Julius put your bag on the front steps. There's no way you're walking through the house right now. I'll get you outside, then you get the hell out of here. You're lucky. I hope you realize that."

"I know," I whispered, feeling something pull in my ribs. "Can you give me an hour to get some shit from my apartment before the boys come to make sure I followed orders?"

"You've got until the morning shift gets here," he said, glancing at his watch. "That gives you about ninety minutes. Then you'd better be on the fucking road out of here."

"I will," I groaned, wincing as we left the garage by the side door and he helped me to the front steps. I found the backpack that Adriana insisted I buy to blend in with the college crowd, my computer inside along with a few of my clothes, the keys to my BMW sitting beside it. Lifting the bag and picking up the keys was the most painful exercise I'd ever done. "Pietro, you know that—"

"I don't want to know anything, Daniel," he said gruffly. "Now go, before my soft side gives way to the rest of me."

Chapter 17

Adriana

I sat in Mom's bedroom, trying not to cry. "It's not fucking right," I mumbled under my breath, looking out of Mom's window to the parking lot of the house. I watched as Daniel limped to his car, sitting inside for long minutes before he got it started, backed out wobbly, and drove away. "It's not right."

"Adriana, right now, I don't think your Uncle is concerned about your opinion of right and wrong," Mom said, trying to keep her voice under control. "To be honest, neither am I."

"Mom, I was just . . ."

"You were having sex with one of Carlo's men in his own house!" Mom yelled, something she hadn't done to me since I had broken the Ming vase Dad had given her when I was eight. "Jesus Christ, Adriana, could you not have controlled your hormones long enough to at least wait until after this Vincent Drake asshole was in the ground?"

I was stunned. Like I said, Mom almost never yelled at me, and she rarely cursed. Uncle Carlo was one thing, but Mom was something completely different. Instead of standing up to her, I just looked down, trying not to cry. I felt like my life was falling apart, and it was all my fault.

She stood where she was, and I was sure she was staring at me for a bit, then she sighed. "Adriana, I'm sorry I yelled. Just . . . sweetie, what a mess this is."

"Like I planned on falling in love with him?" I pleaded, looking up at Mom. "Like I planned on needing him so badly that I seduced him? That's right, Mom. I was the one who invited him into my room tonight, not the other way around!"

She took a deep breath, then sat on the bed. "I guess I'm mostly upset because I saw how you two were together. I knew there was something there, but I kept hoping this issue with Drake would get resolved soon. I thought that you two could at least wait that long, and that you definitely wouldn't be so bold as to do anything here . . ."

I didn't have a reply, except the truth. "Mom, I realized something over the past few weeks. Daniel and I, we've been trying to deny this for a long time. We just didn't know it."

She slid back, still in her pajamas, and leaned against the pillows. It was the same king sized bed she and Dad shared when he was alive, and to be honest, she looked tiny and out of place on it. "I can't be too angry with you," she finally said, lying back. "It was the same with me and Johnny. Oh, by the time you were born, you didn't know it, but your grandfather was so opposed to his Italian son dating a Scotch-Irish girl that he threw fits that shook the walls of this place."

She managed to get a chuckle out of me, and I looked around the room. The Bertoli mansion had been in the family for two generations now. Grandpa bought it in the economic crunch of the nineteen seventies from a former shipbuilding magnate of the early twentieth century. We'd kept it updated, but there was still a lot of history in the house. "Grandpa never did have a problem saying his piece."

"True, but Johnny held his ground," Mom said, smiling

wistfully. "He was so strong, your daddy. A lot calmer than your grandfather, too. Eventually, the old man relented when he saw that Johnny and I were willing to run off if he wouldn't grant his blessing. There was no way that old man was going to let his Vegas buddies have leverage on him with that one, and while I wasn't thrilled that his blessing was due to Mafia business more than true acceptance, it got the job done. Of course, as soon as the old man saw you, he was head over heels about you. You came out with that thick mane of bright red hair, looking the way you did, and you were his little princess right away."

"I'm kind of glad my hair darkened up some though," I laughed, thinking back to some of my childhood photos. "I looked like Pippie Longstocking when I was four."

"I'm glad too," Mom said. "I don't know what you're going to need to do next. I assume you're being honest when you say you love Daniel, or at least you genuinely think you do. And when I think about it, you've had a lot worse quality boyfriends. Regardless of his misgivings, he's a capable man. And I guess I'd be the world's biggest hypocrite to say that you shouldn't fall in love with a Bertoli man."

"Considering you've adapted to the life quite well, yeah," I replied. "You know, since you work with Carlo now and all."

Mom sat up and gave me a look, then lay back with a sigh. "I do. And I honestly don't regret it, adopting this lifestyle. Sure, it was the Mafia life that took Johnny from me, but without it, I'd probably never have had him at all. The fifteen years we had together . . . I'd take that over a millennium without him."

I was about to reply when Carlo knocked on the door frame, changed out of his pajamas and in his business suit. "May I come in?"

"Come in," Mom said, sitting up. "What do you want?"

"I came to talk to Adriana about what's going to happen now," he said, his voice stern but calm. "As I'm sure you saw, I kept my promise. Daniel left the house under his own power, and I have only banished him from Seattle."

"A city of a million people, and you get to decide who can live where?" I said, getting out of my chair. "Who gave you that power?"

Carlo's eyes flashed, but he kept his calm. "I have that power because I'm the only one who is willing to use it. Now, as for you, young lady, you will be escorted to campus today by Julius. Tomorrow, I'll have a more permanent solution, but you will go to class and you will continue your studies. I will not have you dropping out because of that bastard."

"You'd know something about that word, wouldn't you, Carlo?" I said, turning my back to him. "Go to hell."

"Young lady, I've given you a lot of slack because you're my niece, but I will not tolerate anymore disrespect," Carlo warned, his voice dropping to deadly dangerous levels.

I turned and glared at him, but stopped when I saw that he meant business. If I said one more word of how I felt, I'd find myself over Julius's shoulder. My lips tight, I nodded. "Fine. I'll go get dressed, or would you like to have someone make sure I do that too?"

Carlo shook his head. "Of course not. But Adriana?"

"Yes?"

Carlo stroked his chin and fixed me with a level gaze. "Yes, what?"

I blinked, shocked, but a little shake of the head from Mom in the corner of my vision told me not to push the issue. "Yes . . . Uncle Carlo."

"Much better, Bella. We'll discuss this more when you get back from class this afternoon. Have a good day."

I controlled my walk out of the room, although by the time I was halfway down the hall, I heard him and Mom yelling at each other, even though I'd closed the door behind me as I left. As I walked, a crazy plan crept into my mind, one that required a little bit of luck, a lot of guts, and the willingness to abandon everything just to follow my heart. However, by the time I reached my room, I knew I had to do it. The only question was a matter of exactly how and when the opportunity would present itself.

* * *

It took me five days to put my plan into action. The first day was Friday, and I only had one class, with Julius escorting me tightly the whole time. There was no chance to do anything, and when I tried to say that I wanted to go to the library, he shook his head. "I'm sorry, Adriana, but your uncle gave me specific instructions. To class, and back home. If you need something, you can either get it another time or someone will get it for you."

Saturday and Sunday, I was practically a prisoner within my own home, as I wasn't left alone at any time other than to use the shower or the toilet. I spent a lot of time in my room with someone outside my door at all times, mainly because I couldn't deal with Carlo's bullshit any longer.

Even eating meals with him was a chore as I mechanically chewed forkful after forkful of food. I was at least partially reassured when Pietro came to me Saturday morning, after breakfast, and quietly informed me that Kathy had been fired.

It wasn't until Monday that I had the best opportunity to try and implement my plan. Julius had been replaced with Roberto Ciampa, the youngest of Carlo's men who could call himself a full enforcer. He was still pretty raw, and I knew he didn't have the training or skills that Daniel had.

After my second class, I had two hours until the next one, a time that until then, Daniel and I had often spent having lunch, talking, and of course, once we caved in to our desires and took that first step, spent most of the time sharing intimate moments.

Roberto, however, wasn't clued in to the routine, a point I hoped to take advantage of. After class, I pulled my backpack over my shoulders and gave him a half-bored look. "You ready?"

"For what?" Roberto asked, confused. "Isn't it lunch time?"

"It is, but first I need to use the ladies' room," I said. "Let's go to the student union. They've got toilets there."

What Roberto didn't know was how crowded the student union cafeteria got during the lunch rush. When I saw the line outside, I started squirming from side to side, faking that I was about to pee my pants. "I'll go around the corner and use the ones in the fitness center," I quickly said, heading for the door. "Come on!"

Roberto followed until he hit the door that separated the ladies' locker room from the hallway. "Hurry, at least," he griped, looking at the sign. "I can't believe this shit."

"Don't worry, this is usually much faster," I said, darting inside. Quickly heading to the back, I used my knowledge of the locker room and launched my plan.

The locker rooms in the school fitness center had two sets of doors. The outer set was connected to the hallway where Roberto was standing, while another set led to the inside of the fitness center. But, the fitness center had more doors than that leading in and out. I cinched my backpack straps and walked quickly, avoiding the looks of the people working out while I boogied past in jeans and a t-shirt, pulling my hair back into a quick ponytail. I wished I had a ball cap to jam on my head, but I knew that would have looked suspicious since I almost never wear them.

I figured I had three minutes, five at most, before Roberto said screw the rules and found out that I wasn't in the locker room. Rushing down the stairs, I started jogging when I got outside, hoping that I looked like a student who was late for a class or an appointment and not a girl running for her freedom.

The next ten minutes were some of the most stressful of my life to that point. Every time I turned a corner, I was expecting Roberto to be standing there, or to hear him call out my name as he rushed to catch up to me. Luckily, I got away from campus and onto a city bus without incident, not even caring where it was headed. I just needed to put distance between him and myself.

It took me about two hours to get to where I needed, a shopping center with a big box retailer. In that amount of time, my phone had already rung five times before I just shut the thing off and pulled the battery, hoping that Carlo hadn't called the phone company to track the device.

It took me thirty precious minutes to get what I needed, grabbing clothes off the shelves and tossing them in my basket, not even worrying about the sizes other than eyeballing them.

Swinging through the adjacent electronics store, I grabbed two pre-paid phone kits and checked out, heading into the large bathroom near the food court and using the handicap stall inside to change everything I was wearing, even my underwear. I put everything in the shopping bag, which I chucked into the dumpster behind the shopping center, amused that I'd just thrown away three times the amount of money than what I was wearing. Looking down at my jeans, t-shirt with Tweety Bird on it, and white shoes along with a brand new green nylon backpack, I figured I was ready to put the rest of my plan into action.

Pulling out one of the prepaid cell kits, I slipped the SIM card in, confident that the free one hundred minutes of talk time would be enough. The other I left in my bag, hoping I'd never have to use it. Taking a deep breath, I dialed Daniel's phone number from memory and said a quick prayer that he'd pick up.

The phone rang four times, and on the fifth, someone picked up. "Hello?"

I let my breath out in a rush, tears springing to my eyes as I heard the voice that I'd missed for the past five days. "Daniel, it's me."

"Ade?" the surprised voice came back over the line. "What the hell are you doing calling me? You know your uncle will find out!"

"I need to see you, Dan. Please. Where are you? I . . . let's go away together."

There was silence on the other end of the line, and I wondered if Daniel was going to hang up. "I'll come to you. Where are you?"

"I'm at the Westwood Village Shopping Center. Do you

know it?"

"Yes, I'm nearby. I can be there in twenty minutes. Ade, do you realize how insanely dangerous this is?"

I laughed, nodding even as I looked around. "Love is insane. Don't you know that?"

"I'll be there in twenty. Stay inside. I'll call you when I get there."

I was inside the shopping center's McDonald's, holding my lunch in its takeout bag when he called, my cheap phone buzzing in my hand. "Where are you?"

"McDonald's. I'll step outside."

It took us a minute to find each other, both because I looked so different than normal and because Daniel wasn't driving his BMW. Instead, he pulled up in a used white Ford, wearing loose sweatpants, a button down shirt and a ball cap. "Get in."

As soon as I was in the passenger seat, Daniel hit the accelerator, the Ford groaning as he asked the engine to do things it wasn't used to. He made a right turn, and once he was certain we weren't being followed, he looked over at me. "I missed you."

I grimaced. I couldn't help it. Daniel looked like he'd gone ten rounds with one of the Klitschko brothers with his arms tied behind his back. His face was still puffy, the areas under his eyes were black, and he had a bandage across his nose, where it looked like it had been set after being broken. "You look like hell. But I missed you too. Where'd you get the car?"

"You'll see. Let's just say this is a very strange setup I've got right now. We'll be at the house in ten minutes. Try to relax. This is a world you've never really seen before."

"What does that mean?" I asked, confused and elated at

the same time.

Daniel reached over and put his hand on my thigh, his hand warm and comforting. "Adriana, this car, the house . . . well, to put it simply, I'm living with a stripper."

Chapter 18

Daniel

There was, of course, some natural suspicion and discomfort at first when Adriana and Carmen met each other. It wasn't that Carmen and I had anything going on, but I literally had no one to turn to. The Bertoli family and the business was the only life that I'd known. I was lucky Carmen agreed to help me out after I'd pulled a gun on her.

"Hello. I'm Carmen Esperanza," she said, her voice only slightly stiff as she offered her hand to Adriana. I was struck by just how tiny the girl was, as Adriana almost towered over her, and Ade was only five foot eight. "Welcome."

"Thank you," Adriana replied, looking around. Carmen's place was, quite frankly, a dump, but a well cared-for dump. Situated fewer than three hundred yards from the edge of the airport's property, it was in the sort of neighborhood where even Don Bertoli's men didn't come unless they had to. "I appreciate your hospitality."

Carmen's place was a little jewel in the midst of the decaying, high-crime area that she lived. Of course, even a high crime area in Seattle is better off than a lot of neighborhoods in Los Angeles, New York, or other big cities. Still, Carmen saved her money and decorated her little apartment tastefully. Along the windowsill in the kitchen, little flowers potted in cut down milk cartons nestled next to herbs given the same treatment, lending the whole place a pleasant aroma. She'd also decorated the windows with yellow curtains made from old bed sheets, brightening the whole affair.

Carmen gave Adriana a hesitant smile and stepped back. “Daniel asked for my help—I couldn't say no.”

“And just what did Daniel ask you to help him with?” Adriana asked with a small smile, cutting her eyes to the side. “Do I need to kick his ass?”

Her joke broke the tension, and Carmen laughed. “Honey, you should see his torso. That skin of his is still darker than mine in most places.”

Adriana eyes widened, and she turned to me. I thought she'd be angry that Carmen had seen me with my shirt off—she'd helped me wrap my ribs after I spent the first eighteen hours after getting to her place unconscious on her sofa—but instead, she pointed at my shirt. “Let me see.”

“Well, that's foreplay for you,” I joked, but neither of them laughed. Carmen knew the pain I was in. Adriana didn't, but she was concerned. When my joke fell flat, I sighed and started unbuttoning my shirt. When it was fully undone, I looked at them. “A little help?”

Carmen knew what I wanted, and instead of helping me off with my long-sleeved shirt, she took the two tails and tucked them up into the collar, a rather strange configuration but one that allowed Adriana to see the mottled flesh of my chest and back, which I thought had mellowed quite a bit in the five days since the beating in the garage. “My God, and I thought your face looked like hell.”

“I think he kind of looks like he's a walking camo pattern

myself," Carmen said. "But I'm glad that you're here. You can help him with the Epsom salt baths. My *abuela* always said that when it comes to bruising, nothing is better than Epsom salts. I guess we should get this out of the way too—he even soaks in the bathtub wearing swim trunks."

Adriana nodded thankfully to her, then stepped up to me, taking my face in her hands. Standing on her tiptoes, she kissed me, carefully avoiding making contact with my nose. Still, her lips were as soft and wonderful as ever, perhaps even more so since it had been five long, torturous days since I'd felt them. "You wonderful, wonderful man," she whispered. "I wish I could've been here sooner."

I carefully hugged Adriana back, conscious of the pain still in my chest and back, and our kiss deepened until Carmen coughed discreetly. "Excuse me, guys, but we have a lot to talk about, don't you think? Besides, I don't think Daniel is ready for what you two are obviously heading toward."

Adriana stepped back, blushing. "Is it that obvious?"

"Honey, I know all about seduction," Carmen said with a laugh.

We found seats around the living area, Adriana helping me to sit down on the sofa. She took the other end of the sofa while Carmen grabbed a chair from her dining area and sat down.

"First off, Adriana, no offense, but what is a Mafia princess doing in this part of town anyway?" Carmen asked, not aggressively but still concerned. "Am I going to have some of your uncle's men kicking in the door any time soon?"

"Maybe," Adriana said. "I'm not here wearing this discount store crap with his blessing. I ditched my bodyguard and ran like hell."

"So what's with the clothes though?" Carmen asked, curious. "I mean, Daniel's gone on and on about you, and he said you weren't stuck up, but that stuff is right off the shelf. You missed a tag on the jeans, by the way."

Adriana looked down, noticing the little tag on the cuff of the jeans, and pulled it off. "I didn't know if Carlo had put any sort of GPS tracker in my stuff. The only things I still have are my laptop and my cellphone, and I pulled the battery from both of those until I figure out what to do with them."

I gave Adriana a surprised look, which she returned with a raised eyebrow. "What? I've grown up in a Mafia family my entire life. While I may have been somewhat insulated from all of the icky details, I did learn a few things. Just like I know that you and I can't stay here forever, regardless of how nice Carmen is being. And Carmen, thank you. Dan's a handful, even when he isn't being beaten up."

"He is, but he's promised to make things right," Carmen answered.

"I've been trying to analyze the data from Adam's computer when I'm awake," I said, pointing to my laptop. "Thankfully, I copied the whole damn bunch of files onto my computer before we got caught."

Adriana reached out and touched my leg, her eyes swimming with tears. "Even when you were thrown out, I knew you'd stay to protect me. I don't know why, but I just knew it."

"Well, regardless of what you knew, it's time for Daniel's medicine, and then a nap," Carmen said, standing up and brushing off her pants. "And before you give me any more of that macho shit, remember that the doctor at the clinic I dragged you to told me you should be in a hospital. How you even got off the sofa to drive to pick Adriana up, and then made it up the stairs without screaming, I'll never know."

* * *

I was in and out of consciousness for the next twenty-four hours as they insisted that I finish up the last of the pain pills that the doctor had given me. I was pretty out of it when Adriana helped me to the bathtub for my soak, the warm water, aftereffects of the drugs, and my still exhausted state leaving me only semi-conscious.

"How'd you stay awake long enough to come get me?" Adriana asked me as she helped lower me into the water. "Seriously."

"You caught me at just the right time," I mumbled, sighing as the water started to work its magic. I don't know if the myth about the Epsom salts is true, but I was more comfortable in the water than out. Probably because it took at least some of the weight off my aching body. "I was about fifteen minutes from my next pill when you called."

"I'm glad I did," Adriana said, helping me lie back. She rolled up a hand towel and placed it behind my head, the extra comfort helping. "Think you can stay awake enough that you don't drown?"

"I'm good," I said, waving. "But why don't you want to stay?"

"Dan, you still look like a poster child for getting your ass beat, and I know you're in pain, but it's been five days since I last touched you. I don't want to hurt you."

"Mmm, later then," I replied with a little smile. "A little TLC would help all my aches go away. Besides, I need to start stretching things out. I lay around much longer, and Carmen's going to start vacuuming me like part of the rug."

Adriana smiled and kissed my hand, then got up, leaving the bathroom but leaving the door open in case I needed help. I lay back, trying to clear my thoughts, when I heard the two of them talking.

"So you're an art student?"

"Yeah, it's a lot of fun. And you're a dancer at the Starlight Club, right?"

Carmen's reply sounded like she was a little ashamed, which I didn't understand. Like Terry said, she didn't have any hang-ups, and she was good at what she did. *"I . . . I've been doing it for two years now."*

"Why turn red? You put money on your table, you've got a nice place, and you look like a girl who's not planning on doing it forever."

"And the bonus clients?" Carmen asked, causing Adriana to go silent. *"Yeah, that's what I thought. Not too many good men out there want to spend their life with a whore. Not that I do it by choice—some of the men there, you don't say no to, so I pretend to enjoy it."*

I was surprised at the heat I heard in Adriana's reply. *"So you do what you have to do. I'm not one to judge—I grew up in the fucking Mafia. I'm in love with a man who's killed people, my uncle is the Godfather of the whole Sea-Tac area, and my mother is one of his key lieutenants. My entire art school education has been paid for by money made from the family business, which includes who knows how many thousands taken from the Starlight Club over the past ten years. So who needs to apologize to whom? My family made money off your ass. Literally."*

I could hear Carmen thinking about it for a while, then she laughed. *"I guess nobody here is all that innocent."*

Adriana's laughter made me smile, and I was glad to hear the two women start to bond. I let my mind drift, looking at the little yellow ducks that were part of the bathroom tile—a horrendous look, if you ask me—when I heard the two of them laugh again. Carmen took a deep breath, recovering before speaking. *"He did?"*

"Yep," Adriana replied, laughing. *"Seriously, who carries a pistol into the changing room at Nordstrom's?"*

"I'm not surprised. I was actually surprised when he showed up at my doorstep without a gun. He carried that fucking Beretta like it was a teddy bear every time I saw him."

"I know. By the way, he told me about the time he lost his shit with you. I'm glad you forgave him. By the way, how'd he end up here?"

"I was at the Starlight Club, getting ready to go home after a night of work when he staggered in the door, looking like he'd been hit by a truck and then run over. Terry, the manager, was about to throw him out before he realized who it was, and I came up front."

"And what made you help him?"

"If it wasn't for him, I would've never met Adam. He treated me like any other girl—something I've longed for. But I'm guessing that's done now, isn't it?"

"It's my fault, Carmen. I'm sorry I brought this monster into all your lives."

"It's not your fault, Adriana. No one would ever bring someone like that in their life on purpose. I'd like to continue this sometime, but I've got to get ready for work," Carmen said, and I heard her getting up. *"You two relax, and I'll see you in the morning."*

After helping me out of the tub and cooking a light dinner, Adriana and I finally had a chance to talk amongst ourselves. "So what now?"

Setting my fork aside, I wiped my mouth and leaned back into the sofa. "That depends on you, Ade."

"How so?" she asked, setting her fork aside. Neither of us had eaten too much, as her cooking skills weren't really all that great. "Sorry about the sauce. Guess I grew up a little too pampered."

"Don't worry, I'll teach you if you want," I replied. "But as for how so, well, you have a choice. On one hand, we can run. I know some people—independent operators who can get us a fake ID for the right price. We take off, get the hell out of here. Other side of the country, Canada, Mexico, wherever. For me, it's no problem. I have IDs already lined up. You try to buy a plane ticket or cross the border as Adriana Bertoli, and we'll find your uncle waiting for us wherever we go. So a fake ID is vital. That's option one."

"And option two?" Adriana asked, placing her hands on the table.

"We stay," I said quietly. "Drake made this personal for both of us. I don't have too many friends, Adriana. I had Bertoli men who were coworkers, and that is about it except for Adam. To top it off, he's threatened you. I want this guy's head on a plate. And with the data that I got from Adam's computer, I think I can get him. There are some clues that I can follow up on once I'm healed up, and I get myself another weapon."

Adriana thought about it, then shook her head in refusal. "Option one, we run. And we spend the rest of our lives running, both from Drake until he gets caught, and from Uncle Carlo. But if we do option two, we run the risk of being caught by either group, as well as placing Carmen at risk. We can't just keep crashing here, as I'm sure you know. If anything, the manager at the Starlight is going to tell the next guy Carlo sends to pick up his money, and they'll ask her. She doesn't need to be caught in a lie to Carlo."

I nodded. "I know. I was thinking of finding a place we can crash as soon as I'm mobile. Ade, I promised myself as I drove that I'd protect you regardless of the risk."

She blushed and looked down, then a moment later looked in my eyes, a hunger in there that wouldn't be sated by ramen with burned corn. "Then I choose option three."

"Which is?" I asked, turning slightly as she got up off the floor and climbed onto the couch in my lap. "If this is option three, I'm liking it so far."

"Option three is that first, I make love to you until all of the soreness is gone from your body and is replaced by a different kind of sore," Adriana cooed, running her hands through my hair. "Then, we find and kill this asshole, Drake. Finally, I send a message to Mom, telling her I'm leaving. We start a new life, maybe in Tahiti or something."

"I don't have enough saved up to spend the rest of our lives in Tahiti," I replied with a soft groan as Adriana began rubbing my chest through my shirt, "but I'm pretty sure we can figure out something."

Working slowly, she started unbuttoning my shirt, kissing my skin as she exposed it, nibbling under my jawline as I leaned my head back, my hands stroking her arms. "Ade . . ."

"This time, let me take the lead," Adriana whispered, finishing opening my shirt. "I know you're not able to pound me the way we both love it—and yes, I do love it when you put my ankles by my head and slam that huge cock of yours into me over and over until I'm coming and crying because it feels so good. You like it too, don't you?"

"Fuck yes," I moaned, my mind flaring with memories that, combined with the feeling of Adriana on top of me, had me hard as a rock.

"Good, because tonight, I'm going to ride this cowboy hard," she whispered, kissing down my neck until she found my nipples. I'd never had a woman lick my nipples before, but it sent little tingles through me that I was happy to feel. I groaned softly, and she looked up, smiling.

I moaned as she found the waistband of my pants and pulled them down, freeing my cock. "Sorry, forgot my underpants."

"Forgot . . . right," she said with an ironic laugh. "It's okay though. I'm glad—makes it easier for me."

She leaned down and licked my cock, sending chills up my spine. "Someday I'm going to suck this until you give me a creamy treat. But right now, I need it somewhere else. Hope you don't mind."

Adriana scooted back, pulling her t-shirt and bra off, then quickly shucking her loose jeans and panties. Standing there before me in all her nude glory, I was breathless. In all the other times we'd made love, the lights had been dimmed in her temporary room at the Bertoli mansion, where we barely had enough light to see each other.

I'd never seen a more beautiful sight in my life. Her flame red hair cascaded down her back and over her shoulders, ending in the front just at the top swell of her generous breasts, which were creamy and flawless, capped with soft bubblegum pink nipples that were already crinkling with arousal. Her stomach wasn't super lean, but lithe and smooth, with just a hint of red under her belly button from a missed spot the last time she'd trimmed.

The ghostly trail continued to the cleft between her legs, framed by auburn red hair that was just a little darker than her head, beautiful and perfect as her hips flared out before curving back into long, wonderful legs that I thought were the sexiest I'd ever seen. My cock twitched despite itself, and I was left speechless.

“Guess you like the way I look in the light,” Adriana said with a chuckle as she climbed back on the couch. She helped me scoot down some, then swung her leg over, taking my cock and aligning it with her warm entrance.

“Ade . . . wait,” I said, trying to twist to the side and failing as a spear of pain shot up my lower back. “No protection.”

She ignored me, lowering herself an inch onto my cock. Both of us stopped, and my eyes opened wide at the feeling. She paused, her eyes closed and her head thrown back, biting her lower lip and smiling. I'd never seen a more beautiful sight in all my life, and my heart melted again at the sight of her. “Oh God, that's good.”

Opening her eyes as she sank down, she saw the expression on my face. “Daniel Neiman, don't tell me this is a first for you too?”

I nodded, still unable to speak. It felt so good, and she

leaned forward to kiss me. "Well then, I'm glad it's me who gets to give you a first for once," she said, allowing her hips to settle against mine.

She rose, her pussy gripping my cock and massaging it wonderfully before she lowered herself back down, both of us shaking at the pleasure. "I love you."

"I love you too. Now, hold on," Adriana said, planting her hands on either side of my head, grabbing the side of the couch. With a seductive, sexy grin, she started to ride my cock, her pussy gripping me perfectly, my cock caressed as it had never been before.

I brought my arm up. The muscles ached, but the pain was dulled by the passion and pleasure of our lovemaking. I lifted the supple warmth of her breast to my lips, sucking on the hard pebble of her nipple. I love tasting her skin. The way it feels in my mouth is unlike anything I've ever felt before. I nibbled and sucked on the tenderness as she rode me, loving me with all the strength our bodies had.

Pure happiness and pleasure radiated from my cock as Adriana started moving faster and faster, letting herself go and feeling the rise of orgasm inside her. Freeing her nipple, I looked up at her. Her mouth opened slightly in a sort of oval shape and her eyes dilated. "That's it, my love. Don't hold back."

She heard my words but didn't respond, her hips moving faster and faster. Sweat broke out on her forehead as she plunged herself over and over onto me. I tried to help, but my arms were still too damaged and weak to do much more than encourage her—but it didn't matter. I could feel my own orgasm rising within me, my balls tightening and swelling as I rushed toward my climax.

"I'm going to . . ." I grunted, my hips moving out of my control. Adriana nodded, pushing herself harder and faster before freezing, her head thrown back and her hair like fire, a long wail building deep within her chest that peeled out of her mouth with the passion of untold depths. Her pussy clamped down on my cock, and I pushed one last time as my own body pushed over the edge and I held on as best I could. Adriana's legs gave out, and her body sank the last fraction of an inch onto my cock as I tumbled over the edge, claiming her as mine.

We lay, both of us panting at the effort of our lovemaking. "I love you," Adriana whispered. "Forever."

"Ade," I whispered, kissing her hair. "You've made a true man out of me. Before, I was just a boy in an adult body, not ready to commit to any woman. But now that you're in my life, I feel complete and truly a man."

She smiled and snuggled into my chest. "Good, because I'm not letting go of you. I want to spend the rest of my life with you."

I stroked her back and kissed her cheek. "Me too. Adriana, will you marry me?"

She froze for a second, then relaxed, sighing against my cheek. "Of course I will. I hope you don't mind a long engagement, though. I'd like to wait a little while, to see if we can reconcile with my mom, if nobody else. She deserves to see me get married. Besides, it'd give us more time to go on real dates, kind of do the whole regular relationship thing for a while at least."

"I can do that," I said. "Make you safe, reconcile with your family, and then get married. Sounds easy enough when you put it that way."

Chapter 19

Adriana

It took Daniel nearly a week to recover from the majority of his bruises and wounds, during which time he and I spent most of our time in Carmen's apartment. She and I quickly bonded as friends, and I found the spicy, seductive, diminutive Latina a great match. Her life experiences were vastly different from mine, and she was more than willing to open up to me.

"You're up early, aren't you?" Carmen said.

I looked over at the clock and saw that it was nearing nine in the morning. "If you can say that. What are you doing awake? I figured you'd sleep until noon at least."

She shrugged and changed the channel. "Tomorrow I probably will. But I never sleep all that much, although I'll probably try and take a nap before heading in today. She flipped channels again, settling on a game show on some cable channel and setting the remote down next to her. "You know, Adriana, you certainly don't fit the image I had of you."

"You don't fit the image of a stripper either. Well, I mean, except for the bangin' bod."

She patted her overdeveloped chest and laughed. "The best money can buy."

I couldn't help but laugh. "Carmen, I've thanked you a lot over the past few days, but I wanted to ask you something."

"Sure. Go ahead."

"If things work out the way Daniel and I are planning, what's on your agenda after this?"

She shrugged. "Daniel talked to me about maybe getting out of the stripping game, and I told him about my dream of opening my own dance school, but I don't know now. I'm just happy that I'm helping some worthwhile people. Lucky for me, the Bertolis aren't scheduled for another pickup from the Club for another week. Already, word on the street is that the Godfather's losing his shit looking for you."

"I guess he would be." I sighed, feeling a bit of homesickness, but not regret. "Then again, he shouldn't have had Daniel beaten with a garden shovel either."

"Were you really giving him a boob job when they kicked in the door?" Carmen asked suddenly with a laugh. "Damn, that's pretty low, interrupting one of those. And what a mood killer."

"Especially since I was just figuring out how to do it," I added.

We were both laughing when Daniel came in to interrupt. "By the way, we need to start planning on getting your fake ID. And we'll need to go to campus."

"What for?" I asked, then slapped my head. "The registrar's."

Daniel nodded. "If you don't go in, they'll void all your credits. If you want even a prayer of returning to your normal life, you're going to need to go in and fill out the paperwork for a sabbatical."

I closed my eyes and rubbed at my temples, torn by indecision. "Daniel, if we go there, we've got a higher chance of running into Carlo's men. Besides, if we're going to restart our lives under new identities, who the hell cares if I'm listed as on sabbatical or dropped out anyway?"

Daniel reached across the table and took my hands, gently squeezing my fingers. "Ade, I care. I never went to college, and let's be honest, I'll never get the chance, as we explained. For those few weeks that I was taking you around campus, though, you let me get a glimpse at that world, and I saw what it could do for a quality person like yourself. If there is any chance of you going back to school and finishing your degree, I want you to do it. It's that important to me."

I looked into his eyes, moved by his vehemence. I realized that for so long, years even, I'd underestimated him, lumping him in with so many of the other men in the Bertoli organization. Men who not only didn't care about college, but would never have fit in either. In Daniel, I saw the shining example that some of my more liberal classmates tried to hold up as a reason for their pie-in-the-sky schemes, the diamond in the rough who had been denied his maximum potential simply due to bad luck. At least in Daniel, he'd overcome most of it, in my opinion.

"Okay," I said, taking a deep breath and giving him my best smile. "We go in. What's the deadline?"

"We need to go in by Wednesday, I think," he said, tapping his chin. "But we should probably get a Wi-Fi connection. Have you logged onto your school email and sent in the preliminary stuff? There will be some risk with it, especially if your uncle has hired people to put tracers on your email system, but we can work around that."

"How so?" I asked.

"Simple," Daniel said with a laugh. "We go to a coffee

shop. This is Seattle, after all. What else are young hipsters supposed to do but go to coffee shops and cruise the net?"

I laughed and picked up his hands, kissing the fingers. "Daniel, you can be almost anything you want to be. But you, my love, are never going to be a hipster."

We took thirty minutes to drive to a coffee shop, making sure we were as far from Carmen's Georgetown apartment as we could get. We drove south until we found a Wi-Fi spot—not a coffee shop, but a truck stop, of all places. I turned on my computer, taking a moment to realize that I hadn't even opened the lid since the morning I'd run from campus. I had seen Daniel using his, processing and gathering more information on Vincent Drake. I'd seen him tapping at his cellphone occasionally too, more than likely trading messages with his contacts, and occasionally with Drake himself, if I read his expressions properly.

"This is going to take a while. The connection here is slow," I said as the little task bar started loading. "I wonder how many messages I've gotten."

Unfortunately, I was wrong. I had over fifty messages on my email. "Should have remembered that Mom and Carlo are trying to contact me too," I muttered. "Glad we're in a truck stop and not a coffee house."

"Oh, we've still got plenty of money," Daniel said, sipping. "I've been frugal over the past few years. I saved a lot of what I earned."

"How much?" I asked, curious. "I mean, not that it matters, but I'm technically destitute at this point. And you did say we didn't have enough to live in Tahiti."

Daniel leaned in, and I shivered as his warm breath tickled

my ear. "Right now? About three million dollars."

I nearly spit out my coffee and looked at him blankly. "What?"

"Uh-huh," Daniel whispered. "Like I said, I saved a lot of what Carlo paid me. When I said not Tahiti, it was because I don't have enough for us to live in style in Tahiti. Not that we can't take a vacation."

I looked through the messages, which were mostly the same, namely Carlo or Mom asking where I was and to contact them. It wasn't until the end and a new message came from Mom that I really felt it.

Dear Adriana, it began, different from the others, which normally started with just my name or Bella, *I have prayed for the past few days that you are actually reading this, and are not captured or dead somewhere. No mother, regardless of her lifestyle, wants to go through that.*

So I pray that you are reading this, and that you are safe. I understand why you did what you did, and I hope that you are with the man whom you love. I can't say I wasn't angry at first. I know that you tried to tell me.

You tried to explain to me or convince me how much Daniel means to you. I should have been more understanding. You were guided by your heart, which is the same thing I did in marrying your father. If I hadn't, if he hadn't, we'd never have been blessed with you.

So I can't be angry with you anymore. I'm sad, however. I miss my daughter, and want to give her a hug again, or to talk about television, or any of a hundred other things we used to do together. Adriana, if you can at least trust me enough to not try and use this to track you down, can you spare your mother a few words? Just tell me that you're safe, that you're pursuing your dreams . . . and some day, maybe, that we'll see each other again.

I love you. You'll always be my little girl.

Your mother, Margaret

It took me ten minutes to stop crying from the simple message. Daniel put his arm around my shoulders, letting me have my tears. When they were gone, I sniffled and wiped my nose. "We're going in tomorrow," I said softly. "No matter what, Daniel, I want to be able to see my mom again."

"I agree," Daniel replied. "In fact, send her a reply. Let her know you're safe. Then send the message to the registrar's. We can go in tomorrow to sign the paperwork."

When we got back to the apartment, Carmen wasn't as enthusiastic about our plan. "Are you two loco?" she asked, her eyes wide. "Seriously, you're going to intentionally go to the one place where everyone knows you in order to fill out a single piece of paperwork?"

"It's something I have to do," I said, sighing. I'd come to recognize that while Carmen rarely spoke with as heavy a Hispanic accent as she put on for work, she did let it slip a bit when she was emotional. "A sense of completion."

"Oh, you're going to be complete, all right. Completely underground and buried," she groaned, storming back and forth in the living room. "I can't believe you two! Seriously, what sort of Mafioso are you?"

"Two Mafioso who don't want that in their life anymore," Daniel said quietly, and I jerked my head toward him, surprised. He looked at me and shrugged. "I kind of came to that realization over the past few days. Sorry if I didn't mention it to you yet. I guess it was going to be sort of an organic decision."

I thought about it, then nodded. "So you don't want to be an enforcer anymore?"

"No," Daniel said simply. "I want to be your husband."

Carmen stopped her pacing and stared at Daniel, then at me. When I didn't say anything, she shook her head. "Well?"

“Well what?” I asked, then realized we hadn't told her about that either. “Sorry, he asked me a few days ago when you were at work. We're planning on a long engagement though. Think you'd like to be one of the bridesmaids?”

Carmen threw her hands up and walked away, muttering loudly to herself in Spanish, only to come back a moment later, still muttering before pointing at me. “You are absolutely insane. You decided you want to get married to a renegade Mafia enforcer, and now you ask a stripper to be one of your bridesmaids?”

“I asked a beautiful girl who's a good friend and a good person to be my bridesmaid,” I replied evenly. “Think about it.”

“Oh, I don't even need to. I'm in. Now, I've got two hours before I have to go in to work. Please talk me through your crazy plan so I don't have to think about it all night and can have some peace of mind. The boobies bounce much better when I have peace of mind.”

Chapter 20

Adriana

Our plan was simple, but still dangerous for a couple of reasons. First, we had to take Daniel's BMW. While the ghost gray car was known to both Vincent Drake and Uncle Carlo, since the rise in school shootings, campus security had been very strict on traffic control onto and off campus. We'd already had Daniel's BMW checked in, and he had a campus ID sticker in his front windshield. Carmen's Ford didn't, and if we tried to use that, we'd have to spend another ten to thirty minutes at the campus police station, time that we just didn't want to spend on campus.

So Daniel's car it was. Still, we dressed as inconspicuously as possible, with my red hair pulled back into a ponytail and tucked into a ball cap while Daniel looked as much like a bum as I'd ever seen him, in paint splattered jeans, an oversized long-sleeved rugby shirt, and his Jordans, which we'd scuffed and abraded to make them look used. Between the two of us, we looked like totally different people.

Pulling up in the parking lot closest to the front of the registrar's office, Daniel put the car in park and shut off the engine. "You ready?"

"Yeah," I nodded, grabbing my backpack. It was the same backpack I'd picked up in my initial run from home, although with Carmen's help, I'd bought some clothes that fit a little bit better. There was being inconspicuous, and being *too* inconspicuous.

"Come on, this shouldn't take too long."

Part of going on sabbatical involved talking to a guidance counselor, so Daniel and I sat around in the office, waiting for one of them to become available. Finally, just as I was about to lose my mind at the intolerable waiting, one of the counselors came out of their office. "Miss Bertoli? Hi, I'm Tim Drucker. If you can step into my office, please."

Daniel and I got up, and Drucker looked uncomfortable. "Miss Bertoli, it's normal procedure that these meetings are—"

"Are done one on one," I completed for him. "Mr. Drucker, Daniel has been with me on campus for weeks, and is part of the reason that I came in today. He stays by my side."

Drucker nodded, still unconvinced, but the three of us went into his office. The counselors' offices on campus were tiny, practically cubicles with slightly thicker walls. I understood though. The number of students had skyrocketed over the past few years, meaning the administration had to hire more staff. More staff meant more offices, but buildings don't expand at the same rate as enrollment. Still, I did feel a bit cramped as Drucker and I took seats while Daniel remained standing. There wasn't a chair for him. "Would you like to grab a chair from outside, Mr. . . .?"

"Neiman. Daniel Neiman," Daniel answered, his voice flat and robbed of all inflection. It was his Terminator voice, and I had to swallow a smile as Drucker went slightly pale. "And no, I would prefer to stand."

"Oh . . . okay then," Drucker stammered, then turned his attention to me. "Well, Miss Bertoli, I understand from your paperwork that you want to take a one semester to one year sabbatical, is that correct?"

"Yes," I said, putting on my most charming smile. Daniel's intimidating presence urged some things along, but it was the time to gather flies with honey and not vinegar. "After the past couple of weeks, it's just not the right time for me to continue with my studies."

"I see," Drucker said, clearly not understanding. "Miss Bertoli, it's highly irregular for an upperclassman like yourself to take such a long sabbatical. In all honesty, most who do never come back and lose their place in our arts program."

"I understand that, but I feel it's necessary," I said. "No offense, Mr. Drucker, but when this college can't even stop a psycho killer like Vincent Drake from harassing me through the official email channels, I'm having trouble putting my focus where I should have it. Drake violated my safe space, and the college has not done a lot to help restore that. Until he's caught, I'd prefer to not put myself under that sort of unwanted pressure. It triggers me too much."

I couldn't believe the sort of bullshit streaming out of my mouth, and even Daniel's lips twitched in a fraction of a smile before he reassumed his stoic demeanor. I mean, I'm the daughter of a Mafia family, and here I was talking about triggers and safe spaces? What next, a little diatribe about micro aggressions? Still, it was the language that these type of people spoke, and it got through to him with the minimum of explanation.

"I see," Drucker repeated. He sighed and turned to his computer. "Well, it says here that your tuition is fully self-funded—no significant scholarships or grants that require you to do extra paperwork—so this shouldn't take too long. Let me print out the proper forms for your signature, and we should have you on your way. Just a minute."

Drucker tapped at his keyboard, then got up. He had to squeeze past Daniel, who scooted over to let him by, closing the door behind him. As soon as we were alone, Daniel broke down, chuckling under his breath. "Safe spaces? Triggers?"

I smiled back. "Hey, not everyone can pull off the intimidating badass look and get things done like you can. I try it, and I just come off as a bitch that people don't want to work with. No thanks."

Drucker came back a few seconds later with a small stack of papers in his hands, which he quickly stapled together. I couldn't help but reflect humorously on the fact that he had a red Swingline stapler on his desk. It's the sort of little thing that makes me laugh. "Okay, Miss Bertoli, I'm going to need you to sign in three places," Drucker said, taking a pen out of his desk and starting to point at the front page of the documents. "This one says that . . ."

"Mr. Drucker, can we speed this up?" I said, pretending to be scared. It wasn't that hard, once I tried. "The more time I'm on campus, the less safe I feel."

He chewed his lip for a second, then nodded. He flipped to the third page. "Okay. This one says you understand you are taking time off, and that you will get no credit for the classes you are dropping this semester."

I signed, and he flipped more. "This one says that you understand that when you come back, you will have retained your credits, but nothing more. You will have to start right back where you were at the beginning of this semester. Miss Bertoli, again, are you sure? Picking up again when your courses are going this fast and furious is very difficult."

"I'm sure," I said, signing the next page. "What's next?"

He flipped to the last page, and pointed. "This one says that you would lose any scholarships or time dependent grants under this decision, but since you're self-paying anyway, it's just boilerplate."

I signed, and Drucker took the documents and put them in a manila folder. "Okay, Miss Bertoli. I do hope that you feel safe enough to rejoin us soon. The deadline for telling us about winter semester is Thanksgiving. You can do that via email if you wish."

"Thank you, Mr. Drucker," I said, standing. I slipped my backpack on and offered my hand. "I'll be in touch."

Heading downstairs from his office, I glanced over at Daniel. Reaching over, I took his hand, which I had to admit gave me a thrill. It was the first time in public that I'd taken his hand as his girlfriend. "See? Don't worry, we're doing just fine."

"Still have a hundred meters to go," Daniel said. He paused just inside the doors to the outside and pulled me tight for an embrace. "But I do feel better."

We left the building, the bright sunshine dazzling us for a moment, and started across the small grassy area that led to the parking lot. Suddenly, Daniel grabbed my hand, pulling me to a stop. "Damn."

"What?" I asked before I saw it too. Coming toward us, looking as out of place as I would at a Black Panther rally, were two of my uncle's men. Both of them were trying to be quiet about it, but they knew they'd been spotted. "What do we do?"

"Run!" Daniel said, pulling me off to the right. We took off down the sidewalk and away from the two men, one of whom yelled as they took off after us. We rounded the corner, heading deeper into campus, where I hoped that our greater knowledge of the layout would help us lose them.

Unfortunately, our appearance had been anticipated, and I saw another man closing in from the far side of the quad, dressed like a college jock. As he got closer, I saw that it was Roberto. "Fuck!"

"Yeah," Daniel grunted, pain in his voice. He'd just started to get over his beating, and his body wasn't ready for this sort of stress. "Cut left!"

We tore across the grassy area into a tunnel that, if we continued on, would lead to the campus athletic grounds. "Here," Daniel said, reaching down to his pants and pulling out his keys. "When we reach the end, Roberto will most likely be there. You cut left, I go right. Circle around, get to the car, and get back to Carmen's place. If they're still on your tail when you leave campus, get on the Interstate and head north. When you're safe, call me. I'll come to you."

"Dan . . ." I gasped, the air hot in my lungs. "But—"

"They want to kick my ass more than they want you," Daniel said, slowing. He came to a stop and turned to me. "Ade, these idiots still don't understand how strong you are. They think that if they get me, you'll just come back home with your tail between your legs and be the pretty little princess all those idiots think you are. I know, because even I underestimated you. So go, I'll be okay. Come on, three guys? I've dealt with worse than that."

Daniel leaned in quickly and gave me a kiss and a smile. "Now go!"

I could see in his face that he wasn't sure about this plan, but I obeyed anyway. At the end of the tunnel, I sprinted left as hard as I could, heading toward the wooded area that ringed that part of campus. I heard Daniel yell out behind me, and Roberto replied, but that was it as I went hell-bent for leather to the trees.

I didn't slow down until I was within the shadows, surrounded by the pines and bushes. Panting, I leaned against the trunk of one of the bigger pines and looked back, wishing I could see Daniel. Unfortunately, the entire scene in front of me was more or less peaceful. There were students heading to class, a few still looking around, wondering what the hell had just happened, but no sign of any Bertoli men.

I walked quickly through the trees, keeping to the edge of campus as I brought my breathing and heart back under control. Still, I was sweating profusely as I came around to the far side of the parking lot, where I saw Daniel's car. The BMW looked ignored, so I got ready for one last dash. Fifty yards, no more, and then I would be able to get out of there.

I was so focused on the BMW that I didn't hear the footsteps behind me until a fraction of a second before wiry arms, pipe cleaner scrawny but with the strength of the insane, dropped around my waist. "Hello, baby," a reedy, whiny voice that I had dreaded ever hearing again whispered in my ear. "Good to see you again."

I fought against Vincent's grip as hard as I could, but before I could even scream, something was jammed over my mouth and nose. The pungent, almost alcoholic scent hit my brain for a moment, then everything started to go dark. I tried to fight, kicking my legs back, but they were only talking to my brain long-distance, and the force wasn't enough to hurt a fly.

"That's it, mama," Drake said again from the end of the tunnel that was my hearing. "Just sleep. We'll talk after you have a nap."

Darkness followed me next, inky and endless. In it, I could hear laughter, screaming, and in the background . . . Genesis.

Daniel

I hadn't lied when I told Adriana that I could handle three men. Even a week after catching a hellacious beating, I was confident about that. Especially since I didn't need to actually fight them, just evade them. Roberto was the fittest of the three, and I knew that I could outrun him, even as worn out as I was.

What I hadn't anticipated was a fourth. I had literally just stepped onto the sidewalk that bordered the campus when something that felt like a truck blindsided me. Considering that I played football in high school—all conference linebacker, in fact—I knew what happened, but knowledge didn't make the pain of being tackled to the sidewalk any easier. The wind was driven out of me, and I felt my ribs, which had just started to let me breathe without pain again, groan warningly while my nose thudded sickly at the jarring, even if it didn't get hit at all. I wasn't sure if something was broken anew or not, but I certainly wasn't wanting to find out.

"Sorry, Daniel," Julius grunted as he flipped me over. Taking my stunned arm, he yanked my wrist back, and I felt something being slipped over my hand before the zipping sound of the quick-tie told me what was happening. Another yank and another zip, and I was handcuffed just as effectively as if I'd been wearing metal.

A van pulled up, the door opened, and Julius got me to my feet and threw me inside headfirst. I ducked my chin in enough time to take most of the impact on my shoulder and back, but my neck caught some of it, and I was woozy for the next few minutes.

When I could focus, I saw that Roberto had joined us in the back of the van. "Where are you taking me?"

"You fucked up, Daniel, you know that?" Roberto said, giving me an incredulous look. "Bringing her back to campus? Seriously, what the fuck were you thinking?"

"About the value of higher education," I replied, leaning my head back against the bare metal of the van. "Not that you'd understand."

"Not trying to. Now lie there and shut the fuck up. I don't want to have to knock you out," Roberto replied. He didn't say anything the rest of the trip, which through the little I could see in the window, led not toward the Bertoli mansion, but toward the docks. That worried me.

The Port of Seattle isn't the largest port on the West Coast—far from it. Los Angeles, San Francisco, and Portland all have serious ports too, and problems back with the labor movement back in the thirties had shunted a lot of the surface tonnage away from Seattle. Still, it was quite a port and handled a lot of stuff that came into the Pacific Northwest. And of course, ports need longshoremen, and since time immemorial, longshoremen meant Mafia involvement. Carlo Bertoli controlled the longshoremen of Seattle and even owned a couple of warehouses out on the edges of the port, places where he could do some of the more unsavory parts of his business. I'd only had to come here a few times, and each of them hadn't ended well for the person in the position I was now in.

The van pulled into one of the warehouses, and the driver turned off the engine. "Let's go."

Roberto looked over at me. "You gonna walk, or are Julius and I gonna have to drag you out? Makes no difference to me."

"Does it matter?" I asked, then shook my head. "Fuck it, I'll walk."

Roberto nodded and opened the door. Julius, who'd been sitting up front in the shotgun seat, came around, his beagle eyes full of sadness. Roberto, on the other hand, looked happy. I could understand. He was the guy in the Bertoli enforcer group who was closest to my age. With me out of the way, he had the best chance of advancing, of making a bigger impact. Of course, what Roberto didn't realize is that the biggest thing holding him back was that he was pretty much an idiot. Carlo Bertoli was a loyal boss, but he didn't suffer fools lightly. It was why Roberto was kept on the low-level operations and stuff. He just didn't have the brains for more.

Carlo was waiting for me deeper in the warehouse, wearing his work suit and sitting in a hastily positioned office chair with a side table sitting next to it that looked like it had once been a TV tray. He was calm, the sort of calm that I knew meant he was highly pissed on the inside. "Free his hands, then tie them overhead."

I started to struggle until Julius caught me with a knee to the gut that drove the wind out of me while at the same time made my hurt ribs scream in pain. Not a sound other than the explosion of air left my mouth, though, and I was quickly tied up. "Now, I'm going to ask you some questions, Daniel, and you're going to answer them," Carlo said when I was fully trussed. "I don't think you want to refuse answering, do you?"

I stared at Carlo, then shook my head. "You stupid, stupid man, Carlo. What does it benefit you to beat me some more?"

"Where is Adriana?" Carlo screamed, jumping up and kicking me in the thigh. The heel of his shoe dug into the big muscle in my quad, turning it to wood, and I groaned, not worrying about saying what needed to be said. Carlo Bertoli and I had needed to talk for a long time.

"I don't know," I answered when I could talk again. "Why, is she not coming home immediately like you expected?"

Carlo stopped and nodded to Julius, who pulled out an expandable baton. It was one of those nasty ones too, with a body that is mostly a tightly wound spring with a bit of weight at the end. Swing that thing right, and the whole baton flexes, whipping into the body at point of impact. And, the flexed metal leaves a nasty fucking welt. I knew that from personal experience using one, but this was the first time to be on the receiving end. Julius knew just where to hit me too, a full-on shot to my back that mostly hammered into the big muscles of my lats and mid-back. It wouldn't break anything . . . not yet.

"You know, Daniel, I thought you were a smart boy," Carlo continued as if nothing had happened. "You took your first whipping like a man, and according to what Pietro told me afterward, you left like a man as well. I hoped that you would obey the rules and get out of town. Even when whispers came that you were staying with that stripper from the Starlight Club, I let them go. After all, you needed time to rest up, and I'm not one to hold that against a man.

"But when Adriana ran and has done nothing to answer her phone or her email, drops off the face of the fucking planet, only to find out this morning from her own mother than she had run to you? Of all the people in the world, she ran to her lover who left her for a fucking stripper? Oh no, that's too far. Now, one more time, where is Adriana?"

"I . . . don't . . . know!" I replied, smiling. My smile was cut short when Julius caught me with a hook punch that loosened two of my molars, and I spit them out, my grin coming back bloody. At least he hadn't hit my nose, although that too was throbbing. "You can punch me all you want. The answer's going to be the same. I don't know where Adriana is."

"You LIE!" Carlo yelled, picking up a .45 from the table and pointing it in my face. "Tell me!"

I gathered up all my energy and spat, splattering Carlo's face in blood and spit. "Fuck you, Carlo! For fuck's sake, all she wanted to do was have her own life! We fell in love, that's it! I asked her to marry me, you stupid, arrogant wop, and you and your pride are the only things stopping her from still being a part of your life! If YOU hadn't butted your nose into things, I'd still be out there protecting her. If you had just let your fucking pride go and seen that Adriana might actually love someone who is just another one of your Mafia thugs like myself, then maybe we wouldn't be having this fucking conversation!"

The look on Carlo's face pierced through my anger, and I saw his gun waver. "Wait . . . where is she?"

I could see the barrel of Carlo's gun tremble some more

and the doubt creep into the man's eyes. "We . . . I don't know," Carlo said, dropping the gun to his side. "One of my men, they figured that your plan would have you circle around to your BMW, but he's had eyes on the thing from inside the nearest building the entire time, and nobody has approached."

Fear crawled down my spine, and my mouth dropped open, panic starting to grip my insides. "No . . . no, she's supposed to be at Carmen's or heading down the Interstate right now."

Carlo looked at me, and I saw the family man that I'd come to know for the past few years. He set the pistol down and slumped into his chair. "I sent men to the apartment as well, as soon as Julius and Roberto and the others started chasing you. Other than a very pissed off Latina, they found nothing. They're waiting too, and they haven't heard or reported a thing."

I thought and put myself into Adriana's shoes. Cutting left, she would have paralleled the athletic grounds for a while, then come up to the . . . "Oh no."

My tiny whisper got through to Carlo, who looked up. "What?"

"Drake," I whispered, cursing my damn decisions. "The pictures he took of us. He took them from the trees that ring that end of campus. When she cut left, she could have come close to him without knowing it."

Carlo considered my words, then nodded. "Cut him loose."

Julius pulled a knife from his pocket and sawed away at my bonds. When I was free, I still staggered, going to a knee as my leg seized up again. "Let me find her. I know Drake better than anyone else, Carlo. I've been studying him nonstop since I left your house. If anyone can save her, it's me."

Carlo got out of his chair and came over. When I looked up, he had his hand extended, offering me assistance to my feet, which I gladly took. I swayed on my feet, and Carlo looked me in the eye, for the first time in his life not as Don Bertoli, the Godfather of Seattle and Tacoma, but man to man. "You save my Bella, and everything is forgiven. Maybe, just maybe, we'll discuss your relationship."

I nodded. "What changed your mind?"

"Nobody, not even Margaret, has cursed at me in years," he said with a small chuckle. "And nobody has called me a stupid wop since Gianni. You've got balls, kid, and heart. I'm sorry I didn't see that earlier. Find Adriana, Daniel. I need her as much as you do."

"I will . . . Godfather."

Twenty minutes later, I was back in the van, this time seated with Julius in the back. Roberto was driving up front, while the other man, the first driver, had stayed behind to help with the cleanup. Julius looked at me, somewhat in awe. "I ain't ever seen that in all my days."

"What's that, Julius?" I asked, rubbing at my jaw. The adrenalin was wearing off, and the pain of my missing teeth was starting to come through. My jaw was starting to swell too, and I doubted I'd be able to speak much in the next ten minutes or so unless I got some sort of ice on it. Actually, I could use some ice and some pain reliever on a few different areas of my body.

"I ain't never seen anyone stand up to the Godfather and live to see the end of the hour," Julius said, still in awe. "The funny part was, even when you were cursin' him, you were always in control of yourself."

"Glad I came off that way," I mumbled, my jaw getting stiffer by the second. "Gonna need a dentist after this."

"I wouldn't worry about that. If you don't find Adriana, you're going to need a fucking undertaker," Roberto shot back from up front. "Keep that in mind, lover boy."

Julius shot Roberto a dirty look and leaned in close. "You know how it is. Listen, most of us are rootin' for you to find her, and quick-like. You need any help, just ask me."

"Thanks," I mumbled. "Two things. One, I need my laptop from my BMW."

"Easy. I'll make the call now. And second?"

"An ice pack. And some fucking Advil."

Chapter 21

Adriana

I came back to consciousness slowly, with a splitting headache that threatened to turn my brain into scrambled eggs. My throat ached and my nostrils were raw, but at least I was lying down.

"Dan? Babe? I just had the worst dream . . ." I mumbled, trying to get up off the sofa. It wasn't until I was stopped three times that I realized that I wasn't on the sofa at Carmen's, nor was I free to go.

"What the hell?" I whispered, looking down. Across my chest, just under my boobs, and over each of my thighs, right above my knees, were what looked like cargo straps, the kind that you might use to make sure a load in the back of a truck didn't fall off or something. About an inch and half or so wide and nylon, they were bright orange, and despite my best efforts, I couldn't move them. I tried reaching with my hands, but I couldn't find anything to adjust or move. "Help! HELP!"

"Oh my dear, I held the book so tightly. I saw your picture, I heard you call my name . . ." a nightmarish voice said in the dim light of wherever the hell I was, and I paled.

"Vincent?"

"Glad to see you remember me, my love," Vincent said, stepping into my field of view for the first time. "Like the bed I have prepared for you? I had to work hard to make it. It took all sorts of effort to prepare it for you."

"Vincent . . . let me go," I said, trying to be calm. "Let me go, and I won't tell anyone about this. Not even my family."

Vincent giggled, his suit coat taken off and his tie dangling from around his neck, half removed. "Talk to me, baby. You never talk to me."

Great. Fucking Genesis. I decided to roll with it in a language he might understand. "I'm here now, Vincent. Talk to me now, Vincent."

"Why would you listen now, Domino?" Vincent asked, his voice grim and sad. I racked my mind, trying to figure out what the hell he was talking about, until it hit me. *Domino, Parts 1 & 2,* was a pair of songs from their 1986 album, *Invisible Touch.* In Part one, the lyrics are plaintive, as the lead singer seems to sing about an unnamed woman—presumably, in Vincent's madness, Domino—and a one-night stand that changed his heart and his soul forever.

Part two, however, took on a much darker overtone, especially when filtered through Vincent's madness. Lots of lyrics about blood and some pretty apocalyptic stuff, but nothing more than standard Phil Collins's singing about social change.

"Vincent, it's me, Adriana. I'm not *Domino,*" I tried to reply, using my most soothing voice. "You taught me sculpture, remember?"

Vincent giggled, high and manic, and I saw him reach next to him. "Of course I do, baby. That was where you showed me your heart, and where I realized the truth. You were the one meant for me, not that stupid bitch that I called my wife."

"She was with you for over twenty years, Vincent. How

can you say she wasn't for you?"

He backed up and did a twirling, stuttering dance, laughing and singing the song "Cause Jesus He Knows Me."

I wanted to scream, to let my mind descend into the panic and madness that was nibbling at the edges of my consciousness. I was at the mercy of a madman. Instead, I clamped down with everything I could think of. I thought of a trick Angela had taught me, back when I was having problems focusing on my art. "Find your *itten*," she had told me, as we sat around the apartment. "Then you'll be fine."

She told me that it meant 'one point', and it's used in a lot of different ways. Her grandmother used it as a way to say to find that one important thing in your life, the hypothetical thing that if you stripped away all the other things around your life, if you cut away all the bullshit, the thing that comes to you then.

Her words from two years ago came to me now, and I knew the answer immediately. "Daniel," I mouthed, thinking of his strong face with his eyes that took me in with acceptance, humor, and unmatched passion. "Please, I need you."

I kept up my silent prayer the entire time that Vincent had his back turned to me, closing my mouth and putting on an attentive face when he turned around. I had read the crime scene report from both Angela's and Vincent's wife's murders numerous times. Not only was he a cutter, but he was a rapist as well—no doubt two skills that he had developed in his time doing 'enhanced interrogations' in Central America.

"Oh we're going to have such fun," he said when he came back. "You want me to show you some of the games I prepared?"

"I'd like to talk more first," I said, trying to get his mind on his mouth and off my body. "Tell me about your art, Vincent. Please?"

"My art? My art is not something you really want to explore." Vincent howled, like I'd just told the funniest joke in the world. "You think my art is that stuff that I showed you in class, made of clay and metal and wood? Oh, sweetie, you have no clue at all. But I tell you what, let me show you some of my art."

He came over to the side of my bed and touched some sort of floor control, and my bed started to tilt until I was in a semi-reclining position. I could see a television on a cheap table, and with my new angle, I could see some more of the room. It looked like I was in a hotel room, but one that hadn't been updated since about the time I was born.

Vincent turned on the television, the screen lighting up and giving me more light to see with. I honestly wished I didn't, as the room looked like a dump other than my bed/table and the television. Vincent picked up a remote control and stepped back to my side. "Some of these pictures are a little old, so forgive the eighties hair and fashion, but I think it adds to the art, in my opinion."

He had turned on a DVD player, I soon figured out, with a disc full of pictures in the tray. "Here's my first efforts, and while I was happy at the time, as I look back, I realize that I was so sloppy. My use of color and spirit just lacked cohesion."

The picture came up, and I couldn't help myself—I screamed. The image in front of me showed a man, but I couldn't tell much more than that. His face had been disfigured, and it was horrifying to look at.

"I had the same reaction," Vincent said conversationally, as if he were critiquing a bad piece of art. "Far too much emphasis on trying to be complex, to not let the art speak for itself. But I got better."

"It wasn't until my time with the military was done and I had my chance to go to the hospital that I realized what was lacking wasn't my skill," Vincent said, tapping his chin with the remote. "After all, if you gave Leonardo da Vinci a pile of Play-Doh, he wasn't going to be able to create great works of art with it. What was lacking was in my materials. I'd been bottom feeding, just using the scraps that were given to me to demonstrate or to work from so I could advance someone else's corporate shell game. But in the hospital, I was exposed to the idea that if you start with good quality supplies, you have a much better chance of creating good quality work. So, I invested a little bit of money, got some better tools, and upgraded my work materials. It took longer that way, but the results were worth it."

I couldn't help it. It was either cry out or pass out from the horror. I screamed, and Vincent smiled. "And the best part is, my sweet, you're going to help me create my masterpiece."

Chapter 22

Daniel

I was back at the Bertoli mansion, sitting in the dining room, ice packs wrapped to four different places on my body, staring at my computer. I'd been at it for over nine hours, and I was getting pissed. I knew so much about Drake except the one thing I needed most. I needed to know where the hell the bastard was keeping Adriana.

For example, I knew that he was more than just a guy who flipped his lid once and killed two women. While his outburst was greater this time, I suspected that he'd been involved with at least a dozen other murders, stretching back nearly twenty-five years, and that was just in his time after he got out of the military. In each town that he lived in, including Seattle, there was a noticeable uptick in disappearances of young women, with bodies being found months or even years later. While the autopsies normally said that the women had died of exposure, accidentally, or due to some other natural cause, and that any disfigurement to the corpses came from normal decomposition or from small scavengers eating the body, I could tell from the way there were angles and symmetry that those wounds were intentionally inflicted. If I could tell that, any detective worth their salt could too—they must have been trying to not incite panic.

I knew that Drake favored using tools from a company called Sculpture Hut, and that he ordered a lot of it online now that the company had gone to a Web-based presence. I even knew his fucking credit card that he used for placing his orders.

What I didn't know was where in the hell he was right that second. Seattle's a big city, land-wise, and had done a lot of expansion and contraction over the years. Surrounded by the Pacific Northwest, it doesn't take a lot to disappear in Seattle. I needed something to point me in the right direction.

Unfortunately, the pain in my body, combined with the lack of information, was driving me nuts. After looking at the same information for the third time without making any progress, I slammed my fist on the table, rattling the tea cup that was on the other side and sending it tumbling to the floor, where it shattered in a bomb-like explosion.

"I never liked that tea cup anyway," a voice said behind me, and I turned my head, instantly regretting it as my sore neck twinged. Margaret Bertoli stood in the doorway, her hair and face so similar to Adriana's that I nearly cried. She stepped in closer, seeing the pain in my face, and came around to sit down on the chair nearby. "Sorry, I forgot about your neck."

"Not your fault," I replied, rubbing at the sore area. "It'll feel better soon enough."

"You're a pretty horrible liar for a Mafia man," Margaret said with a chuckle. "Besides, I know that jaw has to still be killing you."

"I put some Orajel on it," I mumbled, aware again of the sick throb on the left side of my face. "After I find Adriana, I can go to the dentist and get some nice, shiny porcelain replacements put in."

"How goes the search?" she asked. "Carlo told me he has

every man in our employ out combing the city. Still, it's a big damn city."

"With a lot of places someone with military training could hide," I finished. "And this guy—he's good. I've gotten to know more about him than perhaps even the cops they have on his ass, and he scares me. One on one, I'd have his ass for breakfast, but right now, he has the advantage. I have to find him, not wait for him to come to me."

Margaret nodded. "If you were him, what would you do?"

I blanked for a second, then sighed. "I don't know. I'm not a psycho. I'm not like him."

She shook her head and put her hand on mine. "Don't limit yourself. Being married to Johnny, I saw both the wonderful man and the dark side of him over the fifteen years we were married. I came to understand it, and it's why, even after his death, I stay with the Bertoli family. It's more honest than the lie the rest of the world tells itself sometimes. Turn on the TV and listen to what normal people tell themselves. They hear about crimes, the horrible things that monsters like Drake do, and they tell themselves that they can never understand them. They say that they could never do the same, and that only someone aberrant would do such things. But the truth is different. We all have that monster inside us, the voices inside our heads. Most of the people out there refuse to accept it. They refuse to accept that your ancestors were the same people who perpetrated the Holocaust, while ancestors of the Bertolis thought that crucifixion was quite a normal way to treat undesirable people. The Irish and Scots . . . we engaged in the wholesale slaughter of each other, uniting only when we hated the English more than other clans. This idea that we call civilized culture is a relatively new thing, overall. Within the Bertoli organization, we accept that dark animal side, and by accepting it, we've been able to have greater strength and control over ourselves. So don't deny that side of you. Accept it, knowing that when you are done with it, you can put it away."

I thought about it, then nodded slowly. "I'll try."

"In the meantime, though, can you answer another question for me?" she asked, her voice different. She sounded both concerned and happy at the same time.

"Sure. Whatever you need."

"Were you two going to invite me to the wedding?" she asked lightly. "Or was I going to find out through email?"

I smiled and let my head hang. "We were going to wait on the wedding," I said softly. "She wanted to try and reconcile enough that you'd be able to come."

Margaret smiled and leaned over, kissing me on the cheek. "Thank you . . . son. Now, when you find her, we can have the wedding here, and not at some cheesy hotel."

I chuckled, then stopped, a lightning bolt of inspiration flashing through my mind. "Hotel. Hotel . . . shit!"

"What?" Margaret said, excitement dawning in her face from the sound of my voice. "What did you think of?"

"Adam did a complete background on Drake, and he was going to check out everything, but outside of his house, there wasn't anything. But his wife . . . there!"

"The Vista Pine Motel," Margaret said, reading over my shoulder. "What is it?"

"An old motel on Route 99, south of SeaTac," I said. "It's in his wife's name. It's been sitting in probate the whole time. The cops went through right after the murder and didn't find anything, but if I were to try and kidnap someone . . ."

"Let's go," Margaret said, standing up and offering me a hand. "I'll drive. You armed?"

"No," I replied. "Carlo's men did a smart job of that."

Margaret nodded, then shrugged. "There's always some guns somewhere in this house. We can get you something from the kitchen safe."

I took her offered hand and lurched to my feet. Going to the kitchen, she opened the safe there and pulled out two pistols. "Which do you prefer, 9mm or .45?"

"Forty-five," I answered. "Beretta."

"Always buy Italian, Daniel. Don't you know that? Here." She handed me the forty-five handle first, and I took it. It was nice, one of the newer pistols from Beretta's Cougar line, not my preferred model, but still damn good. "Good enough?"

"Good," I said, checking the magazine. I had eight rounds of gleaming brass inside, with hollow point rounds. If I put one of these into him, the fight would be over. "Come on. What are we driving?"

"The Gran Turismo," Margaret said, pointing. I was impressed. She normally drove much more conservative cars, but the Maserati Gran Turismo Stradale was different. Sleek, powerful, with feminine lines and that touch that just differentiated it from its competitors. "Need help into the passenger seat?"

"No, I'll make it," I said, limping over and ungainly dropping into the passenger seat. "See?"

She started the engine up, and I couldn't help but grin at the rumbling power under the hood. This was one sexy car.

"Think you can peel this thing out?" I asked, buckling in. "I can navigate."

"Watch me," she said, slamming the gear stick forward and jamming her foot to the floor. "Johnny took me on a couple of trips to Europe. I got to drive cars like this on the Autobahn. Hold on—we're going to break some traffic laws."

According to what I checked out later, the distance from the Bertoli mansion to the Vista Pine Motel was thirty-seven miles. If you follow the traffic laws, driving that would take you between forty-five minutes and an hour.

For Margaret Bertoli, driving to find her daughter behind the wheel of a car with four hundred and sixty horsepower, racing suspension and near super-car status, she nearly ripped street signs off in her wake as she tore down Interstate 5. I wanted to navigate, but I was so focused on trying to just hold on as she took curves and corners at nearly suicidal speeds that I barely had the presence of mind to call Pietro. "Pietro? Yeah, it's me. Mrs. Bertoli and I are checking out a lead. The Vista Pine Motel, it's a closed down motel near SeaTac. Yeah, I'll send you the address. Get some men over there before us if you can. What? FUCK!"

"What is it?" Margaret said through clenched teeth as we passed a semi before quickly cutting back in to swerve around a minivan in the passing line.

"Pietro says they don't have anyone near SeaTac right now," I said. "Everyone is in the downtown and University areas. They figured that he'd keep her close by, as much as he was able to get onto campus."

"Then we get there first," Margaret said. "You take the lead."

I stopped, then turned to her, surprised. "You're going in with me?"

"That's my daughter," she said, her voice filled with steel. "There's no way I'm not going in after her. Besides, I know how to handle a gun, Daniel."

I said nothing, my thoughts my own as she jerked the steering wheel to the right, this time into the breakdown lane, to go around a pair of cars in the two lanes before cutting back over. "You do realize we just passed a cop."

"By the time he gets that piece of junk up to speed, we're going to be off the Interstate," Margaret replied through clenched teeth as we approached the off ramp. "Hold on, this'll be fast."

My ribs groaned as I was thrown against the side door as we took the right turn getting off the Interstate at seventy, sliding part of the turn like a drift racer. "You should be a pro at this," I hissed as I tried to find a comfortable position again. "And get a five-point harness system."

"Don't worry," Margaret said. "Only a mile to go. Get ready."

We pulled up into the parking lot, which was weedy and cracked, one of the few eyesores in an area that looked like it had been undergoing rejuvenation for a while. Heading to the back, I saw a van and held up my hand. "Stop here."

"Why?" She said, but still doing what I asked.

"Because if that is Drake, and he's got Ade . . . if he sees a vehicle, he may kill her before we're even out of our seats. We go in on foot."

My cellphone rang, and I picked it up. "Yeah, Pietro?"

"We have men coming. They'll be there in ten minutes,"

Pietro said, his voice calm and composed. "What is your status?"

"We're at the motel," I replied. "I'm going in."

"No, Daniel. Hold for backup," Pietro said. "This Drake is to be taken alive."

I took the phone away from my ear and hung it up. "Pietro says wait. I'm not going to disobey him directly by saying no, so if anyone asks, my phone lost reception."

She nodded and took the phone from me, putting it in her purse. "You ready?"

"Just a second," I said, and winced. When Margaret leaned over to see if I was okay, I chopped her in the back of the neck, knocking her out. She sagged against the door, and I swallowed my disgust at my actions. "I'm sorry, but I'm not going to risk you just to get a little backup. I need to do this one alone."

I got out of the car, closing the door softly behind me, and raised the pistol next to my head. I was sore, hurt, stiff, and barely functioning after being without sleep for so long.

Good enough. I went in.

Chapter 23

Adriana

My mind was numb, horror struck as Vincent's mental torture wore me down. I was tired, the sun had set hours ago, and the only light that filled the room came from the television, which had shifted from Vincent's gory slide show to an equally macabre scene, which my mind only compensated for by calling it Home Movies from Hell.

After getting bored with just his still photographs, Vincent had turned to videotaping as well, a process he explained to me that involved wearing a small camera on his head while he did his deeds. "GoPro has been my friend, although I've found that there are better options," he explained as he started the video. For hours now, I'd been terrified over and over as I was forced to watch.

I was beyond caring anymore. My mind was too horrified by it all. Instead, I let loose the truth that had been boiling inside me, figuring I had nothing to lose. "You . . . you're a sick son of a bitch, Vincent. Not an artist, but a sadistic rapist psychopath."

"And Van Gogh cut off his own ear as a present," Vincent retorted. He sighed deeply and paused the video. "I had such high hopes for you, Adriana. After seeing your work, I hoped that you could be the woman who would understand me, be my partner and join me in making such art that the world would always remember our names. I see you're just like all the others, though. Well, if you can't be a partner, you can at least be a fine set of materials to create my latest masterpiece."

I struggled, but the straps holding me to the table had absolutely no give to them, and Vincent knew exactly how to tie me down. He didn't even need to tie my arms—he was that confident. "There's no way you're going to get those free."

"Come close enough, and I won't need to," I hissed. "I'm going to tear off your balls. Then I'll let my family do what they do best."

Vincent laughed, leaning his head back. "You mean your uncle, the Godfather of Seattle? Please. That pudgy old fuck couldn't save you even if he tried. I spent nearly two months right under his nose—hours a day—within rifle shot of you, and the best you could do was to have some dumb lunk of a bodyguard hang around with you."

I laughed, hilarity replacing my horror. "I'm going to enjoy watching Daniel give you the ending you deserve."

"Maybe from heaven," Vincent said, finding the adjustment switches on the bed again. He flipped a switch, and the bed flattened out and lowered slightly. "Just the right height."

Vincent walked over to the DVD player, taking out his disc of horrors and putting in another. He hit play, and I winced as Genesis began playing at nearly deafening levels. "Greatest hits!" Vincent yelled, turning to me. "Ain't it *great*?"

He pulled off his shirt, revealing his toaster rack chest and pot belly before shucking his pants. How a man so out of shape had the strength to do everything he'd done still surprised me. There must have been some truth to the idea of 'crazy strength.'

Nude, Vincent knelt once again, picking up a bag that looked like a soft sided carpenter's tool kit. "Can't forget my tools."

I figured I was getting ready to die, and if I was, I wanted to do it on my terms. "That's your main tool? I've seen bigger on Michelangelo statues," I said, looking between his legs.

I wanted him angry. I wanted him pissed off. If I was going to check out of the world, then damn it, I was going to do it my way.

He turned red, and I laughed harder.

"Shut up!" Vincent screamed, reaching to his side and grabbing a pistol. "You can't laugh at me! You can't!"

I opened my mouth to bray laughter into his face when the door to the room blasted open and a miracle burst into the room. Daniel had his weapon drawn, but he was pointed the wrong direction as he stumbled into the room. Vincent had a second to react, and he did, squeezing a shot off that clipped Daniel between his shoulder and his neck. Daniel dropped to the floor, out of my line of vision, and I screamed in fright and in hope. "Daniel!"

Chapter 24

Daniel

I felt bad about knocking Margaret out, but as I tried to make my way quietly down the row of rooms in the motel, I put my regret aside. While she had guts and a lot of reasons to want to put a bullet into Vincent Drake, she also didn't have any training that I knew of. Since I'd known the woman for twenty years, that meant quite a lot.

And Drake was trained, no doubt about it. I had seen the man's work, and while it seemed that he favored knives and other sorts of slicing weapons, he used guns too. I didn't need to worry about Margaret's life while trying to save Adriana.

As I approached the room closest to the van parked near the end of the building, I heard music. While I wasn't quite sure, as I got closer, I heard the unmistakable sound of Phil Collins's singing and knew I had the right place. I checked the safety on the Beretta and got ready.

I tried to look in the window of the unit, but it had been boarded up, probably to reduce the noise that leaked from the building. I knew for sure that inside, the sound of the music would be deafening, which I took as a measure in my favor. I quickly went over my mental checklist of how to bust down a door and sweep a room, and I took a deep breath.

Now, normally, if you're going to kick down the door on a room with a known armed occupant, you want two people, one to check each direction, especially if the asshole inside knows that you're coming. I put my ear to the door, trying to hear something but the music was just too loud.

"Shut up!" I heard Vincent scream, clearly on the edge of losing control. *"You can't laugh at me! You can't!"*

I used the scream to time my kick, driving with as much force as my right leg could muster. Unfortunately for me, my thigh muscle was still more cramp and knotted tissue than actual effective muscle, so a kick that should have shattered the door barely broke the lock, and I had to lower my shoulder to charge the rest of the way through, stumbling as I did.

This meant that when I went through the door, I had my gun down and I was looking to my left. I started to bring my gun up when I heard Adriana gasp, and I started to turn. I heard an explosion, and my neck was suddenly on fire and my right arm turned to lead. Instead of continuing the turn and staying in the line of fire, I rolled with my stumble, hoping to get the hell out of the way.

I got to a knee and pointed my pistol back the other way, but some sort of table was in the way, and I couldn't see Drake at all. Instead, I could see a cascade of red hair draped over the side of the obstruction, and at least I knew where Adriana was.

A sound to my left caught my attention as a door slammed, and I staggered to my feet. Adriana was strapped to the table, and I didn't see anyone else. "Where is he?"

"He went toward that door," Adriana said, her voice quavering. "Daniel . . ."

"I'll live," I said, even as I felt the blood start to soak my shirt and drip down my chest. I saw that Adriana was held to the table by some cargo straps, and I didn't have the time to try and work the catch, which was most likely on the underside of the table. Instead, I grabbed a knife out of the toolkit that Drake had left on the table and handed it to her. "Here. Can you cut yourself free?"

"Yeah," she said. "But Dan . . ."

"It ends tonight," I said, starting out the door Drake had gone through. I had to be careful. He knew this property much better than I did. Still, at least Adriana was now behind me and Drake in front of me. Much better than it had been.

The blood was rushing through my ears as I stepped into the dark hallway, seeing the open door to the outside. I guessed that the door was a late addition, or perhaps the room wasn't a guest room but instead a manager's quarters back when the motel had been in operation. It didn't really matter, as I had my pistol in front of me. My right arm was heavy, the shock of being shot still blasting the nerves, so I used two hands, my left hand steadying my right as I worked my way down the hallway, not rushing but not being overly cautious. I knew that if he was going to try and ambush me again, he'd do it when I came out of the room.

I saw him as soon as I came out, his nude body nearly glowing in the moonlight. "Drake! Vincent Drake!" I yelled, leveling my pistol at him. "Stop where you are!"

I would have squeezed a shot off at him, but he was already just beyond the maximum range I'd trust for making an open shot with a pistol at night, and I was wounded and using an unfamiliar Beretta. I didn't want to give it away.

He turned, his face sweaty and glistening in the pale white light, madness clear even at the distance he was. "Well, hero, you got me," he said, laughing. "Whatcha gonna do about it?"

He whipped his pistol up, faster than I thought a man his age could move, and I barely dove out of the way as he fired two shots that bounced off the concrete behind where'd I'd been just an instant earlier. I fired into the air, not caring if I actually hit him but just trying to give him a reason to give up his relatively stable position. Hitting the ground hard, I rolled as best I could to my belly, my arms up and looking for a firing angle.

He was already on the move, charging at me with his pistol outstretched, his grin nearly stretching from ear to ear. "Yeah! Hooo-raaa!" he hollered as he ran, squeezing the trigger. His first shot hit the asphalt inches from my head, and I knew I had only one chance. "Die!"

"You first," I whispered, squeezing my trigger. The Beretta kicked in my hand, harder than I'd expected, and I realized that my arm was really losing sensation, the forty-five feeling like I was firing a shotgun pistol or something. Thankfully, my shot took him high in his chest, right below his collarbone area, and he stopped, dumbfounded.

He coughed, then sank to his knees. The hollow point round had done a number on him. He realized he was dying, and he looked up at me. "Nice shot."

I squeezed the trigger again. I sagged as his body collapsed, the pain, shock and blood loss finally overcoming me, and darkness crept across my vision. At least Adriana was safe.

* * *

I came to when I felt a pair of hands tugging at my shirt. "Come on, I can't get you up on my own."

I blinked, trying to figure out where that voice was coming

from. It sounded like it was on a long distance line a million miles away, but it was familiar. "Adriana?"

"Yeah, you big, stupid, brave, wonderful lunk," she said, pulling on my left arm. "Come on, we've gotta get out of here."

"So tired . . ." I said, not knowing what was going on. "Just wanna sleep . . ."

"Yeah, yeah, you can sleep at home. In fact, you can sleep in my bed if you want, but we've gotta get out of here. Come on!"

I staggered to my feet, still not sure what was going on, but tried to lean on Adriana as she started walking. Unfortunately, I was too heavy, and she was also staggering, bumping into the door frame and hissing in pain. "Dan, I need your help."

"I've got him," another voice said, and I had to blink. I had two angels with me, it seemed, two Adrianas, who each took a side of me and helped me through the room and out the door. I was glad for the wonderful silence. The music had been splitting my head, it was so horrible. I was never going to listen to Genesis again, that was for sure.

"Mom, when did you get here?" Adriana asked as the three of us made our way toward Margaret's car. The walking was clearing my head, or perhaps just that Margaret's pulling on my right side was jostling my bullet wound, and the pain was waking me up.

"She drove," I said, not walking much better but at least able to focus. "I kinda knocked her out before coming in to get you."

"You hit my mother?" Adriana asked. We reached the car, and Adriana pulled open the back door, sliding me into the seat. "Why?"

"Didn't want to get her killed," I whispered as Margaret closed the door and went around to the driver's seat. I was glad that the GT had a back seat. I'd have never been able to sit in the front seat with my bullet wound. "Sorry. Guess the whole mother-in-law, son-in-law thing is off to a bad start, huh?"

"You told them?" Adriana asked, and Margaret chuckled.

"Honey, it was what got your uncle to not shoot him in the head," Margaret laughed. "Now hold on, we're getting out of here. This may not be the best part of Seattle, but still, the cops should be here soon enough. I'd prefer not to answer questions. Pietro will have men here in a minute to torch the place."

I nodded, suddenly tired again. "Okay."

"We'll get you to the hospital soon," Adriana said, and I shook my head. "What?"

"No hospital. Home," I replied, drifting off. "I can get patched up there. Take . . . take me home."

Chapter 25

Adriana

Patched up wasn't the word to describe what we ended up having to do with Daniel. In the end, Uncle Carlo called in a doctor—one who made house calls, took cash, and kept his mouth shut—to seal the hole. "He took it in his trapezius muscle," the doctor said as he washed his hands afterward in the kitchen. "It was a through-and-through. He's lucky though. Another inch or so toward the neck, and he'd have gotten his carotid or jugular cut. He'd never have gotten off the floor."

"Thank you, Doctor," Carlo said, giving the man a thick envelope. "Your services are, as always, appreciated."

"No thanks necessary, Godfather," the doctor replied. "It's an honor to be at your service. Now, make sure that wound stays bandaged, and leave the IV in for the rest of the night. Then, for the next five days, give him those antibiotic pills I gave you. He's going to need to sleep a lot. He's been through hell. And not just from the gunshot either."

"Yes, well, that's a family matter," Carlo said. "Thank you. He'll get the best care we can provide."

The doctor left, leaving Carlo, Mom and me alone in Daniel's bedroom. He was lying on his bed, his neck and shoulder wrapped, his eyes closed. The doctor had given him a shot to let him sleep, to let his body recover. I sat on the edge of the bed, looking down at his bruised but peaceful face.

"He fought with honor," Carlo said, standing next to the bed. His voice was soft, almost in awe as he looked down at Daniel.

"He's as Italian as you or me," I said softly, tracing his eyebrows and feeling the tears coming to my eyes. "Maybe not by blood, but he's been part of our family since he was a baby. He's a good man."

Carlo hummed and turned his eyes to me. "I owe you an apology."

I turned my head and looked at him, nodding slightly. "You do. I owe you one as well, though."

It was the most compromise I was willing to offer. Sure, I had been wrong to ditch his bodyguard, but Carlo had been much further in the wrong having had Daniel beaten and turned into the walking bruise that I saw days later in Carmen's apartment. Still, families were brought together and relationships were mended by forgiveness, even if I wouldn't forget. I got off the bed. "Uncle, I'm sorry that I wasn't up front with my relationship with Daniel and that I ran away from home. Please forgive me."

Carlo gulped and looked to the sky, then back at me with tears in his eyes. "Oh, Bella, there is nothing I need to forgive. It is I who begs your forgiveness. I tried to run your life as if you were still a little girl, and not the beautiful, wonderful young woman you have become. I insulted you, I insulted the man you love, and in the process, I nearly lost the most important thing in my life. I am so sorry, and I promise that no matter what, I will support you and your decisions from now on."

I felt tears in my eyes too as I came around the bed and embraced my uncle, hugging him tightly.

We stayed that way for a moment before releasing each other. I blinked and wiped at my eyes. "I forgive you. But there's someone else who must forgive you too—Daniel. He's going to be part of my life, and unless he's willing to accept your apology, we can't be part of this life anymore."

Carlo opened his mouth to protest, then nodded. "You are right, of course. When he wakes up, let me know. I will come and speak with him, man to man."

He turned and left the bedroom, leaving me and Mom. She'd been silent since the doctor finished his stitching, standing with her back against the wall, a growing bruise forming on the side of her neck. "You doing okay, Mom?"

She stood there for a moment, then smiled, laughing until she was nearly crying. I understood and went to her, where we held each other for a long time, crying and laughing and holding each other. "Adriana, oh, my baby."

"I'm okay," I said, still crying and laughing. "How's your neck?"

Mom let go of me and chuckled, rubbing her neck. "He knows exactly where to put someone down, that's for sure. Considering he's knocked me out and called Carlo an arrogant wop, I'd say he's got more guts than anyone else I've ever known."

"He called Uncle Carlo an arrogant wop?" I asked, amazed. "And he didn't get shot over it?"

"He was about two seconds from it, according to what I heard," Mom told me. "When he wakes up, maybe he can tell you the story."

"I'd like that," I said, looking back at him. "If you don't mind, I think I'm going to sleep here tonight. Not with him—he needs his rest—but on the floor next to him. He protected me for so long. He beat back the demons that threatened me. I think it's my turn to protect him for a while."

"I agree, honey," Mom said. "But first, let him sleep, and you and I will get some dinner. I think there are some leftovers in the fridge."

"As long as we eat here," I said, indicating the space in front of Daniel's bed. "He even had a TV in here. What a wonderfully luxurious living situation."

Mom looked around the tiny broom closet-sized space and chuckled. "I think you might be marrying a monk."

"Yeah, of the Shaolin variety," I joked back. "Come on, let's get some food. I bet there will be a report on the fire at the motel on the super early morning news, and I'd like to watch."

* * *

In fact, the news reports were already on the cable networks, as it had been a relatively slow news day otherwise. While I ate some leftover pizza and Mom ate some lasagna, we got to watch as the fire department struggled with two pumper trucks to get the blaze under control. "Wow," I commented, munching on a piece of bell pepper, "Pietro really outdid himself with the pyrotechnics."

"He was rushed. Better to do too much than not enough," Mom replied. "He probably had to focus on the bed you were kept and the room itself. That's a lot of accelerant in a really short amount of time."

Daniel stirred behind us, mumbling in his sleep, and we both turned to check on him. He quieted after a moment, and we watched the news story continue.

"In another shocking development, police found the body of a nude man outside the hotel as well. Reports are still preliminary, but sources are telling us that the police suspect that the body might be that of Vincent Drake, the suspect in two recent murders. Please note—these reports are preliminary, and the police are not confirming or denying anything at this time."

"Guess we're going to have to get the lawyers on this one," Mom said, taking the last bite of her food. "I'm pretty sure the cops are going to want you to make a statement. You might want to start going over the particulars now. A lot of stuff has gone on, and not everyone is going to be willing to keep their mouths shut. The university, for one. The cops are going to want to know why you took a sabbatical, all that kind of thing."

"Uncle Carlo can't get this all swept under the rug?" I asked, curious but unafraid.

Mom shook her head. "The police won't be chasing this too hard. Drake was a murdering psychopath, but they will still want to make sure all their paperwork is done right. Drake had military connections and who knows what else. The people who made this monster are going to want to make sure their asses are covered, so as long as they know they won't have someone chasing them down and that Drake is well and good in the ground, they'll keep their noses out of it. Still, they will have questions."

"And I don't want to give them a reason to keep poking around Bertoli business," I said. "That's a lot of stress."

"Which I am sure you will handle well," Mom said, relaxed. "You're a Bertoli, and less than an hour ago, you got the Godfather of this entire area to tearfully apologize to you. I'd say you've got the nerve."

* * *

Mom was right. The next day, after I had crashed for six hours from sunrise until noon, I was invited down to police headquarters to make a statement on Vincent Drake's death. Daniel was still sleeping, but Mom promised me that she would stay by his side, so I changed into my best clothes and went down with Uncle Carlo and his lawyer, a guy named Dominic Petruzelli, whom I'd met occasionally but never had the chance to seriously talk to.

As Uncle drove—something totally unlike him—Dominic briefed me in the back of the car. "Miss Bertoli, I strongly stress that you only answer questions related directly to Vincent Drake's murder. The police have no reason to ask you about why you went on sabbatical or your rather—ahem—public display of running away from your uncle's employees."

"So what am I supposed to do? Plead the Fifth?" I asked, incredulous. "Won't that just make me look guiltier?"

"The law is not about what people know, but what they can prove," Dominic replied. "The Seattle police, I am sure, know more about your uncle than they will ever tell us. They are probably also quite sure that someone affiliated with your uncle was involved in killing Drake. However, what they suspect, what they know, and what they can prove in a court of law are three entirely different things."

Carlo chuckled up front. "Listen to him, Bella. The man knows what he is talking about."

The interview was conducted by two detectives, Fritz and Taguchi, who obviously knew who I was. However, they weren't the cops I'd met before who worked Angela's murder case. "Hello, Miss Bertoli. Would you like a coffee?"

"No thanks," I said. I took a chair while Dominic sat down next to me. "I did ask Mr. Petruzelli to join us today, guys, just to make sure things are on the up and up. What can I do for you?"

"Why would you have a lawyer if we just asked you to come down so we can clear up some details about Vincent Drake's death?" Taguchi asked. He had a sort of faux hawk look, with the sides of his head nearly shaved while the top was about two inches long. To me, he kind of looked like a rooster. "That makes no sense to me."

"It makes no sense to me that a man who killed two people, looked like Mr. Potato Head, and was on the wall in every police station from here to Sacramento was able to get within two hundred yards of me on a regular basis and was killed at an abandoned motel less than a mile from a police station," I replied evenly. I nodded to Dominic, who reached into his briefcase and took out a digital recorder, which he placed on the table and turned on. "Now, I'm not interested in pursuing the Seattle PD for being incompetent, or for putting my personal safety at risk. I just want to make sure I'm not turned into some sort of scapegoat by someone looking to cover his own ass. That's all."

Fritz and Taguchi exchanged a look, and I knew that I'd won. Despite what they'd said, they were hoping to use the investigation to get something, some sort of angle that they could use to pry at the Bertoli family. They weren't going to get that from me.

Fritz sighed and opened his case file. "All right then, Miss Bertoli, can you tell me . . ."

The interview took two hours, and at the end, I could see that both cops were cracking. Each time they strayed from anything other than the time surrounding when Vincent was killed, Dominic was there, shutting them down. They tried tricking me. They tried cajoling. In the end, they were both nearly crying, they were so frustrated. I realized that Dominic was right. Fritz and Taguchi knew what had happened. They knew that Mom had driven her Maserati in the area of the fire. They didn't have a shot of the license plate though, because of a supposed weird trick of light that didn't allow the traffic cameras to get a clear image. They knew that a Beretta had been used to shoot Drake. They knew that Drake had also fired his own pistol, having dug a bullet out of the burned wall. They knew that someone had been strapped to a table. They were sure I'd been kidnapped, and they were sure of so many things. They knew. They *knew.*

But they couldn't prove a damn thing. Maybe in the future, if Daniel's DNA was ever logged, they'd be able to fix him to the crime scene. Maybe, if some cop wanted to track it down and some prosecutor was willing to run the risk of taking a man who killed a multiple murderer to trial. But until then . . . they could prove nothing.

The afternoon sun was low in the sky, the day still bright and clear when I walked out of police headquarters with Dominic. Uncle Carlo dropped us off to head to work, promising that he'd send a car if we wanted it afterward. "You handled yourself like a pro in there, Miss Bertoli. Sure you haven't done this before?"

I smiled and looked at Dominic out of the corner of my eyes. "Now, Dominic, after all that talk you gave me about suspecting, knowing, and proving, are you really going to ask me to confirm something to you?"

He chuckled and shook his head. "No, not at all. But if I

may say, Miss Bertoli, you have the guts and brains of your father and uncle. If your cousins don't want to take over the family business, you might entertain the idea of doing so yourself."

I shook my head, still smiling. "No thanks. I'm perfectly happy being a budding artist. Now, if you don't mind, I'm going to take the public transportation back home. It's been a long time since I felt safe doing that, and I'm going to enjoy the experience."

Chapter 26

Adriana

I felt out of place wearing the blue cocktail dress. It had been so long. "Mom, I wish we could skip this," I muttered as she fussed with my hair. "It's a family dinner, not a dinner with the President."

"It's your engagement dinner, sweetie. Besides, Carlo's boys came back from college for this. And you might as well humor Carlo. I know he's been looking forward to this part of your life for years. I bet he already has a speech all prepared for your reception." Mom was wearing a nearly identical dress in deep wine red with her best heels. "To tell you the truth, I've been looking forward to it too. Actually, if I remember right, Carlo now owes me a dollar, too."

"Oh, why's that?"

Mom blushed, then laughed. "When Tomasso was born, you were still only two, so you probably don't remember, but Johnny and Carlo, they made a bet as to which of their children would get married first. With Tommy and Angelo growing up so handsome, and you being not so much a social butterfly as just independent, I was wondering for a while."

"Tommy and Angelo aren't social butterflies, Mom," I replied with a laugh. "They're players, maybe even more than Daniel was."

"And look how that turned out," Mom reminded me.

"You have to admit that it kind of caught all of us, you included, by surprise."

"Surprise? Sure," I said, picking the string of pearls up from my changing table and putting them on. It felt nice to be back in my old room, and not the interior *safe* room I had been using. For one, I had windows and light. "But in a lot of ways, it kinda feels like fate, if you know what I mean."

"I do," Mom said. "You two were good friends when you were little. Even back then, he looked out for you when other people might try and tease or make fun of you. I guess in that way, things never changed."

We left my room and went downstairs to the grand dining room. It wasn't used often. After all, the table could hold twenty-four, but with Carlo, Mom, Tommy, Angelo, Daniel and myself, it was more than the normal dining room table could hold too. "You know, Mom, we need to get a smaller table, or maybe something we could do outside. Say, something for twelve or so?"

"Why?" Mom said with a grin. "Give it a few years, and there'll be enough for more of the table to be filled. What with Tommy and Angelo eventually finding girlfriends, and then your . . ."

"Whoa Mom, talking children already?" I asked, flabbergasted. "A little early to be talking about that, isn't it?"

"It kind of happens when you get married, especially as amorous as you two are," Mom replied, her smile widening until it was nearly laughter. "But I'm not trying to pressure you. Just saying."

"We can discuss that later, Mom. Let's get me through college first."

I took my seat at the table, second from the right side. We were following a pretty formal arrangement, with Carlo and Mom at the head of the table. Daniel would be to the immediate right, next to Carlo, while I would sit beside him. Tomasso and Angelo would sit across from us, Tomasso closest to the corner. All the men were wearing suits, and I had to remind myself that I was in company because Daniel looked so handsome. The bruises had faded, the bandages had come off, and while he was sporting an impressive new scar on his shoulder, he was back to his normal self.

"You look beautiful," he whispered to me as I took my seat, causing me to blush slightly.

"The sentiment's returned," I whispered back, and cleared my throat, looking at Uncle Carlo. "Sorry."

"No reason to apologize, Bella," Carlo said. "Before we sit, I'd like to offer a toast to you and Daniel. Despite the roadblocks, most of which I will admit I was more than responsible for, you two found love. Bella, for years I wanted you to find the perfect man, when I never realized that he was already right in our house. Salud."

Everyone raised their glasses, and we took a sip. Carlo continued. "Daniel, I already apologized to you in private, but I think that deserves a repeating here and now. You came to my house, and you have lived your entire life as an honorable man—even when I didn't realize it. You fought for, you bled for, and more importantly, you have loved this family. It is my honor, and I most humbly request that you accept my blessing on the engagement between you and Bella, and I offer you a place in our family."

"It is my honor to accept, Godfather," Daniel replied, his face shining. "If Mrs. Bertoli also offers me the same, of course. No offense, but it's her daughter, after all."

We all laughed as Mom raised her glass and the toasts were complete. We took a seat, and Carlo lifted the lid on the serving platter, a beautiful roast that was certainly not in the Italian tradition. "What's this?" I asked, surprised. "I'd expected something more . . . Italian."

Tommy laughed and set his wine glass down. He looked a lot like Dad did when he was young, with thick, lustrous brown hair that had just a hint of wave, hazel eyes, and a thick build that reminded me a little bit of a wrestler or bodybuilder. He didn't have Dad's height, though, topping out at only five foot ten. Still, his good looks and natural charm let him be quite the ladies' man.

"We can enjoy some sophistication from the other cultures that are going to make up our family, can we not?" he asked in his accentless voice. While Carlo had hung onto his Italian accent, Tommy's only came out when he spoke Italian. "Of course, I tried to convince Papa here to do haggis and sauerkraut, but that was a no go."

"That's good, Tommy. I'd hate to drink you under the table again," Daniel teased back, smiling. "Remember that trip to Vancouver?"

Tommy's smile disappeared, and he set his glass down. Mom laughed. "It's going to take some getting used to, Daniel being able to talk back to you two. I'm actually glad. Gives you someone your age who won't care about telling you when you two get out of line."

Angelo nodded, not happy but accepting it. He'd always

been the baby of the family, and at nineteen, was just coming into his adult body. "Honestly though, it is surprising that you'd be the first of us to settle down, Daniel. Not that you aren't a great guy, but just . . . you were pretty one-track minded. Well, two tracks I guess."

"I still am," Daniel replied. "Actually, I'll whittle it down more now. I'm one-track minded. What can I do to make and keep Adriana happy?"

"And that is a mantra that I think you should live by the rest of your days," Uncle Carlo said, taking the carving knife and slicing up the roast. "In fact, Daniel, I also wanted to tell you something else tonight. I thought I'd save it for after dinner, but why not now?"

"What is it, sir?" Daniel asked, a bit concerned. I shot Mom a questioning glance, and she returned it with a shrug. She had no idea what was going on.

"Daniel, I ask much of my men, especially my enforcers. And while you obviously proved your dedication and courage with rescuing Bella, you still showed a rather disturbing streak of not obeying orders. And that, I can't have. So . . . you're fired."

"What?" Daniel, Mom, and I all said at nearly the same time. I added, despite the fact that Daniel and I had talked about this exact subject with Carmen in her apartment, "Uncle Carlo, that's not fair!"

Carlo held up his hands until we quieted down. "Will you let me finish? Daniel, you're fired as an enforcer. However, I did have a discussion with Pietro, and he thought of a new way that the Bertoli family could expand our enterprises without running afoul of the law. So, we're going to look at starting a private security firm. Of course, it's going to start relatively small—bodyguards, security escorts, stuff like that. But, I think with the right man in charge of the company, it could grow to be quite profitable. Daniel, can you think of anyone who might be good at this?"

"It might need a team, sir," Daniel said, his smile returning. "After all, someone would need to stay behind and run the office side of things while others are running all over the place pretending to be Kevin Costner."

"God, that movie sucked," Angelo grumped, then took a bite of his roast. "At least the roast is good."

Carlo ignored his youngest son and nodded in agreement with Daniel. "Oh, of course. I was thinking . . . maybe a staff of two or three to start? President, secretary, and then the field operatives? Also, I wouldn't want to risk the money all myself, of course. I was thinking a man who might be willing to buy in fifty-fifty with me? That'd make him co-owner and managing partner, of course."

Daniel chewed his roast and nodded. "I can think of some names. Let's talk after dinner."

"Tomorrow," I interjected. "You two can talk business tomorrow. Tonight, it's all about family, remember?"

* * *

After a late dessert, Daniel and I went back to the dining room arm in arm while the rest of my family scattered to their own bedrooms. "You know, I nearly punched Angelo when he said he and Tommy decided to hire Genesis to sing at our wedding," I said, causing Daniel to laugh. "Well, I was going to."

"I know you were," he replied, patting my hand which was

entwined in his arm. "I'm still not sure if he knows you aren't really going to castrate him."

"He'd make a good *castrata*," I said with a giggle. "He's got such a good singing voice. You know, he's used that at least once to get into a girl's pants."

"Hmm, maybe I should try that," Daniel said, stopping. He shook his head and turned me to face him. "Adriana, would you give me the honor of a dance?"

"Here?" I asked, surprised. "It's the middle of the dining room."

He went over to the recessed nook where a stereo system had been installed. It was a bit older. It used CDs for the most part, but it had good quality, and when I heard the beautiful strains of Puccini, my heart melted.

"How'd you know?" I asked as he crossed the floor to me. "I've always loved Puccini at the balls."

"We were meant to be together. All those little things you mentioned, I never forgot them, even when I pretended to everyone that I had," Daniel said, taking me in his arms. "Sometimes, I even believed that lie. But the little things, like Puccini, or that you prefer to sleep on your left side, I never really forgot. Now I don't need to tell myself to forget anymore. I can just love you."

We started moving slowly in a dance that wasn't classical in the strict sense. Of course, I'd had lessons. I knew how to waltz and tango and foxtrot and all that other stuff. But Daniel hadn't, and instead he moved with a natural, flowing grace, the two of us making it up as we went along. My feet felt light on the floor, and I glided across the polished wood, and when I saw Mom stick her head in about halfway through some music from *La Boehme*, she smiled and closed the door behind her, turning the lock and making sure we were undisturbed. I leaned in closer to Daniel, letting my head rest on his chest. "Daniel?"

"Yes, Ade?"

"Take me . . ."

Daniel surprised and thrilled me by spinning me around and picking me up, carrying me over to the table before setting me down. "Daniel!"

"We had dinner here. I think this is a great place for a real dessert too," he growled, his hands running over the satin of my dress and cupping my ass. "You don't know how sexy you look in this damn thing."

His hands were insistent, caressing my body even as he started to peel my dress off, his mouth claiming mine in a fierce, possessive kiss that left me breathless. "Whew, am I going to get this every time we have to take a few days off from sex?" I teased when I could breathe again. I slid my hands inside his suit jacket and slid it off his broad shoulders, starting to undress him as he was undressing me. "If so, I'm going to have to call a one-week pause right before our honeymoon."

"Why?"

"So you can rock my world." I laughed, grabbing hold of the two halves of his shirt and yanking. Buttons flew off, clattering across the table to drop to the floor, and I darted my head forward, kissing and licking the skin of his chest. It'd been over a week since we had a chance to make love, first with recovery from his injuries, then dealing with the cops, before finally just getting caught up in everything, including my cousins coming back from college to visit. I was hungry, and not for gelato.

Daniel ripped his tie off, leaving him in just his suit pants as he hiked my dress up, lifting it above my waist as our fiery passion overcame our hesitancy and desire to hold back and make it last. There would be time for that later.

Pushing away from Daniel, I gave him my sexiest look and slid off the table, turning around and bending over. "Take me."

I trembled as he lifted my dress all the way up again, exposing my ass to the night air. The weather was starting to cool off some, fall was coming, and I felt goosebumps break out on my skin, delicious and sensitive. "Sexy."

I felt heat rising to my face, and I looked back at Daniel's appreciative gaze. "I was kinda hoping I'd get lucky tonight."

"Grab the table and don't turn around," he replied, his blue eyes blazing with desire, "and you'll get lucky for sure."

I did as he said, trying to grip what I could on the table as I felt him run his hands over the exposed curves of my hips and ass, shifting around until I felt his warm breath on my skin.

He lifted my panties out of the way, and before I could take a breath, his tongue darted in between my pussy lips, quick and rapier-like, stabbing me open and thrilling me. His nimble tongue snaked deep inside, licking my inner folds and setting my nerves on fire with pleasure. I was vulnerable, with his hands pressing my thighs into the table and his weight behind me, but I didn't want to move. I was secure and safe with him, protected.

The aroma of my arousal came to my nose, and I trembled, feeling my orgasm building inside me. I pushed back, burying my ass into his face as he licked and tasted me, desperate for more. "Dan . . . oh Dan . . . fuck me baby. Make me come."

I couldn't make out his mumbled reply, but he brought his right hand between my legs, gathering some of my moisture before finding the hard nub of my clit and rubbing it in a feather-light stroke. My eyes flew open, and it felt so good I felt like my heart would explode. My fingers clawed at the table as I trembled on the edge of coming, but he kept me frozen there, caught in agonizing ecstasy, until I couldn't take it any longer. "Please . . ."

"As you wish," I think he said, his tongue leaving my pussy to quickly stroke against my clit, the sensation pushing me over the edge. My feet curled up off the ground and my body convulsed, thick, guttural moans ripping from my chest as I came. I can't say it was the biggest orgasm I'd ever had, because each time Daniel and I made love, each orgasm felt like the biggest, and each one was completely different. This was almost relaxing, forcing me to let go and give in to him and to our love.

I was just starting to come down to earth again when I felt him behind me, and the sound of him opening his zipper came through over the sound of Puccini that was still playing on the stereo. It had nearly filtered out of my consciousness when he was feasting on me, but now, with the head of his cock pressing against me, I was aware of everything, from the sound of the violins and horns to the weave of the tablecloth underneath me, but most of all, the blunt tip of his massive cock at my entrance. "Give yourself to me, Adriana. Show me what you want."

I lowered my feet back down, happy for the high heels, which let my legs stretch up enough that I could push back, impaling myself on him and filling my heart with happiness. I kept pushing, not caring if I was being stretched or about the slight edge of pain that came from having him so deep inside me again after such a long time without him, just knowing that I needed that connection, that completion.

I whimpered when I felt my ass tickled by the soft tuft of trimmed hair at the base of his cock, and I wept softly in joy. "That . . . that's what I want."

He took my waist in his hands and pulled back, pausing for a moment, only the head of his cock inside me before thrusting back in, driving me against the table with his force and passion. He had gone without sex for that time too, and he was on the edge of losing control. I had never felt sexier, knowing that it was me who was making this wonderful man overcome with lust.

Daniel pounded into me, my hips pressed into the hundred-year-old oak of the table as Puccini's music sang about love and romance and the mysteries of the world. The impact of each thrust shook the table, and I was swept away on the wave of his desire. Throwing my head back, I cried out, tears of happiness trickling down my face as he grabbed a handful of my hair and kept going, his breath huffing in and out of his chest.

He let go of my waist, and suddenly, a small crack filled the air as he smacked my ass, the heat and sting mixing with the heady explosions of pleasure inside me, driving me insensate and wild. I was overloaded, my body clenching and pulsing with wave after wave of pleasure as Daniel's cock filled me over and over.

Another orgasm built within me, and I threw my all back into him, trying to match him thrust for thrust until we were overwhelmed. I was coming, so hard I couldn't even make a noise, and my breath was locked in my chest as my entire body rushed higher and higher, until I was almost certain that I would die due to being unable to breathe. I didn't care—it felt so great, and I was almost disappointed when air flooded back into my lungs and time returned to the world.

I was drained, my legs shaky and my throat raw from crying out, even though I didn't know I had been doing it. I sagged against the table, sweat making my dress stick to me and my chest heaving in long, shuddering gasps. "Tell me it feels better the more we do this."

"I don't know," Daniel asked, "but we have the rest of our lives to find out. Shall we?"

"Let's."

Epilogue

Adriana - One Year Later

"You're working for whom?"

Daniel checked his Beretta and shrugged, making sure his suit was ready for work. "Come on, honey. Just because we don't like his music, it's not his fault. That would be like blaming Gaga for Tommy's drunken dancing at our reception. You didn't seem to get mad at her though. In fact, if I remember right, you were pretty buzzed when she went to Carlo's house for dinner with the family."

I had to admit, going to the family manor to have dinner with a Grammy award winner was a pretty cool experience, especially coupled with the fact that she had raved about my artwork. Now, I was only six months from graduation and I already had five orders for pieces. "Still . . . Phil Collins?"

Daniel laughed and pulled his jacket on. "Sweetheart, it's for one night only. He's flying in town for the environmental awards dinner the governor is holding and flying out immediately afterward. It's an easy five grand. He's just making a speech and then glad-handing."

I grumbled, but nodded. "Okay, okay. At least he's not singing, and you did get me a seat at the table."

"Exactly," Daniel said with a smile. "Just think—how many millions of dollars will be surrounding you, all, I'm sure, eager to meet the artist who is catching the attention of the entertainment set? Why, if you play this right, you might end up meeting Banksy."

"Ha ha ha," I replied, wincing afterward. "Ouch, kiddo, hold on there."

Daniel came over and ran his hand over my now noticeable baby bump, his face in a sort of soft awe. "He's getting big."

"He's going to be like his daddy, I'm sure of it," I said, feeling the baby inside my womb shift again before settling down in a comfortable position. "Mom says she hopes he has my hair though. I think she just wants the redhead gene to get passed down another generation."

"I was thinking maybe this one could be blond, and then our second can be a redhead. A girl, with beautiful green eyes like her mother," Daniel said softly, wrapping his arms around me and hugging me carefully. We still made love often. The doctor had very clearly said it wouldn't hurt the baby. We just had to be more creative with how we did it.

"You are the most romantic man in the world, you know that?" I replied, kissing his nose, then his lips. Our kiss deepened, until we let go, both of us sighing, and Daniel discreetly reached down to readjust himself in his pants. It was those little things—I don't even know if he did them consciously—that helped me still feel beautiful even as my body changed.

"It's easy when I'm married to the world's most beautiful woman," he said, his eyes open and honest. That, more than anything else, helped me. In the nearly eight months since opening Neiman Security Consultants, he'd been able to be bodyguard or consultant to some of the world's most famous. He'd guarded pop stars, media personalities, models, politicians and businessmen all over the Pacific Northwest, and still, I could see in his eyes that none of the women he met measured up to me. The one-time player and enforcer for the Bertoli Crime Family had become the most dedicated husband in the world, and I couldn't be happier. "So what are you going to do in between now and when Carlo comes around to take you to the benefit?"

I chuckled and stepped back, straightening his tie. He was in his blue suit, with a black tie and white shirt—very conservative, but very imposing. He knew with that look, his Terminator act was easy to do, and that was half the job. "Carmen's going to come over about three o'clock and help me with a bath and massage. She says she's got a new oil that's guaranteed to not give me stretch marks when our little one gets bigger. I don't know if I believe it, but it can't hurt."

"How is school going for her, anyway?" Daniel asked, sitting down and putting on his shoes. She'd recently gone back to dance school, and was working part-time as a massage therapist in a rehabilitation clinic Uncle Carlo was invested in. "Well, I hope?"

"She's doing great, she says. And she's happy that Carlo is sponsoring her while she works part-time at the clinic. She didn't think he was being serious."

"You know him. If he says something, he usually means it," Daniel said, finishing his left shoe and going to his right. "Especially since the clinic lets his men do rehabilitation and other things for free. No hanky-panky though."

"Still, I bet the boys love getting a back rub from her," I said with a laugh. "She's got good hands. Among other things men like."

Daniel finished his shoes and got up, coming over and

kissing me again. "Well, tell her that I think she's doing an amazing job so far and wish her the best."

"I love you."

"I love you too. Unfortunately, gotta go."

I nodded and kissed his nose again. "Say hello to Phil for me, and that I'm looking forward to tonight. If anything, you've got some interesting stories you can tell him about us and his music."

Daniel laughed and walked to the door of our house. It wasn't anywhere near the size of the Bertoli estate, but it was our own. He walked out, closing the door behind him. The early fall day was brisk, but he showed no signs as he got into his brand new work Mercedes sedan and started it up. He waved, and I waved back. "I love you. Both of us," I whispered to myself.

Daniel drove off, and I watched him go before walking back to my studio in the back of the house. Carmen was due in an hour or so, and in the meantime, there was painting I wanted to do. A painting full of light. And joy. And most of all, love.

If you enjoyed this book, please take a moment to leave a review. Thank you for Reading!

Made in the USA
Middletown, DE
18 June 2016